Love... Among The Stars

Sometimes, the hardest part of becoming a success is keeping a straight face...

Jamie & Laura Newman have recently become quite the successful - and mildly wealthy - couple, thanks to the fact they've managed to write a series of popular romantic comedies together. This has come as a *complete* surprise to the hapless pair, and is - needless to say - a turn of events neither is in the slightest bit equipped to deal with.

They get invited to posh events where they feel endlessly out of place, have long lost relatives turn up out of the blue, raise an aspiring diva for a daughter, and go on holiday to exotic places they really have no place being. It's enough to make anyone crawl under the nearest rock.

If you're Jamie, you also get to turn 40 - and there's not a damn thing he can do to stop it. As for Laura, well let's say that just because you *can* afford to purchase expensive beauty products, it doesn't necessarily mean that you *should*.

'Money can't buy you happiness' as the old saying goes. Nor can it stop the Newmans being *the Newmans,* with all their quirks, eccentricities - and the uncanny ability to embarrass themselves in public at the drop of a hat.

LOVE... AMONG THE STARS is the fourth book by Nick Spalding about Jamie & Laura, and is full of the warts-and-all, laugh out loud comedy you've come to know and love.

D1464964

By Nick Spalding:

Fat Chance

Love... From Both Sides
Love... And Sleepless Nights
Love... Under Different Skies
Love... Among The Stars

Life... With No Breaks
Life... On A High

Blue Christmas Balls
Buzzing Easter Bunnies

The Cornerstone
Wordsmith: The Cornerstone Book 2

Spalding's Scary Shorts

Click link to buy Nick's books at Amazon UK
Click link to buy Nick's books at Amazon USA
Click link to buy Nick's books at Amazon AUS

Nick's Website
Nick on Twitter
Nick on Facebook

Chapters

Laura's Diary
Tuesday, February 16th

Dear Mum,

Here's what went through my head as I stared into the mirror this morning: *'Oh good fucking grief, I look like a banana'*.
Last night I went to bed a successful and largely happy woman in her late thirties, and today I woke up as a tropical fruit - popular with children for its taste, and with adult males for its highly amusing phallic shape.

Now, obviously I haven't *really* turned into a banana overnight. If that were the case, you wouldn't be reading this, as bananas have no opposable thumbs with which to hold a pen. I make the comparison because my face has turned the same colour as the average bunch of Fyffes.

As I stare at myself in the mirror with mounting horror, I realise that vast areas of my skin have gone a disturbing shade of yellow.

I tell you what, if you don't like the banana comparison, let's chuck a few more in for good measure: I'm as yellow as a sun ripened lemon, as yellow as a squeezy rubber ducky, as yellow as a sunflower in full bloom...

And the reason for this new, disturbing hue?

A £150 tub of fake tan Jamie bought me for Christmas.

Yes, you heard that right. A *one hundred and fifty pound* tub of fake tan (or 'refined bronzing solution' as the manufacturers choose to call it). I'd read all about it on the internet back in November. Invented by a small but excruciatingly expensive Swiss perfumery, this stuff was supposed to not only banish your wrinkles to the pits of the nearest hell, it was also meant to give you the kind of healthy tan that can only otherwise be achieved with several months in the equatorial midday sun. For the princely sum of £150 I could buy myself a tub of *'Riche Femme Bronzée No.1'* and kiss both wrinkles and pale skin goodbye!

...or rather, Jamie could buy it for me for Christmas - which is exactly what he did, bless him. If there's one advantage to having a bit of money in the bank these days, it's that your husband can occasionally splash out on hideously overpriced beauty products without wincing too much.

I was delighted to open the small golden box that the tub came in on Christmas Day, and promised myself I would use it as soon as possible. Which, in other words, meant it got put in the bathroom cabinet and completely forgotten about until last night when I discovered it again during a clear out. Needless to say I was delighted. With a book launch coming up the next day in London, a nice bit of wrinkle disappearage and instant tan would go a long way to making me look dazzling while I pretended to fit in with a load of book industry types.

So, confident that any product which costs that much *must* work perfectly every time, I slathered the greasy concoction all over my face and body, and went to bed safe in the knowledge that I would wake up the next day miraculously younger and browner.

This morning I still have crow's feet, and my body is resolutely *not brown*.

It is however, yellow. *Very yellow.*

'I'm dead,' I whisper to myself as my eyes widen to take in the full glory of my newly bananarised flesh. '*I am fucked beyond measure.*'

'Mum! You're swearing again! That's naughty!'

My head whips round to see a small accusatory finger pointing at me. This is connected to my bright-eyed and bushy-tailed daughter Poppy. At least I think her eyes are bright. I can't quite tell, given that they are currently narrowed in disgust at her mother's use of such bad language.

I'm about to apologise to my irate child, but she doesn't give me the chance, as she's just realised that her mother is now bananarised. Her mouth goes wide, she gives a sharp intake of breath, and points her finger at me again, this time in shock. 'Mum! Why are you so yellow?!'

'Is it that bad?' I respond forlornly. I had hoped that the yellow tone to my skin was only obvious close up, but Pops is standing a good ten feet away and can still see that I have apparently picked up a nasty case of beauty product related jaundice.

'What happened, Mum?!' she squeals in horrified fascination.

'Your Dad bought me some make-up,' I tell her, unconsciously blaming Jamie for this mess, despite the fact that the blame clearly lies at the feet of whatever Swiss twat concocted this horrible goop. 'It was supposed to give me a tan, but it's turned me into a banana.'

Poppy gasps and lets out a high-pitched giggle. 'You do look like a banana, Mum!'

I sigh and put my hands on my hips. 'Not a lemon then?' I reply. 'Just a banana?'

'A lemon as well!' Poppy screeches, and giggles anew. Then, a sudden realisation hits her and a hand flies to her mouth. 'You're at a party tonight!' Another sharp intake of breath. 'What's Dad going to say?!'

I cross my arms. 'What your father has to say about this is the least of my worries, young lady.'

Poppy walks over to me, grabs my yellow hand, and starts to rub at my skin. 'It won't come off,' she points out helpfully.

'Not like that it won't,' I agree. 'This is going to take several hours, and more cleanser than you can shake a stick at.'

Poppy pouts. 'But you're still taking me to the park today, before I go to Grandma's aren't you?'

'If I can get this stuff off I will.' I bend down and kiss her on the forehead. 'You don't want to be pushed on the swings by a giant lemon do you?'

This sends her into another fit of hysterical laughter, as she no doubt pictures herself being propelled forward on a swing by an enormous lemon, with a blonde Laura Newman wig perched on top of its head.

'Go make yourself some breakfast, Pops,' I say to her, reaching for my strongest cleanser. 'I'll be down once I've had a go at de-lemonising myself.'

Poppy's hands go to her hips. 'But I want porridge today, Mum,' she says, the pout returning to her otherwise gorgeous features. The amount of times this pout has appeared on my daughter's face has increased in recent months. I'm starting to worry that Jamie and I are creating an entitled monster. But what else are you supposed to do when you become successful than lavish presents on your offspring? Especially when they are, by your choice, an only child?

—

'You can have cold cereals this morning sweetheart,' I say in a conciliatory tone.

'I want porridge Mum!'

'I said, you can have cereals *Poppy*,' I say in a sharper tone - one that can turn into an *angry* tone, should that pout not disappear with its owner within the next few seconds.

Poppy goes to open her mouth, sees her mother's expression, and her natural gift for self-preservation kicks in. Without another word, she leaves the bathroom. I do hear her feet stamp loudly as she moves down the landing, but I let her off as my attention is now thoroughly back on the job at hand.

With hope in my heart, and a look of determination on my face, I pull out the cotton wool pads and go to work.

An hour later I'm exhausted.

And still yellow.

Okay, the bright vibrant shade I was when I woke up has calmed down a bit, so I'm now more of a *sickly* yellow, but I am still nonetheless a woman of supreme yellowosity.

'Bugger,' I moan at the mirror, and bang the bottle of cleanser down in disgust.

If I can't rub the horrible stuff off, I'm going to have to cover it with something.

Luckily I'm approaching 40, so have more foundation in my make-up cabinet than *seven* 40-year-old women would ever need.

Twenty minutes later, I am back to what roughly equates to my natural skin tone - on my face, neck and visible extremities anyway. I had planned on wearing my little black cocktail dress to the party tonight, but as that would expose a healthy amount of leg - which would need make-up all over it to hide the yellowness - I mentally change my plans and opt for the dark blue strappy gown, and black bolero that's been gently gathering dust on the far left hand side of my wardrobe for the past year.

I kind of wish that wearing a bag over your head to high profile social occasions had become a recent fashion statement, but it sadly hasn't, so I will have to make sure the cover-up is the most convincing it can be before I step out of the door.

Step out of the *hotel* door, that is. I remember that I still have a two hour drive up to the city to endure later, after I've dropped Poppy off at Jamie's mum's for a couple of days.

Oh, but that's not really what you'll be doing, is it, you pretentious bitch? the ugly little voice in my head pipes up. *You won't actually be doing any of the driving yourself, will you?*

This voice has been echoing through my head ever since the first book in the Love... series sold quarter of a million copies. It's only got louder over the past eighteen months, as more books have come out - to similar or greater success.

I won't be driving to London later this afternoon, because Watermill Publishing has laid on a car for me. It won't be a Rolls Royce or anything, but even the prospect of a Mercedes thrills and disgusts me in equal measure.

You should be *disgusted,* the voice intones. *A couple of years ago you would have scoffed at the idea of being driven around like a right lah-de-dah. Now look at you.*

Oh sod off, I tell the voice, before stamping out of the bathroom and going downstairs to see what kind of mess Poppy has gotten herself into with the Kellogg's variety pack.

I can't help the fact that Jamie and I have stumbled into a successful writing career, can I?

Writing was never my dream, it was always Jamie's, but when he suggested I take joint credit for Love From Both Sides, I was more than happy to do so - after all, half the stories in it were mine. And besides, it's good for a couple to have a hobby they can do together, isn't it?

How was I to know it would sell so many sodding copies? And that in only a few years I'd be a pretentious lah-de-dah bitch on her chauffeured way to a Valentine's Day book launch in London?

I have been consumed by a combination of wide-eyed amazement, guilt, and smug satisfaction for quite a while now - and it's frankly starting to get on my nerves. At turns, I either love myself or loathe myself, and the sudden change that occurs between the two is giving me mental whiplash.

As I enter the kitchen, I try to shake myself out of this unhelpful train of thought, and concentrate on things more mundane and down to earth - like clearing up the small lake of milky cornflakes that Pops has left on the breakfast bar.

You sure you're happy cleaning that up? the voice says, just when I thought I'd got it under control, *or should we just call out a cleaning service to do it for you, you over-privileged witch?*

I draw in a long, deep breath, and let it out as slowly and calmly as possible.

What with the yellow skin, deep seated sense of guilt, and impending book launch, today promises to be something of a nightmare.

But first, there's Jamie's mother to deal with.

Since our upturn in fortune, Jane Newman has changed somewhat. A self-absorbed woman who values material possessions, you can only imagine what her reaction was to learning that her son and daughter-in-law had become more well off than she.

Every time we see her now, there is a barely suppressed twitch in one corner of her eye, and her lips pinch together as if she's having to swallow something extremely sour. Which, I suppose, from her point of view, is exactly what she's doing.

My relationship with Jane has always been fairly fractious over the years - not least because I once caught her shagging a fitness instructor. That fractious quality has certainly not diminished with my newly fledged publishing career.

It has *changed* though. She can no longer look down her nose at me, much to her dismay. When I was a struggling chocolate shop owner, I'm sure it was very easy for Jane to convince herself I was beneath her. She can't think that anymore, thankfully. Instead, she has embarked on a campaign of pointing out each and every physical flaw I have, in order to bring me down a peg or two. In Jane's mind, I've gone from a poor, working class scumbag who isn't good enough for her son - to a rich over-achieving megalomaniac, who inexplicably is *still not good enough for her son.*

I don't know whether it's a change I'm particularly happy with, but at least it's something different.

'Oh, you look tired Laura,' is the first thing out of her mouth as she opens the front door.

I heave a familiar sigh. Thanks to the strategically applied foundation, at least she doesn't know that I am in fact a tired looking banana.

'Afternoon Jane,' I say wearily, and look down at Poppy, expecting her to follow suit.

This doesn't happen. Poppy is instead glaring at her feet in no uncertain terms.

I heave another sigh. Pops is not happy about being left behind while I swan up to London to join Jamie at the party, and intends to show the world her displeasure with this silent demonstration. 'Say hello to Grandma, Poppy,' I tell her, noticing with some satisfaction the look on Jane's face as I do so. This is not a woman who enjoys the concept of being called 'Grandma'. Not in the slightest.

'I said, say hello to your *Grandma*, Poppy,' I repeat, emphasising the word just enough to start the twitch going in Jane's eye.

"ello, 'randma,' Poppy eventually mumbles.

'Hello Poppy!' Jane replies with mock enthusiasm. 'We're going to have a lovely time!' She bends down and takes Poppy's hand. 'We're going to order a pizza, and watch all your favourite Disney cartoons!'

Poppy perks up a bit at this. 'Okay Grandma!' The opportunity to guzzle down a slice of Texas BBQ and watch *Frozen* for the eightieth time has apparently stirred her from her malaise. Jane and I might not get on, but I can't fault her dedication to my daughter. This earns her a pass every time as far as I'm concerned, no matter how much she comments on my stubborn chin spot, which keeps cropping up every few months.

Jamie's mother looks over my shoulder to the car waiting in the driveway. She spots the driver, a twenty something lad called Kyle, who is currently playing on his iPhone and is therefore oblivious to the world around him.

'Do you have time to come in?' Jane asks.

'No,' I say, shaking my head. 'I have to get going if we're going to beat the London traffic and get to the hotel in good time.' We were originally leaving an hour later, but I moved the departure time up when I realised I'd have to spend a good half an hour in the hotel just reapplying the ruddy foundation.

Jane sniffs. 'Nice hotel, is it?'

'Yes,' I reply, not offering any further information.

'And why isn't Jamie with you?'

'He had to go up yesterday for a meeting with our agent, Jane. We told you that.' About four times, as I recall. Jane is well aware of why my husband isn't with me today, but if she admitted it, she wouldn't be able to say the following:

'Ah, I see. It's such a shame he couldn't be with you. I almost feel like he's being kept away from me, because of all this book stuff.'

She says *book stuff* but she means *me*, of course. As far as Jane is concerned I am directly responsible for everything that denies her the chance to fuss over her successful child.

I try my hardest to smile without cracking my make-up. 'Well, the book business keeps us busy,' I say.

'Yes. It does seem to.'

Jane pauses, and squints at my face. Here it comes.

'I see you're still having trouble with that spot. Did you try the cleanser I recommended?'

Sometimes, I wish I'd never met Jamie Newman.

'I did Jane yes. It has helped.' With the spot that is, not with the removal of fake tan, unfortunately.

'Well, keep going with it. I'm sure it'll clear up soon.'

'Thank you.' I'm trying very hard not to grit my teeth. I am resolutely failing.

'Bye bye, Mum!' Poppy says from below. I can't be sure if she's deliberately trying to break the tense atmosphere, but I wouldn't put it past her.

I bend down and administer a kiss to her forehead. I really do hate to leave her behind like this, but these idiotic book launches leave no room for a hyperactive seven-year-old girl. 'Be good for Grandma,' I tell her. 'Dad and I will be back tomorrow afternoon.'

Her eyes widen. 'Can we go for KFC!?'

'That stuff isn't good for you, Pops.'

Her little face crinkles up. 'But I love it.'

I hesitate, then smile and nod. 'Yes, of course we can honey.'

This is another prime example of parental guilt leading to an over-indulged child, but I just don't have the time right now to argue with her - damn me and my stupid highfalutin' job.

I kiss Poppy again and stand up. 'Thank you for taking care of her, Jane.'

'My pleasure, Laura. It's the least I can do as a good and caring Grandmother.'

There's a veiled insult there, I just know it, but my watch says three o'clock, and I have to get going. I issue another goodbye to them both and walk back to the car. Kyle sees me coming, stops playing Angry Birds, and fires up the Audi's engine.

As the car pulls away, I wave at my little daughter, who waves back at me from the doorway. Right now I would cheerfully trade a night dressed in an evening gown for an evening in pyjamas with my little girl in front of the TV. Even if it did mean that Jane was also there, pointing out how many blackheads I've got.

I didn't tell Jane the name of the hotel we would be staying at this evening. It might have sent her into apoplexy.

The Dorchester is the type of hotel I would never stay at if I had the choice, because I am not insane. This is not necessarily an opinion I hold due to how expensive it is, but simply because its levels of poshness are so beyond my sphere of experience that I can't possibly have a nice time staying in it, for the constant fear of looking completely out of place.

'Nice hotel you're staying at, Mrs Newman,' Kyle the driver remarks as we pull up to the expansive front entrance.

'Yes!' I say, rather too quickly. 'It was the publisher's idea, not mine!' I add just as fast, making sure to let Kyle know that I am not a complete arsehole.

The car door is opened by a middle-aged man, dressed like an extra from My Fair Lady. He offers me a million pound smile from under his large peaked green cap, as he beckons me out of the vehicle. 'Good afternoon, madam,' he says, trying his best to get into my good books, but failing miserably for the use of the word 'madam'.

'Afternoon,' I reply and get out of the car in as demure a fashion as I am able to. Being demure is not entirely possible in a pair of faded jeans, hooded duffle coat and high heels, but I give it my best shot anyway.

Kyle has got my suitcase out of the boot, and he places it next to my feet with a flourish. I go to take the handle at exactly the same time as the My Fair Lady reject. We're both so swift and determined to be the one to get purchase on the suitcase that his hand inadvertently covers mine, and for one fleeting and excruciatingly awkward moment, I'm holding hands with a tall grey haired doorman in a jacket with more buttons down the front than is strictly necessary. 'Sorry!' I tell him, and whisk my hand away. I just can't get used to this level of personal service. The last time someone took my suitcase on the way into a building I was about to give birth.

'Not at all, madam,' Peaky says with that same ingratiating smile.

'Goodbye Mrs Newman,' Kyle says. 'Have a good time at the party.'

'Thanks Kyle!' I blurt, grateful for the distraction from the embarrassment of unintentional handholding. 'Bye!'

Kyle gives me a smile and makes his way back to the driver's seat. Peaky takes a firmer grip on my suitcase and holds out a hand towards the hotel lobby.

I try my best to return the million pound smile, acutely aware that mine is probably more like three items for a quid in Poundland, and make my way towards the entrance.

The Dorchester's lobby couldn't be more opulent if you fired the Queen into it with a bazooka, and I spend a few minutes idly gazing round at the marble columns and chandeliers, as the concierge sorts out my reservation on his computer. Peaky has thankfully been replaced with a much less terrifying young Indian man called Muresh. His grey porter's outfit is far easier to deal with than Peaky's enormous green buttoned down jacket and rigidly pressed trousers. I don't need Muresh's help of course, I can yank the suitcase along quite happily myself; but this is a swanky London hotel, and by Christ, in swanky London hotels you *will* obey the rules - and allow another human being to carry your suitcase, no matter how perfectly healthy and able you are to do it yourself.

'You're in room 216, Mrs Newman. Your husband's been enjoying the room since yesterday. He went out a bit earlier, but told me to tell you that he'd be back around the time you checked in,' the whip thin concierge says, handing me the electronic room key. 'Muresh will show you the way.'

'Thanks very much,' I tell him. The concept of Jamie 'enjoying' a hotel room conjures up all sorts of disturbing imagery, but I push it to the back of my mind as I feel my suitcase whisked away from my side.

Muresh, a man so practiced at this stuff he can probably do it unconscious, is already beetling off down a long corridor so ostentatious you'd have to reload the bazooka and shoot the rest of the royal family down it.

I take off in hot pursuit.

Muresh calls the lift, and in no time at all, I'm being whisked upwards. The little Indian man has obviously gone to the same institute of smiling technology as Peaky, as he also gives me a million pound grin while classical music wafts out of the hidden elevator speakers.

I try to smile back, but it dawns on me that I don't know if I have any cash in my purse, and the smile dies on my lips.

This is a *disaster*.

Poor old Muresh will quite rightly be expecting a tip for his services, and I don't know if I have any bloody money on me with which to supply him with one. I can't exactly start rummaging round in my handbag right now; it would look tacky as hell. I'll just have to wait until we reach the room and hope I've got an adequate amount to satisfy him.

The walk down the corridor to my room is now an exercise in tension and anxiety. I'd like to admire the vastly expensive fixtures and fittings, but all I can picture is Muresh's disappointed face when I have no tip to give him.

He pauses outside the door to a room and indicates to me to pass him the electronic room key.

Oh good grief, this is just ridiculous now. Pulling my suitcase along is one thing, making me stand there like a twat while he performs the simple task of opening a hotel room door is quite another.

'Don't worry, I can do it!' I tell Muresh and leap forward, key in hand. I confidently swipe it through the card reader before my porter has a chance to object.

Bzzt, goes the reader, and a red LED lights up on top of it to indicate the key card has not been read properly.

I have another go.

Bzzt.

And another.

Bzzt.

Muresh tries to take the key card from my hand. 'Please,' he says, almost imploring.

'No! No! I can do this!' I assure him, and try the card again.

Bzzt.

'Oh, for fuck's sake,' I mumble angrily under my breath.

Bzzt.

Bzzt.

Bzzt.

'Please!' Muresh repeats, a little more frantically.

I suck air in over my teeth and hand him the card. Muresh offers me the patented Dorchester smile, *turns the key card around the other way,* and swipes it through the reader.

Bing!

Green light.

Bugger, fuck and twateration.

Muresh has the decency not to look at me, and simply rolls my suitcase into the room. As he does, I catch a glimpse of my home for the next 24 hours and fall instantly in love. You should never stay in a hotel room that looks nicer than your own house. Nothing good can ever come of it.

My delight is slightly tempered by the fact that Jamie got here a day earlier, and has ruined the place somewhat by liberally sprinkling his clothes and electronic entertainment devices around it with no regard for the carefully thought out feng shui.

Muresh plants the suitcase neatly next to the wall and turns to give me another smile, this one tinged with a healthy degree of expectancy.

This is the moment I've been dreading. Will I make Muresh's day? Or will I have to see his face crumple in a barely concealed mixture of disappointment and loathing?

Let's see what I've got in my purse, shall we?

Hmmmm.

So, which do you think would be worse? Giving Muresh the £2.36 I have in very small change, or a book of 12 first class stamps - with two and a half stamps left in it (Jamie is always too rough with those things). How about the picture of the three of us taken on the Gold Coast two days before we left, or my library card - which was out of date seven years ago?

I panic, and give him the change and the book of stamps, figuring that they have enough face value to bring his tip above the £3 mark.

18

For a fleeting second, Muresh looks like someone has just taken a shit in both his hand *and* his mouth, before he covers up his disgust magnificently.

'Thank you so much,' he tells me, through a barricade of shiny white teeth. Translated: '*Wow, thank you very much. I bet two quid in coppers and some stamps was a real stretch for you, what with that job as a successful writer. I had JK Rowling in here the other day and she only stumped up £1.73 and a chocolate frog.*'

Muresh decides to throw a return insult back in my direction by picking the book of stamps out of his hand with two pinched fingers and handing them back to me.

'Thanks?' I offer, which is not the usual response you make after having a tip rejected, but in these dire circumstances, there is little else I can do.

My towering shame is given relief when Muresh backs his way out of the room, shutting the door as he goes. I hear him stamp off down the corridor, no doubt to go tell every other member of the Dorchester staff that the woman in room 216 is a right bitch, so feel free to spit in her breakfast and forget to leave fresh towels.

For the first time that day, since I discovered I was a banana, I am left gratifyingly alone. A swift look at my watch tells me it's coming up to 6pm, so I'd better get a wiggle on. According to the text Jamie sent me in the car on the way up, another chauffeur driven car will be here in an hour to pick us up for tonight's shenanigans, which gives me fifteen minutes to shower, ten minutes to get dressed, twenty minutes to agonise over whether I should wear the bolero jacket or not, and just quarter of an hour to reapply foundation to all the bits I need to, and put on the rest of my make-up.

Aaargh!

It'll be close, but I think I can just about make it happen - if I'm very lucky and pray to the dressing up fairies hard enough.

The shower is wonderful, and I sacrifice five minutes dressing time for continued use of the massage function. This results in a rather hurried donning of underwear, tights and evening gown, but I get away with just one small ladder on my right thigh and a couple of bent teeth on the dress's zipper.

Bolero related agony is far worse than I thought it would be, given that I look super cute with it both on and off. In the end, practicality wins the day, and I decide to wear it, given the fact it's February and three degrees outside.

So now it's just the matter of the foundation and make-up.

Still, I managed to do it pretty fast this morning, so all I have to do is be confident, controlled and liberal with application, and I should be fi -

Where's the fucking foundation?

I rummage around my expansive make-up bag, but no foundation is to be found. I then frantically up-end the bag into the sink, but *still* no foundation is to be seen.

The next thing up-ended is my handbag onto the chair... then my suitcase onto the bed... but still no luck.

A grisly, awful realisation hits me.

You left it in the bathroom at home, you silly bitch.

I can picture the large tube of skin salvation right where I left it - stood next to the toothpaste and sun cream in my bathroom cabinet, a good eighty miles away from me and my yellow tinged skin.

With an involuntary whimper I pelt back into the bathroom to see if I have anything that might do the job instead. In an ideal world I'd at least have some concealer knocking about, but damn the make-up companies for coming up with foundation so good that you don't need any these days.

In fact, the only thing that I have here in the sink that can be slathered right across my skin is the sodding £150 fake tan that got me in this mess in the first place.

With a cry of unholy rage, I hold the tub of sickening goo up in one hand and shake it angrily. This doesn't appease my wrath, so I throw it with all my might back into the bedroom - right at the soft, fluffy pillows in front of the headboard. I have the aim of a blind drunkard in a force ten hurricane though, so the tub misses the bed and strikes the bedside lamp instead, knocking it off the table. The lamp hits the carpet, crumpling the lampshade and blowing the bulb, while the fake tan continues its trajectory into the wall behind, where it smashes open, spraying thick blobs of the horrid muck all over the wall.

'Oh fuckery biggins!' I scream at the top of my voice.

It is at this moment the main door to the hotel room opens, and in walks Jamie Newman. Or rather, in walks a pale, grey shadow of what was once Jamie Newman. He's holding a Costa Coffee in one slightly shaking hand. 'Hey baby,' he says in a cracked voice as he walks in, 'Er... are you okay? I hope you managed to get checked in alri - '.

Jamie comes to a shambling halt when he sees me standing in the bathroom doorway, a look of combined shock and rage on my face. He then notices the broken lamp, and the blobs of fake tan that are beginning to slide down the wall towards the most expensive carpet either of us has ever stood on. 'What the hell's going on?' he asks in amazed horror, his bloodshot eyes widening. His face then crumples into confusion. 'Why is your face so yellow?'

I simply don't have the words. I just don't have the current mental capacity to form a coherent response. Instead, I look at the blobs of fake tan still sliding their way inexorably to the floor - and the triple digit cleaning bill that will inevitably be coming our way - and start to cry. Then my brain puts two and two together, and makes a rather inevitable connection.

I point an accusatory finger at my husband. 'You! This is all *your* fault!'

'What the hell have I done?'

'You... you bought me that bloody fake tan!!'

Yes Mum, I know it's a completely unreasonable thing for me to say, but in times such as these, when you've made a series of stupid mistakes that are no-one's fault but your own, it's vital for your own sense of self worth that you find a scapegoat as soon as possible.

This is the real reason why most women choose to get married.

Love you and miss you. Your yellow daughter, Laura.

XX

Jamie's Blog
Tuesday 16 February

If I close my eyes and think very hard, I can picture the exact moment when the weekend started to go tits up.

It was on Thursday night, so not actually the weekend proper, but within spitting distance.

It was the fourth Jack Daniels and Coke.

Definitely the fourth one.

Not the third, because I'd had a big meal and there was no way just three Jack Daniels would send me down the slippery slope towards total inebriation - even if they were all doubles.

Nope, it was definitely the fourth.

I should have stopped as the liquid touched my lips, but instead I ploughed on, safe in the knowledge that somebody else was footing the bill. And, much like the top of the first rise you encounter on a rollercoaster, as soon as I'd swallowed a good half of the fourth Jack Daniels, I was cresting the rise and starting the fast plummet down towards Chundertown.

The plummet would end some three hours later, with me hugging the porcelain back at The Dorchester, and wishing I was a thousand miles away from my stomach contents.

It was all Craig's bloody fault.

My literary agent is Scottish.

Mash 'literary agent' and 'Scottish' together and you come up with 'functioning alcoholic'.

The man doesn't need an excuse to throw back enough booze to pickle the average sized human being, so it came as no surprise that he wanted to hold a meeting with me and my editor in a London restaurant famous for its enormous selection of alcoholic beverages.

Having known Craig for two years, I go to the meeting absolutely determined to stay sober for once. I do not want a repeat of the *belly-dancing incident*, no matter how much it made Laura laugh at the time.

Also, our editor Imogen is going to be there, and while I have a close enough relationship with Craig that I don't care if he sees me belly dancing on a table, the same cannot be said for Imogen. She's a nice woman, but is strictly all business, all of the time.

This is exemplified by the fact that when I reach the restaurant, she is already seated and waiting.

For once I'm actually on time, a fact I would be more proud of, had I been the first to arrive.

'Evening Imogen,' I say as I sit down in the plush leather booth by one of the arched windows that looks out onto the West London nightlife.

'Hello Jamie,' she replies with a tight smile. 'Did you get the email about the orphans I mentioned?'

For a moment I'm completely confused. Is Imogen asking me to contribute to some sort of charity effort? Or does she actually want me to adopt a couple of Sudanese refugees? I know Laura and I are doing alright these days, but I'm not sure Poppy would take well to -

Then my brain kicks into gear and I realise that Imogen is talking about a typesetting term for books, where the first line of a paragraph begins at the bottom of the page and looks a bit untidy. 'Yeah, yeah I got it. Tell them the changes are all fine with Laura and me.'

'Excellent,' she beams. You can tell that the world is a happy place for Imogen when people don't put up much of an argument.

'Have you been here before?' I ask, wanting to steer the conversation away from typesetting issues before my eyes glaze over - as they are wont to do in such circumstances.

'No. This is a first for me. You?'

If Imogen knew me well, she wouldn't have to ask that question. The chances of finding Jamie Newman in a restaurant called *Maruga* - famous for its enormously overpriced steak, aforementioned alcohol selection, and preponderance for attracting upper middle class twats by the thousand - are usually non-existent. This is not a pond I am comfortable swimming in. But Craig's footing the bill tonight, so he gets to decide where we eat, I suppose. When he gets here, I'll have to ask him what *Maruga* means. I'm fairly sure it's the name of one of my old He-Man action figures, but I can't see them naming a plush London steakhouse after him, no matter how many points of articulation he had.

Speak of the devil, and he shall appear.

You can always tell when Craig has entered the room, even if you're sat facing the wall with headphones on.

'I'm sat with them!' he roars at the maître d from the doorway. 'Those two over there!' he adds, pointing right at us. 'The table's booked under the surname Chambers!' You'd be forgiven for thinking that the maître d was either hard of hearing or foreign, given how loudly Craig is talking at him. Neither is the case though. The guy seems to be able to hear perfectly well, and his nametag says Brian.

Brian knows better than to engage with this Scots madman any longer than is necessary, and allows him past.

As Craig weaves his way towards Imogen and I, I can't help but notice how he seems drawn to the bar like a small planetoid caught in the gravity well of a passing black hole. People sitting at other tables shrink back a little as Craig passes them. He is six foot two and looks like he can toss three cabers at once. If he hadn't decided on a career in literature, a job as the model for the bloke on the shortcake tins would have been a no-brainer.

'Evening you two!' he says as he reaches us. Thankfully for our eardrums, he's managed to modulate the volume of his voice a touch. Off comes his black trench coat with a flourish, and before you know it Craig is sat next to me with the drinks menu in hand. 'Have you not ordered any booze yet?'

'Er, no.' Imogen replies. 'We were waiting for you.'

Craig waves a hand. 'Ah, you silly buggers. Never wait for a drink, that's what I always say.' He looks across the restaurant to a likely looking waitress. 'Hey love! Can you come over here and get us some drinks?!'

I cringe in my seat. The last time I tried to order a waitress over like that I ended up with minty discharge and utter humiliation. I simply don't have the build or demeanour to get away with it. Craig, on the other hand, channels a mixture of Sean Connery and Frankie Boyle on a good day, so he most definitely can.

'What would you both like?' he asks as the slightly stunned waitress makes her way over, in much the same manner as a puppy approaching a fully grown dog.

'A lime and soda water for me,' Imogen replies, eliciting the merest raise of a Craig Chambers eyebrow.

'I'll have a Diet Coke,' I say in a rather meek voice.

'You what?!' Craig responds, eyes narrowing.

'I mean I'll have a Jack Daniels and Coke,' I say with a squeak.

'A double?'

'Yes?'

'Good man!'

Look, I know I sound pretty pathetic. You don't have to tell me. This is simply what happens when I'm confronted with males who are considerably more alpha than me. The unintended emasculation would bother me a lot more, were it not for the fact that Craig has secured Laura and I several lucrative publishing contracts, no doubt partly due to his explosive personality. There's every chance he just turns up at the publishers door and shouts at them until they agree to print the bloody book. I don't think he negotiates, so much as scares his opponent into submission.

I'm not complaining though. If my bank balance likes Craig Chambers, then I bloody well do too.

…even if it means drinking a double shot of Tennessee whisky before I've even had so much as a starter.

Fast forward about an hour and a half and we rejoin Jamie Newman just as that fourth double hits his stomach. It has followed garlic mushrooms for starters, eight ounces of fillet steak for main, and a chocolate brownie for pudding that was so sweet, I could almost feel the diabetes fairy tapping me on the back and coughing politely in my ear to get my attention. You'd think that lot would soak all the alcohol up.

Nope. Nothing could be further from the truth.

Imogen had a tuna niçoise salad and some balled melon, while Craig basically ate everything else on the menu.

He has also drunk seven large measures of Glen Fiddich - but appears to be only mildly inebriated when compared to me.

I know I'm in trouble when the waitress brings around the coffee menu and it takes me a good twenty seconds before I can focus my eyes on it.

'So Jamie, how are you feeling about tomorrow night? Looking forward to it?' Imogen asks. Thus far this evening the conversation has largely been around the subjects of contract wording, production deadlines, marketing strategies, and other such dry topics, so I'm quite surprised to hear her come out with a question that's actually about such a squishy, non-business thing like *feelings*.

'Hmmmm?' I respond, my voice inexplicably rising in register at the end like a swanee whistle.

'The book launch? Tomorrow night?'

'Oh yes! Yes! I am... I am... '

I am what? Happy about it? Terrified? Lackadaisical? Insouciant? Borderline psychotic?

I leave the response hanging in the air, because if nothing else, I am far too fucking drunk to form a coherent sentence.

'He's really looking forward to it. Ain't you Jamie?' Craig interjects, and slaps me on the back with one broad hand. Such is the size of Craig's hand, and such is the strength of his friendly slap that I emit a loud burp in much the same manner as a newborn baby.

Imogen looks horrified, and even Craig's eyes widen under their bushy dark eyebrows. 'Better out than in, son!' he opines with a roar of laughter.

Needless to say I am disgusted with myself, even in my current foggy state of mind. Burping at the dinner table is reserved for when you're five years old or on a stag do. It is not something you do in a dinner meeting with two people you're in business with. It's just not bloody professional.

The publishing industry is also a very small world, and I'm sure before the week is out, everyone in it will know that Jamie Newman is a galloping drunkard, with the table manners of a pig.

Some may argue that this would just make me like every other writer in the world, but that is beside the point.

I am hugely embarrassed, and want to leave as swiftly as possible.

Craig has other ideas though, and orders me an Irish whisky - the complete and total bastard that he is.

I sip this like it's hot brown poison, until the clock hits 10pm.

'Well, this has been a lovely evening,' Imogen lies - unless she has a penchant for watching two men get shit-faced over medium rare cow parts. 'But I'm due in the office tomorrow at 8am, so had better be going.'

I take this as my opportunity to leave as well. 'Yes! I agree. I'd like to go get some sleep as I have to... '

Dammit!

I don't have *anywhere* to be tomorrow! I'm a sodding *writer*. Craig can quite comfortably keep me here until three in the morning, pumping booze into me, and I have absolutely no excuse to get out of it, other than the fact I'm a total lightweight.

'No problem, Imogen. It was nice to see you again,' says Craig, a man still capable of being perfectly charming even with a bottle of 15 year old single malt sloshing around in his guts. Bastard!

He rises elegantly from his seat.

I try to follow suit, managing to clout my knee on the bottom of the table as I do so. 'Ow! Fuckery biggins!' I cry in pain. I don't usually borrow any of Laura's curses. It only tends to happen when I'm blind drunk and not feeling all that creative.

'Are you alright?' Imogen asks.

'Yes,' I wave off her concern with a limp waggle of my wrist. 'I'll be fine. Absolutely fine. Fiiiiiiine.' In an effort to brush off my latest act of drunken clumsiness I throw my arms open wide and move towards her. 'Now, come here and give us a kiss.'

What?

Fucking WHAT?

Did I really just ask my editor - a woman I have only ever known in an entirely professional capacity - to give me a ruddy *kiss*? Like we're long lost relatives, or best buddies who won't be seeing each other for a year, because one is travelling in the Orient?

The faux pas is *enormous*. A ten story, luxury faux pas, with 24 hour room service. It's the Dorchester Hotel of faux pas.

I stand there with arms outstretched, ready to give Imogen a sweaty hug and kiss. In my ramshackle, drunken state I look less like a person offering their goodbyes, and more like an extra from The Walking Dead going in for his lunch.

Poor Imogen doesn't know what the hell to do. I can see it on her face. On the one hand, I'm sure she has no desire to embrace me, if for no other reason than it will bring her closer to my apocalyptic breath. On the other though, I am one of Watermill Publishing's more successful authors, and I'm sure employees of the company are encouraged to be *nice* to successful authors, no matter how badly they're behaving.

Self preservation gives way to the desire to keep seeing a paycheck, and Imogen reluctantly moves forward and puts one awkward arm around my shoulder. Her worried face hovers just in front of mine, one cheek proffered in my direction.

I have to go through with it now, don't I? If I reject her sacrifice, it will just make things ten times worse. I pucker up my lips and go in for a peck on her cheek. Sadly, I'm so bastard drunk, I stumble to the left as I do so, and end up planting the kiss on Imogen's ear. She recoils in barely concealed disgust. 'Okay then!' she says in a high-pitched tone. 'I'll be off now! Goodnight Jamie! Goodnight Craig!'

The poor woman can't move through the busy throng of Maruga customers quick enough. I watch her go with bleary-eyed regret, knowing full well that I will be getting a new editor soon.

I look back to Craig, to discover that he is staring at me in wide-eyed Scottish horror.

'Oh boy, Jamie. Oh boy!' He roars with laughter and sits back down. 'You know, I've read all your books and thought you might have been exaggerating about the stuff that happens to you, but you bloody weren't, were you?'

I slump back into my seat, rubbing my knee as I do. 'Nope,' I reply in a forlorn voice. 'If anything I've underplayed quite a lot of stuff.' A thought occurs. 'At least I didn't try any belly dancing this time.'

This sends Craig off into a gale of Highland laughter. Sadly, this also draws the attention of our waitress for the evening, who comes over to see if there's anything else we'd like. I would like to order a taxi, a bottle of Tramadol and a loaded shotgun, but Craig unfortunately gets to her first and orders us both a nightcap. I start to protest... but give up before I've even got my mouth halfway open. There is no possible way on Earth that Craig will let me leave tonight without consuming at least one Bailey's Irish Cream liqueur.

'Bottoms up, Jamie!' he exults, and throws the entire glass of creamy liquid back in one go. 'Here's to your book launch tomorrow!'

Oh yes. That's right, isn't it? This is *Thursday* night, and *Friday* night is the most important night I've had in a long time. Of course, the perfect preparation for it is to get captain bladdered the night before and kiss your editor's earlobe.

I throw the Bailey's down my throat with resignation and feebly hold the empty glass up. 'Yay,' I say in an equally feeble voice.

'What's the matter? You don't think it'll go well?' Craig asks.

'Well Craig, well, the thing is... the thing... the thing is... '

The thing is I'm absolutely busting for a piss. I have no idea how I feel about the book launch, but I do know that if I don't get to a toilet soon, the crotch of my trousers will be a lot darker and wetter. 'I need a wee,' I tell Craig. I could have said 'slash' or 'piss', either would have been more alpha, but as I think I've already established, around Craig I am most definitely beta, so what's the point in trying to prove otherwise?

I rise from the table - managing to avoid another knee related injury this time - and stumble off in the general direction of where I think the toilets are. Having never been to this restaurant before I have absolutely *no* idea where the toilets are located however. I have to be rescued from trying to take a piss in the kitchen by a passing waitress, who points me in the direction of where the facilities actually are - right back across the other side of Maruga, behind where Craig and I are sat.

As I shamble past my agent again, I give him a little wave. He responds with the kind of unsure smile you'd usually see someone make when his dog starts chewing on its own foot.

In the toilet I discover a row of clean white urinals... and blessed relief.

I'm halfway done, when a short, fat little man of about 50 comes in, and stands a couple of urinals down from me. I ignore him completely of course, as is right and proper.

I can hear him start to urinate too, so he's obviously not a man who suffers from the legendary stage fright. I return to contemplating the wall in front of me, which is decorated in an attractive aqua marine marble effect that I think would look lovely in the bathroom back home.

'Excuse me?' says my fellow urinator.

I turn my head slowly in his direction. 'I'm sorry? Were you talking to me?' I ask, unable to believe that this could be the case. Men simply don't have conversations at urinals. It is most definitely not right and proper.

'Yes. Sorry to interrupt, but you're not the fellow who writes those books, are you? Only you look like him. You were on Lorraine a couple of weeks ago with your wife.'

Oh good bloody grief.

'Um...'

There are two ways I can handle this. I can feign ignorance. After all, I'm a bloody author, not Tom Cruise. My books are the things people recognise, not my face. I can lie, and pretend I don't know what the fat little fella is on about. Or, I can fess up and hope he doesn't want to engage me in a lengthy conversation about grammatical syntax and character development.

I'm too sodding drunk to lie convincingly, so opt for the latter. 'Yeah... that's me. The book writing bloke. On Lorraine with m' wife.'

I knew agreeing to appear on TV was a mistake that would bite me on the arse - I just wasn't expecting it to happen at a urinal.

'I thought so!' my new friend says, as he finishes up and zips his fly.

The man has the good courtesy to let me do the same, before thrusting out his hand. 'My wife and I are big fans of your work,' he says.

Now then...

We have what might be considered a 'social situation' here. One where hygiene plays an important part.

When I was much, much younger and could handle my drink better, I briefly dated a girl called Odette, who was French, and modelled herself on Avril Lavigne. About all I can remember of Odette was her penchant for woollen beanies, wearing too much eyeliner, and energetic hand jobs. She always insisted on washing her hand afterwards though, for fear of walking around for the rest of the evening with what she called 'willy fingers'.

Odette would also refuse to go anywhere near any boys who had just come out of the toilet, unless they could prove to her that they'd washed their hands. Odette neither approved of, nor tolerated willy fingers to any degree.

If she were in my position now, she'd turn white with horror.

This man - this *stranger* - is asking me to shake his hand, even though he undoubtedly suffers from first degree willy fingers, having only just popped his gentleman back into his trousers.

What's worse is that I am *also* suffering from chronic willy fingers, having only just done the same thing.

I can either take the bull by the horns - and the man by the willy fingers - or insist that we both go wash our hands first.

This is a fan of my books, though. I have no idea how many of those I've actually got, so I make it a goal in life to never offend or upset one, just in case it starts a chain reaction that ends in my complete and utter failure. This sounds totally irrational I know, but there's a streak of irrationality in any writer if you peel back enough layers.

And fuck it, I'm pissed anyway. A light case of willy fingers shouldn't be too much of an issue for a man well into his cups like I am.

'Pleased to meet you,' I say, and take the man's hand with barely a grimace.

'And you!' he replies with enthusiasm, pumping my hand up and down in his own. 'The name's William Walker. Of course I already know yours, Mr Newman!'

William Walker.

William 'Willy Fingers' Walker.

It's so utterly perfect; I wish I'd written it in a book.

Fuck it, maybe I will.

'Well, as I said, it's nice to meet you Willy... I mean William.'

Now please let go of my hand so I can wash it.

Thankfully he does so, allowing me to scuttle over to the sink. 'Can I get a picture?' Willy Fingers asks before I can start to wash my hands. He produces an iPhone from his pocket and gives me an expectant smile.

Oh, *fabulous*. Now I get to have a selfie taken with a man whose penis I've technically just touched by association. My eyes are also bloodshot from all the booze Craig has pumped into me, and my hair is thoroughly dishevelled for much the same reason.

But never upset a punter, right?

I attempt to look happy for the picture, which is very difficult, given that I've been plagued with two man willy fingers for a good half minute now. William has no problem looking happy, and gives it his best Cheshire Cat as the flash goes off.

'Thank you so much, Jamie!' he tells me. 'My wife will be amazed when I tell her!'

My wife will be rolling in the aisles mate, so I think you'll get the better end of the bargain on that one. 'Pleasure,' I tell him with a drunken slur.

'I won't disturb you any longer,' Willy Fingers says, before making his way back out of the toilets, leaving me to ponder what the hell just happened.

I give my hands a thorough wash, and shamble back to the table, where Craig is merrily making his way through another Glen Fiddich on the rocks.

'Feeling better there, are you?' he asks, swilling the ice around in the glass.

I unconsciously look down at my hands for a second. 'I think so.' I then glance at my watch and decide it's time to make a stand. 'Craig, it's been a lovely evening but I want to... want to get a good night's sleep before t'm'rrw.'

'Ah, you must have time for a last nifter?'

I hold up an unsteady hand. 'No. No. Thank you. No. No. I'm quite fine. Quite, quite fine.'

'Fair enough! I'll get the bill, and we'll get out of here.'

I am *amazed*. Craig has capitulated. And all I needed to do was get stinking drunk to be brave enough to stand up to him. Given that the whole reason for standing up to him was so that I *didn't* get stinking drunk, it's a bit of a moot point, but we'll try to ignore that fact, and hold on to the last sliver of pride that wasn't washed away with the willy fingers.

London when you're shitfaced is an odd place. In any normal town, by the time you reach that state, the evening is usually winding down, and most people are going home. Not in the capital though. It's quite possible to drink yourself into a stupor, and still be able to keep on drinking well into the early hours.

I don't think I'd have the stamina to live here. I don't know what would give out first, my heart or my liver. I can understand why local people use cocaine. You need the bloody stuff just to get to last orders.

The cab pulls up to The Dorchester Hotel, and the door is opened by a doorman who looks positively delighted to be greeting a blind drunkard at just gone 10.30 on a Thursday night. I don't quite fall flat on my face as I get out of the car, but it's a close run thing.

'G'night Craiginin,' I say to my agent from the kerb. He chuckles and waves to me, before the doorman shuts the car door. We both watch the cab speed away into the West London night.

I turn and look at the doorman with a wide-eyed expression of amusement. 'Thas a very nice peaked cap you have there, my friend.'

'Thank you, sir.'

'Can I have a go on it?'

'I don't think so, sir.'

'Are you sure? I think I'd look smashin'. '

'Shall we get you to your room, sir?'

'Thas probably a good idea. This is after all, the Dorchesser 'otel. The las' thing you want is Jamie Newmanan stinking up the place, eh?'

'Let me get the door for you sir.'

'Than' you, my cappy friend. Thas very, very kin' of you.'

I stumble through the large doorway and am forced to shield my eyes from the scorching bright lights inside. It's not actually scorching in the slightest, but I find rampant inebriation brings out the worst in my photosensitivity.

At the counter, the young blonde haired concierge sees me coming and steals himself. 'Good evening, sir.'

'G'd evenin.' I fumble around in the back pocket of my trousers for a good four and a half hours (at least I'm sure that's what it felt like to him), before producing my room key card. I hold the mighty plastic oblong aloft in one proud hand. 'Now then! Can you please tell me what room I am in? I have to confess, I'm a little forget... forgetful this evenin'.'

'What's your name, sir?'

'What?' I don't really want to give him my name. It's one thing to be an anonymous drunkard standing in the foyer of one of the most expensive hotels in the country, it's quite another to have your identity known as you do so. 'Can't you jus' run this thing through the compuper?' I giggle expansively. 'Compuper. I said compuper didn' I?'

'You did, sir.'

'Iss not a compuper is it?'

'No sir.'

No sir! It's a compuTER!'

'That's right sir.'

I lean on the counter. 'You know, you're very good at remainin' polite when you're talkin' to a pissed twat. Well done you!'

'Thank you, sir. We receive extensive training. I will still need your name, sir.'

'Alright Charlie, keep your hair on.' The guy's nametag reads Serge, but he looks like a Charlie to me, so fuck it. 'My name's Jamie Newman.' So that's it, my name is out of the bag, and Charlie here will go off and tell all his friends how much of a drunk that writer bloke is.

I do have a cunning plan though, to throw him off the scent. 'Yes, my name is Jamie Newmananan, but I most certainly do NOT write books!'

'Is that right, Mr Newman?'

'It is! The name is a comple' coindicince... a comple' cosindidence... a comple' cosidernence. It's not me.'

'Of course, Mr Newman. You're staying in room 216, with your wife I believe.' One of his eyebrows imperceptibly arches as he says this. I get his meaning, even in my shambolic state.

I tap my nose. 'She's no' comin' until t'm'rr'w Charlie. Everythin' is absoluley fine.'

'I'm delighted to hear it.' Serge holds a hand out. 'The elevators are that way, Mr Newman. Have a good night.'

'Than' you Charlie. I certainly will. G'dnight to you too.'

Luckily, I manage to resist the temptation to give Serge's earlobe a kiss, and walk my way cautiously over to the lift.

A mere three quarters of an hour later, I open the door to my hotel room. I would explain why it took me three quarters of an hour to get there, but I can't remember for the life of me. There may have been a pot plant involved.

Precisely thirty two seconds after that, I am fast asleep on the bed, with my face buried in the pillow.

I stay that way until 4 in the morning, when the chunder fairy pays me a visit and I have to go and speak to God on the porcelain telephone for half an hour.

The morning dawns bright, sunny... and like Hell on Earth.

My eyeballs are stuck together, my tongue is 93% carpet, my head throbs like a hammered thumb.

This is not a hangover, this is a hangallthewayaroundandbackagain.

Other than to secure a glass of cool refreshing water - a process which takes me a good ten minutes - I don't stir from my comatose state until midday. I would probably still be lying there now, were it not for the phone call from my glorious wife, checking up on me.

'So... hungover then?' she asks, hearing my tone of voice. Shame fills every pore. I'd promised Laura I'd be a good boy.

'No! I feel fine sweetheart!' I try to say as brightly as possible. The charade might have worked, were it not for the fact that I sound like Barry White after smoking a packet of menthols. 'I'm just off down the gym in a minute!'

The bark of laughter that comes down the phone is so loud, I have to move the earpiece away from my ear for a moment. 'Okay Jamie,' Laura chuckles. 'You have fun at the *gym,* and I'll see you this evening.'

I decide not to press my luck. 'Okay. What have you got planned for the afternoon?'

'Oh, not much. Not much at all,' Laura responds, with a mumble that lets me know she's doing something she doesn't want to talk about. I've been with my wife for a long time now, so I can tell from her tone that the thing she doesn't want to talk about is quite, quite embarrassing. I would get into it more, but I have to go and shave the carpet off my tongue before braving lunch somewhere.

I say goodbye to Laura, get off the bed... and try my hardest to start functioning like a normal human being. I have a book launch tonight, so I'd better at least be able to fake it for a few hours.

The rest of the day goes by in something of a haze, thanks to a heady combination of Anadin Extra and strong, hot coffee from the nearest Costa. In fact, the coffee is doing me so much good that by about 5pm I am able to sit in the cafe itself, slowly digesting a slice of banana bread while I make my way through the fifth latte of the day. This takes me through to six, when I know Laura is arriving at the hotel, so I order another coffee and amble back to The Dorchester with caffeine flowing satisfyingly through my veins as I do so. My stupendous headache has even softened to a dull thud at the back of my head - a marked improvement from earlier in the day.

I am even able to raise a smile at the prospect of seeing Laura as I swipe the room key card to number 216.

'Oh fuckery biggins!' I hear Laura scream from inside the room. My hand pauses ever so briefly on the door handle.

If you back away now son, you can be at Heathrow Airport in an hour, and on a plane to Belize in two, my cowardly brain tells me.

Luckily for my continued existence, my hand is having none of it, and opens the door to see what awaits me inside.

'Hey baby,' I say as cheerfully as possible. 'Er... are you okay? I hope you managed to get checked in alri - '

I spot Laura's hunched form in the bathroom doorway and the words die on my lips. Then I see the broken table lamp, and what looks disturbingly like lumps of warm poo sliding down the wall behind it. 'What the hell's going on?' I ask, looking back at my wife, who has moved towards me, so that I can see her face properly.

Laura is yellow.

Laura is *really, really* yellow.

Why is Laura yellow?

...

Hang on.

Is she yellow?

Is she *actually* yellow? Or is this hangover worse than I thought?

I've never heard of unchecked alcohol consumption causing hallucinations like this, but I suppose it's possible.

'Why is your face yellow?' I ask, hesitantly. If she says 'what are you talking about?' in response, I'd best be making my way to the nearest casualty department.

Laura doesn't come out with this, but what she does say is so, so much *worse*.

'You! This is all *your* fault!' she shrieks, one finger pointing at my poor, hungover face.

'What the hell have I done?' I bite back loudly, setting off the headache again.

'You... you bought me that bloody fake tan!!'

'What?!' I say in utter confusion.

I don't get a follow up answer. Laura points a shaking finger at me for a moment, before storming back into the bathroom, slamming the door in my face as she does so.

In a mere thirty seconds, my world has gone from gentle, caffeine soaked calm, to violent, blood pumping confusion.

I would be surprised by this rapid turn of events, but then I've been married for nearly ten years now, so it's pretty much par for the course.

Laura's Diary
Wednesday, February 17th

Dear Mum,

So, let's recap: I am an idiot, and my husband is an alcoholic. My face is bright yellow, his is pale grey - and both have to show themselves at a party in less than an hour, to celebrate the launch of a book neither of us look remotely capable of writing.
Excellent.

'It's not that bad, baby,' Jamie tells me, as he pops two more Anadin into his mouth and finishes doing up his tie. I am once again struck with sublime jealousy that he can be ready for a night out in under five minutes, even with a perishing hangover.

'Really?' I reply, not believing a bloody word.

'No! In a certain light you can hardly tell your skin is a bit... er... *lemony.*'

'In a certain light, eh?'

'Yeah. In a certain light.'

'Would that 'certain light' be not very much light *at all*, Jamie? Possibly even *no* light? Possibly pitch *fucking* black?'

Jamie grimaces. There is simply no good way out of this conversation for him, and he knows it. 'Honestly, it's not that bad...'

He is saved from having to lie anymore by his phone going off. He answers, and listens to what the person on the other end is saying for a few moments. 'Okay mate,' he replies. 'We'll be down shortly.'

Jamie ends the call, and looks back at me with mild fear in his eyes. 'The car's here, sweet. We kind of have to go?'

'Yes! Yes!' I say, flapping my hands at him. 'Just let me have one more look in the mirror.'

Which, no matter how hard I wish it, is unable to show me anything other than a woman in her late thirties with what looks like a severe case of jaundice.

She does look dynamite in the dark blue gown and bolero though. Even her knobbly knees are behaving themselves, hidden as they are behind the pair of opaque tights she was lucky enough to pick up in Next last weekend.

Maybe, just *maybe*, these elements will detract from the colour of my skin enough for people not to notice it.

Hah! Who am I kidding?

With one last despairing sigh, I attempt to rearrange my face into something resembling the appearance of a good mood. 'Come on then, husband of mine. Let's go hob with the nobs.'

Jamie takes my arm and we leave the safe confines of the Dorchester hotel room, our yellow and grey faces now on display for the world to see.

The first person out of the seven billion on this planet to notice my little issue is Kyle the chauffeur.

'Good evening, Mr and Mrs Newman. You both look lovel - you both look very nice. Looking forward to the party?'

He's good, but he's not *that* good. The shift from 'lovely' to 'very nice' is a self evident downgrade, one that not even a practiced chauffeur can hide. 'Yes, we are!' Jamie says a little too brightly.

Kyle's eyes linger on my face just a bit longer than they need to. 'Let me get the door for you, Mrs Newman,' he eventually says.

'Thanks,' I say drily and get into the car with some relief. In here, for the next twenty minutes at least, no-one will be able to see what I look like. Except Kyle in his rear view mirror of course, which he starts to glance into as soon as we've left the kerb outside The Dorchester. The look on his face is one of mild befuddlement.

I take Jamie's hand. 'I don't think I can do this. I look ridiculous.'

'No you don't. You look fine.'

He's lying, but the soothing tone of his voice takes the edge off a bit.

By the time we reach Watermill Publishing's Soho offices, I'm relatively calm, having spent the interim period sat in the back of the car, whispering motivational phrases under my breath to psyche myself up. Most of these consist of a load of old blather from those stupid posters - like it not mattering what's on the surface, it's the person inside that counts; or, if you act like you're confident, then you'll *be* confident.

Unfortunately I can't think of one that goes: it doesn't matter how much of a yellow clown face you have, you still have a heart of gold, and don't let anyone tell you otherwise. But then we arrive, so there's no more time to mentally prepare myself anyway.

Kyle gets my car door again, assiduously not looking at my face as he does so.

The second person to spot my problem is the girl at the reception desk of Watermill Publishing. I walk towards her across the glass and marble floored atrium, just waiting for her to look up and notice us coming.

When she does I am treated to an expression that I'll have to get used to over the next few hours. There's a brief look of polite recognition, followed by a creasing of the forehead in confusion, rapidly followed by wide-eyed surprise when she realises that the person she's talking to is quite clearly a looney. Finally, we get a smattering of guilt, as she realises that I probably have something wrong with me and she shouldn't be judging too harshly.

'Good evening, Mr and Mrs Newman,' the girl says, clearly having been told we were coming. 'The party is being held in our conference lounge on the seventh floor. I'll sign you in. If you'd just like to take the lift over to your left, you'll be greeted when you arrive.'

'Thank you Kate,' Jamie says, and I whip my head around to look at him. I'm not a jealous woman, but the receptionist is in her mid-twenties and annoyingly pretty. She doesn't look like Pacman either, so the fact that my husband is on first name terms with her raises the suspicion monster from its deep slumber.

'Kate, eh?' I say to him as we cross to the lift.

Jamie catches sight of my expression and sighs. 'She's a big fan of the books, dear. I know her name because she had me sign her copy of Love From Both Sides yesterday.'

My irrational jealous is immediately quelled. Kathy has gone from being a potential love rival who needs her eyes clawing out, to a valuable fan who I love and adore, all in the space of one short explanatory sentence.

In the lift, my nerves take hold again. People are going to laugh at me. They may even point when my back is turned. From now on I shall be known as Laura 'Pacman' Newman, the yellow faced maniac who writes romantic comedies with her long suffering alcoholic husband.

'Seriously Jamie, I don't think I can do this. It's going to be far too embarrassing!'

'You'll be okay,' he disagrees. 'We'll both be okay.'

'*Both?*'

'Well, yeah. I am feeling pretty rough, sweetheart.'

'Don't you dare try to compare my yellowness with your self-inflicted hangover, Jamie Newman,' I chide, and squeeze his hand tightly. 'Oh, think of something to get us out of this! I can't do it!'

But it's too late. The lift is slowing, and any second now the doors will go ping.

Jamie looks at me for a moment, then his eyes widen. 'I've thought of something!'

Oh God, no. *Oh no, no, no, no.*

When Jamie Newman 'thinks of something' it's usually time to batten down the hatches and prepare for the worst.

'Jamie, I don't think you can do anyth - '

Ping!

Too late!

The lift door opens on a cool, brightly lit marble floored corridor. Off to the left is a large glass door with Watermill Publishing's logo etched into it. Next to the door is a standee of the cover for Love Under Different Skies. Beyond both is a throng of smartly dressed people, all awaiting our arrival. My stress levels rocket.

'Stay here for a moment,' Jamie tells me.

'Why?'

He waves a hand at me as he leaves the lift. 'Just stay here. Trust me!'

My knobbly knees start to quiver. It's bad enough when Jamie says he has an idea, the fact that he's now expecting me to trust him as well is a sure fire sign that my life is about to take a turn for the idiotic.

I stand still in the lift for a good minute or so, willing my knees to stop knocking, and my face to stop being so yellow. Neither prayer is successful.

Suddenly, the brightly lit corridor beyond the lift dims slightly, in a very eerie fashion. I breathe a sigh of relief. Satan has obviously decided to come and claim me as one of his own, saving me the yellow faced humiliation I am about to endure.

It's not Beelzebub who enters the lift though, it's my smug looking husband. Mind you, there's every chance that if Lucifer did decide to pay me a visit, there would certainly be no more terrifying a visage to use than Jamie Newman looking smug and self satisfied.

I am in a *lot* of trouble.

'Right! I've sorted it,' he says with a grin, and goes to take my hand. 'Come on, everything's fine.'

I refuse the proffered hand and narrow my eyes. 'What have you done, Jamie? Why have the lights gone down?'

The smug grin increases in smugness by three hundred and twenty eight percent. 'Photophobia.'

'What?'

'*Photophobia.* That's what you've got.'

'Have I?' I reply in complete confusion.

'Yeah! It's when you're sensitive to light. I just told everyone that you're suffering with it at the moment, and asked that the lights be lowered so it doesn't hurt you. I figured that in the low light, no-one will be able to see that your face is yellow, and even if they do spot it, they'll put it down to light sensitivity.'

I stand there for a moment digesting this.

I am completely dumbfounded.

It's *brilliant.*

My husband has actually come up with a fantastic and plausible way to hide my yellow face, without causing me embarrassment or personal injury.

This must be some kind of miracle.

I look at the roof of the lift, expecting choirs of heavenly angels to descend any second now to serenade us both.

'You're surprised, aren't you?' Jamie says knowingly.

'Hmmm?' I say in wonder.

'You're amazed that I've come up with such a good plan.'

'Well, yes Jamie. Yes, I am. You're normally an idiot.'

His face crumples. 'That's a bit harsh.'

The look of wonder is replaced by ire. 'So is telling two Australian hippies that I can't have a proper shit in their house!' I still haven't quite let that one go.

Jamie has the good grace to look sheepish. 'Ah. Good point.' He clears his throat. 'Shall we get going?'

I take his hand. 'Yes, we shall. And thank you, sweetheart. I feel a bit better now.'

The old Newman charm makes a triumphant return as Jamie smiles, kisses me gently on the cheek and says 'My pleasure, baby. Anything for you.'

I've been married to this idiot for a long time now, and I still love the fact his kisses can make my heart flutter.

Jamie leads me out into the corridor and through the large glass door, where we are greeted by a hundred happy looking individuals.

At least I think they're happy. In the relative gloom I can't quite make out their facial expressions, but I'm going to be positive here and assume that they are pleased to see us.

Cringingly, we then receive a short round of applause from everyone gathered. The enthusiasm of the clapping varies, according to how much money the individual is making from our book sales. I see our agent Craig smacking his hands together with great aplomb, while several others at the back of the crowd are showing far less vigour. I can only assume that they are the poor schmucks who actually have to do all the work around here, and would much rather be at home right now watching Netflix.

Thankfully, this squirm inducing exercise is brought to a halt when we are approached by Craig, and Peter Hincham, the head of the company. Hincham is the kind of man who looks like he should be in a Hugh Grant comedy. Not one of the main cast you understand, he's a bit too non-descript for that. But there is no doubt in my mind that he'd provide a cracking cameo as the eccentric uncle, or the kindly antique store owner who tells the hero which direction the love of his life has just run off in.

You probably don't need any more description of Peter Hincham than that, but just in case - he has wavy grey hair, is wearing a maroon waistcoat underneath his Hugo Boss suit, and his fingers are stained with forty years of heavy tobacco usage. You couldn't get a man more different from our towering agent Craig, who beams magnificently as he reaches us.

'Glad you're here at last!' he booms, then contrives to look concerned. 'Hope you're not feeling too bad, Laura.'

I affect a slightly pained squint. In for a penny, in for a pound, as they say. 'No, no. It's okay. I just can't stand in bright lights for too long.' I hold up a hand to the dim arc sodium strip lights above our head, shielding my eyes slightly. I'm going comprehensively overboard here, but what can I say? I'm getting a flair for melodrama in my old age.

'Pleased to hear it!' Peter Hincham chimes in. 'We would have hated for you to miss the event Laura. You are, after all, the star of the show!'

Flattery will probably get you somewhere Peter, but not quite as far as you'd like, I'm sure.

It is at this moment that the most important person in the entire building approaches me... the guy with the plate of drinks. I swiftly grab a glass of white wine, and try my very best to hide myself completely behind it. Jamie blanches as soon as he sees the arranged alcoholic beverages. 'Have you got any orange juice?' he asks, and is delighted when a girl enters from stage left carrying a plate of softies.

'All ready to do a little speech guys?' Peter asks.

'Sorry, what?' I reply, nearly spitting out my wine.

'A speech? I did ask Jamie if it was okay...' Peter replies, looking to my husband for affirmation.

Jamie's lips purse, and all the good, hard work he accomplished with the photophobia has now flown merrily out the window, thanks to the fact that he has neglected to tell me that we have to stand in front of this lot and speak.

'Jamie, should you have told me about this, do you think?' I hiss under my breath.

'Er... um... ah... '

Oh, for fuck's sake.

Craig, who may be a bull in a china shop 99% of the time, is still capable of tact and diplomacy when necessary. 'Never mind, Laura,' he says, putting one arm around my shoulder. 'I'm sure Jamie can do the speaking for the both of you, if you'd like him to.'

'I can?' my husband responds with a slight whine.

'Yes. Yes, *you* can Jamie.' I tell him firmly.

'Great!' Peter exclaims and rubs his hands together. 'Thank you very much.' He cranes his head over one shoulder, and looks over to where a contingent of small Oriental men are standing near the drinks table. One tiny woman is also with them, nursing a small glass of water and pretending to look interested in what's going on. 'We've got some important folk here this evening. Mr Sakamura is here from Rokuko Holdings.'

Peter says this as if it's meant to mean anything to us.

'Who's that?' Jamie enquires, peering through the gloom.

'Rokuko have just bought a large stake in Watermill Publishing. Mr Sakamura is very excited by his investment. He's even brought his wife along tonight, which just goes to show how proud he is,' Peter explains. 'His money couldn't have come at a better time, what with the economic climate, and the whole ebook thing... ' he trails off, as if talking about it gives him physical pain.

'Ah, I see,' Jamie says with a nod. 'Then I'll try my best.'

'Thank you!' Peter responds, genuinely pleased. 'I'll introduce you to him after your speech.' He glances at his watch. 'Speaking of which, shall we get it over and done with so you can enjoy the rest of the evening?'

'Yes please!'

My husband is eager to get things under way. I, however, am not. You see, Jamie may have been volunteered to do the whole of the speech alone, but he is to public speaking what Pol Pot was to the Cambodian tourist trade. I am not looking forward to what comes next.

'If I could have everyone's attention!' Peter calls over the crowd, immediately ending the variety of hushed conversations that were going on in the room. 'Thank you. We're all delighted to be here tonight to celebrate the launch of the third book in the Love series. It's fantastic to have the writers Jamie and Laura Newman here this evening, and I think Jamie would like to say a few words to you all. Jamie?'

Peter moves aside as a small ripple of applause breaks out. Jamie moves forward, and for a moment I think I'm going to avoid embarrassment, but then he reaches out a hand for me to join him. I suppress a growl of discontent, and reluctantly go to stand next to him. I know the lights are low, but I still don't want to be in front of a crowd of onlookers as little miss banana face.

'Hello everyone,' Jamie begins, which is as good a start as any. 'Thanks for coming.' Also fine. 'We're delighted to be here this evening.' A lie, but only a white one. 'Even if I'm a little hungover

---

and Laura has turned into a vampire.' Yep, there we go. Not three sentences in, and Jamie has screwed the pooch already.

There are a couple of uncertain titters from the crowd.

'It's lovely to be here, so we can thank you for coming to launch our book with us.' Okay, that's better again. Let's just hope the references to his drinking problems and my skin issues were just minor aberrations on the smooth path to a successful speech.

'They say you should always picture a crowd naked when you're talking to them,' he continues. 'If you're feeling nervous that is.' Jamie looks at me. 'To be honest with you though, Laura's about the only one here I'd like to see naked!'

Oh, fuck me.

Jamie has decided he's going to be funny. Disaster is imminent.

He points at the girl with the soft drinks. 'And maybe that girl over there, eh? Ha ha!'

Nobody is laughing, least of all the poor bitch Jamie has just singled out for his perverted attentions.

My husband realises that the crowd is not with him on this one, but instead of shutting up, he instead ploughs onwards with this feeble line of comedy. 'I certainly wouldn't want to see old Craig our agent with no clothes on!' My hand goes to my forehead. 'Or anyone here who's fat!' Facepalm. 'Or over fifty!' Double facepalm.

I suppose it was inevitable that I'd have to step in and take over at some point, but you like to think in life that things can change every once in a while. I had hoped that at the age of nearly forty, Jamie would be able to stand in front of a small group of people and make a short, sensible speech without insulting anyone, but it appears that I am comprehensively wrong.

'I'm sorry everyone, my husband gets a bit tongue tied when he has to speak in public,' I smoothly interject. 'Why don't you let me say a few words, *darling*?'

Jamie's left eye twitches a couple of times. 'Yeah... maybe you should. Thanks,' he replies slowly, and hands the floor to me.

'What I think my husband was trying to say,' I start, attempting to polish this turd a bit, 'is that we're very grateful to see you here this evening, and that it feels quite humbling to have all of your support.' This gets me a few appreciative nods, so I know I'm on the right lines. 'While Jamie and I write these books, they wouldn't see the light of day without your hard work, and it's very important that we - '

I'm interrupted by the sudden glare of the overhead lights ratcheting up in intensity by several notches. Everyone in the room is forced to shield their eyes to adjust, as the general ambience goes from the soft gloom of an Italian bistro, to the harsh arc sodium glare of an operating theatre.

While this brings a short and unpleasant wince from everyone gathered, it marks a far darker turn of events for yours truly. The hideous yellowness of my face is now on display for all to see and gawk at. I might as well start charging 50p to come up and have your picture taken with the half banana woman.

What's more, Jamie has of course told everyone that I am suffering from photophobia, so I'd better do something right now to back up the charade, or I'm going to make him look like a liar.

I turn my head away from the lights as swiftly as possible.

This doesn't feel like it's enough to convey how bad my fictional photophobia is, so I also make a hissing noise as I do so. I'm meaning to sound the same way a person does when they put their hand into scalding hot water, but what I actually sound like is Christopher Lee at the end of Dracula, when Peter Cushing pulls the curtain aside to let in the glorious Transylvanian sunlight. I have gone from erudite public speaker, to evil creature of the night in a few split seconds.

Jamie sees what I've done and decides to make the whole thing worse by throwing his arms around me and barking 'will somebody please turn down the lights! My wife!' He screeches this in such a high pitched, tremulous voice that anyone would think my face was melting right off and into the carpet.

'Somebody turn the bloody lights down!' Craig roars, picking up on Jamie's panicked tone.

'Get me to the bloody toilet Jamie,' I whisper to my husband from my hunched position. "And calm the fuck down before somebody calls an ambulance!"

'Sorry! Just trying to sell the illusion!'

'I think you've sold it, bagged the damn thing up, and followed the customer home to watch them insert it. Now get me to the toilet!'

Jamie does as he's told, shielding me from the crowd as we trot swiftly across the room. We hurry down a corridor and I slam the door to the ladies open, disappearing inside without another word, leaving Jamie to handle the concerned partygoers.

The lights in the toilet are pretty bright, but at least I don't have to worry about pretending they are burning my face off. With a sigh of relief, I lean against the long row of marble sinks and take a deep breath.

'Photo *bloody* phobia,' I mumble. 'What a great excuse Jamie,' I admonish to my absent husband. What had seemed like a great idea to begin with, has now turned comprehensively sour, and left me conducting a vampire based pantomime for a hundred publishing people. I turn to the mirrors behind the wash basins and let out a sharp intake of breath as I am confronted once again with just how bloody yellow my face truly is. They had better have lowered the lights out there again, otherwise I'm not coming out until everyone else has left.

The sound of one of the cubicle doors being unlocked makes me jump. From it emerges a small oriental woman, who I remember as the wife of the Japanese fellow who's just bailed out Watermill Publishing. She is wearing a smart black power suit, and looks deadly serious about the entire universe. She regards me quizzically for a second.

'Mrs Newman. I am pleased to meet you,' she says in perfect English.

'Very pleased to meet you too, Mrs... ' I'm going to have to take a punt at it. I just hope I get it right. '...Mrs Sakamura?'

I don't think I pronounce it correctly, but she doesn't take me task on it. 'How are you feeling?' she asks.

I wave a hand. 'Oh, you know...' I reply, as if every woman on the planet knows what it's like to stain your face yellow with bad fake tan and pretend you're Nosferatu just to cover up your embarrassment.

'I am sorry I missed your speech,' she apologises.

'No problem. No problem at all!'

The Japanese lady then looks up at the bright lighting above, then back down at me. 'Your condition has improved, it seems. We were concerned when Mr Newman had the lights in the main room lowered.'

Now, there are two ways I can go with this. I can either continue to bullshit, and dig myself an even deeper hole, or I can stop messing about and be honest. This little woman looks as sharp as a tack, so I choose not to drag the charade out. 'I haven't got anything wrong with me,' I admit. 'I just made a mess of using some very expensive fake tan, and it stained my face this colour.'

She folds her arms. 'Ah, I see.'

I offer her a lopsided smile. 'I've gone through the entire day with this horrible yellow face.' I sigh again. 'I look like Miss Pacman.' I look back up at Mrs Sakamura. 'I guess you'd know about that though,' I add, with a rueful chuckle.

Right, before we go any further Mum, let's get one thing really clear:

I was *not* making a reference to the colour of her face.

I was making reference to the fact that Miss Pacman was a video game invented in *Japan*.

It may sound like I am suggesting that this woman knows what it is like to go through life with a horrible yellow face, but what I am actually *saying* is that her being Japanese means she would of course be familiar *with* Miss Pacman.

I am *not* a hideous racist who should be locked up at the nearest opportunity!

Good. Now that we've got that sorted out between us, let's see if Mrs Sakamura realises the same thing, shall we?

'What did you say?' she utters in shocked disbelief.

'What?'

'About my face?'

'What?'

'You think I have a horrible yellow face?!'

'*What?*'

I replay the last ten seconds in my head and immediately realise the extent of my faux pas. I throw both hands up and start waving them frantically back and forth, shaking my head as I do so. 'No! No! I didn't mean... I wasn't saying... '

Oh God! What the hell do I say!?

'I don't think you have a horrible yellow face!' I say, and try to smile apologetically. The terror won't let me though, and I just look

---

like I'm having some kind of seizure. 'I think your face is a lovely shade of yellow!'

Mrs Sakamura's face darkens even more.

'No! No! I didn't mean that either!'

Oh God, oh God, oh God.

'It's just that Miss Pacman is Japanese, isn't she? And you... you are also Japanese. And, and all I meant was, was that you would know *about* Miss Pacman *because* you are Japanese.'

'I'm Korean.'

Oh fuck me. My life is over.

My eyes go wide. My mouth contorts into a tight circle of horror. My buttocks clench and my toes curl. 'I'm so sorry! I'm so, so sorry! I just thought you were Japanese because your husband - '

'Has a yellow face as well?' she retorts, one foot tapping angrily on the toilet floor.

'No! Because you're married, and, and... '

'Because only Japanese yellow faces can marry other Japanese yellow faces?'

I slam both hands against my sides. 'That's not what I said!' While I am still mortified by my unintentional double dose of accidental racism, I am also getting a little bit annoyed that this woman is putting words in my mouth. 'Look. I am sorry if I offended you Mrs Sakamura, but I assure you I didn't mean to. Neither did I mean to stain my face yellow. I would like to say that it's been an extraordinarily strange and taxing day for me, but if you've read any of my books, you know I'd be lying.'

The little woman glowers at me for a moment, and then her eyes narrow. 'Did you really buy a swimsuit with Beach Whore written on it?'

'Yes,' I reply with a roll of the eyes. Here we go.

'And that fajita thing... '

'All true, I'm afraid.' I'm on familiar ground here. If I had a penny for every time I've had this conversation, I'd have enough money to buy an even more expensive brand of fake tan.

'The job interview?'

'Yep. Sick everywhere, I was.'

Mrs Sakamura's expression has gone from one of righteous indignation, to a look of curious pity. I'll leave you to decide which is worse. 'I think I should return to my husband,' she says carefully.

'Yes, you probably should.'

'Will you be alright?'

'Yes, I'm sure I will.'

'Perhaps we'll talk again later.'

'I should think so, yes.'

Mrs Sakamura walks back towards the door to the toilet. As she opens it, she nearly runs right into Jamie, who has apparently been lurking in the corridor beyond. The lights outside have been lowered again.

'Oh! Hello! Sorry!' he exclaims, holding the door open to let her by. As she passes, the little woman gives Jamie a quick look of mild distaste.

He watches her go and looks back at me. 'Let me guess. The fajitas?'

'Yep.' I rub my eyes and shake my head.

'Er, I've got the lights back down.'

'So I see.'

'Are you coming back out then?'

I suck air in through my teeth, pull a couple of small creases out of the front of my dress, and slowly walk over to my husband. 'Jamie. I think I already have material for the next book.'

'How so?'

'I just racially abused a small Korean woman twice in the space of a minute.'

'Is she Korean? I thought she was Jap - '

'Leave it!' I put a hand up to his face. 'Just leave it.' Giving his cheek a gentle pat, I leave the ladies toilet and venture back into the gloom.

In actual fact, the rest of the party goes quite well Mum, all things considered.

I do have to speak to the Sakamuras again at Peter Hincham's insistence, but it goes reasonably well. I catch Mrs Sakamura staring at me the way a botanist would stare at a particularly large and aggressive looking fungus, but it really doesn't bother me that much. At least she isn't calling the police and having me arrested for a hate crime.

By 10pm I'm more than ready to leave, so am very grateful when Peter wraps the book launch up with a short speech, before sending everyone on their way. It was the happiest I'd seen anyone look that evening - including myself.

'You know what I think, Jamie?' I say to my husband in the car on the way back to The Dorchester.

'What's that, sweetheart?'

'I think there's a part of me that knows these silly events are coming up, and subconsciously tries to sabotage it to stop me from going.'

'Why's that?'

'Because I just don't fit in, and my brain knows it, even if I don't.'

'Oh great,' he replies witheringly. 'If you don't think *you* fit in, then I haven't got a hope in hell.'

I look out at the passing London nightlife and reach a profound and rock solid conclusion. 'I need a bloody holiday.'

Jamie smiles. 'I couldn't agree more.'

'But first... Kyle?'

The driver looks into the rear view mirror. 'Yes, Mrs Newman?'

'Take us to the nearest 24 hour chemist please.'

'Why are we going there?' Jamie asks quizzically.

'Two things Jamie. Cleanser and concealer.' I look back out of the car window again. 'And if neither of them work, I can always wear the plastic bag they come in over my head.'

It took three days for the yellow to fade completely Mum.

My face is as raw as an uncooked turkey, but at least I won't have to cower in the corner every time I see someone from Asia coming towards me. Whether they are Japanese *or* Korean.

Love you and miss you,
Your pink daughter Laura.

XX

Jamie's Blog
Friday 26 March

I'm on holiday in one of the most beautiful places on the planet, and I should be more relaxed than a pot smoking sloth.

Thousands of pounds have been spent to fly me, my wife and my daughter to the Maldives. I should be enjoying every single second of it. The island is gorgeous, the service is tremendous, the facilities are top notch, and the alcohol is free.

So why am I sat eating breakfast on our final day here, with a nervous twitch in one eye, rapidly rising blood pressure, and a tension headache forming behind both temples?

I'll tell you bloody why:

I want that fucking pedalo.

Yes, you heard me right. I am a twitching ball of nervous tension because of a giant plastic boat with pedals. The kind you get on boating lakes across the United Kingdom, beloved of ice cream wielding children and cackling grannies alike.

The whole idea for a holiday started to ferment in both our minds the night of that horrible book launch fiasco at Watermill Publishing. In fact, the very next day I was on the iPad looking at likely destinations via the magical gateway to all things holiday related - Expedia.

Given that I'm still not used to having a fair amount of disposable income, I start small.

'How about Magaluf?' I shout through to Laura, who is busying herself in the bathroom with some hardcore facial scrubbing.

She pokes her lather covered face around the door frame. Through the suds I can see a look of disapproval on her face. 'Magaluf, Jamie? A place crammed to the rafters with Brits on the piss and Club 18 to 30 reps? Where the gross national product is venereal disease? No thank you. Keep looking.'

And keep looking I did, for an entire week. Sadly, every suggestion I made fell on deaf ears. Funnily enough, Laura's protestations were stronger the closer the destination was to the UK. If it was a short haul flight and relatively inexpensive, she didn't want to contemplate it. It was only when I started to suggest locations more than a five hour flight away that she started to get excited, particularly if those destinations were in the tropics. But still we could not come to an agreement.

'Africa?'

'Hmmm. Bit too unsettled these days, don't you think?'

'Caribbean?'

'Too touristy.'

'Florida?'

'*Way* too touristy.'

'India?'

'What, with your sensitive bowels and my complete lack of spice tolerance?'

'Antarctica?'

'Stop being silly, Jamie.'

Laura may have thought I was being silly, but I really was starting to run out of options. I decided to stop suggesting destinations in the hope that she'd come up with one. She did a few days later, when I returned home from the pub late one evening to find a stack of holiday brochures on the coffee table, all advertising the Maldives.

'You've got to be kidding me,' I say to her in an incredulous voice, as she comes back into the lounge from the kitchen.

'I was just doing a little light reading,' she replies innocently.

'A little light reading? There are seven... no, *eight* brochures there Laura. Nothing involving a stack of books a foot tall can be described as a *little light reading*.'

'It looks lovely,' she says with a sniff as she sits back down on the couch.

'Oh, I'm sure it does, given that you have to sell at least two body parts to afford to go there.'

Laura rolls her eyes. 'Oh, unbunch them Newman. It's not like we're strapped for cash these days, is it? If we can't enjoy the fruits of our writing labours, then what's the point?'

'I agree, but we're not E.L James, sweetheart. Just because we got a mention in the Sunday Times, it doesn't mean we can afford to go swanning off to the most expensive place on the planet.'

Laura huffs and folds her arms. 'I wish you'd just think about it.'

'I have. Enough to know it's too pricey. Find somewhere a bit more reasonable baby, *please*.'

I'm surprised by the level of my own resolve, but thankfully Laura doesn't push the issue any more that evening.

She does however do something *colossally* underhand and sneaky - she gets our daughter involved.

A couple of days later it's my turn to tuck Poppy in for the night. She climbs into bed and gives me a sleepy look. 'I want a bed time story, Dad,' she says, and rubs her eyes in a manner that is so adorable it should come with a health warning.

'Really? You haven't wanted a bed time story in a long time, sweetheart,' I say a bit perplexed. Poppy is at the age now when she can quite happily read herself to sleep if she wants to.

'I want one tonight though, Dad.'

Well, I'm hardly one to refuse my charming little daughter anything, so I reach towards her bookcase and my fingers hover over the selection of children's books therein. 'What do you fancy then?'

'Not one of those, Dad. I've got a book under my bed.'

'Okay,' I reply and reach under the divan base. My fingers close around a slim A4 sized volume, and I pluck it from its hiding place, ready to send my little girl off into her slumbers with a spell binding rendition of whatever children's classic she has chosen.

'Oh good grief,' I utter as I look at the waving palm trees and white sandy beaches emblazoned on the Kuoni cover. 'You want me to read to you from a holiday brochure?' I say in a deadpan voice.

'Yes,' Poppy replies, having the good grace to lower herself down further under the covers.

'And this is something that you've arrived at on your own is it? With no help from your mother?'

'Yes.' Now all that is visible are her tiny fingers, innocent blue eyes and mop of blonde hair.

'Now, now Poppy. You know lying is bad.'

Her head instantly shoots back out of the covers. 'But it looks really pretty Dad!'

'Does it really?'

'And... and... it has... ' My daughter's face scrunches up, as if trying to remember something she's been coached to say. '...an all including packet, with a wide range of wines and a la kazam food.'

'Do you possibly mean an all inclusive package, with a wide range of wines and à la carte food?'

Poppy blinks a couple of times. 'Yes?' she says uncertainly.

I sigh. 'Would you like to go here, Poppy?' I ask in a sinking voice.

Poppy sits bolt upright. 'Yes Dad! It's got big fish, and really blue sky, and canoes we can go on, and Mum says I can build as many sand castles as I want - '

My daughter comes up short, realising that she's let the cat out of the bag.

'Mum says, eh?'

She shakes her head back and forth. 'No. No. No.' She then takes a deep breath and looks up at the ceiling for a moment before fixing her gaze back on me. The smile that then beams across her face is pure Dad kryptonite. 'There are sharks as well, Dad! And clown fish just like Nemo too!'

'Laura!' I shout downstairs. 'This is a decidedly unfair tactic, you know!'

'What ever do you mean, Jamie?' my wife replies, from where she's been standing in the hallway outside the bedroom this entire time.

'Honestly woman, employing your poor sweet innocent daughter as emotional blackmail is just beyond the pale.'

Laura holds out her hand and points. 'But look at her excited little face, Jamie. How can you possibly refuse such a thing?'

I turn back to Poppy, who is deliberately affecting a look of such barely contained glee that I'm surprised the top of her head isn't steaming.

Giving my wife one last look of disgust, I flip the brochure open. 'Alright, alright. Which hotel would you like to hear about, Poppy? The one with an infinity pool that will bankrupt me in weeks? Or the one with the spa jacuzzi that will bankrupt me in days?'

In the end, we choose (or rather, *Laura* chooses) a hotel that comes with both infinity pool *and* jacuzzi, ensuring that I will be sucking off my bank manager for years to come, to prevent us being turfed out of our house.

Okay, I'm exaggerating, but I am not a man used to such extravagance. Spending the kind of money on a holiday that I'd usually lay out on a new car does not come easy.

'You can relax a bit, you know,' Laura tells me on the drive to the Kuoni shop in town. 'We can afford this. We really can.'

The look of mild anguish I give her says differently.

'I know things have been tight in recent years,' she continues, 'but they're not anymore. You just need to accept that, sweetheart.'

Which is my real problem here. I've had so many years of struggle with finances that I just don't know how to cope with the idea of *not* having to struggle anymore. It's a completely alien concept to me. I say as much to Laura.

'I know, baby,' she replies, patting my hand where it rests on the gear stick. 'It's okay though.'

'I hope so.'

'It really is. Besides... ' Laura tilts the rear view mirror so I can see Poppy in the back. The look of exuberant delight on her face is now so extreme that I swear I can see the steam coming out of both ears. '...look how excited your daughter is.'

'Excited... or about to have an accident, I can't quite tell which.'

'Eww! Dad!' Poppy says, nose crinkling.

An hour later - and several thousand pounds lighter - I emerge from Kuoni in a daze. We are now booked into the nearly unpronounceable Milwadi Wimbufushi Resort on the even more unpronounceable Miladunmaduru Patkani Atoll. It appears that the more money you spend on a holiday in the Maldives, the less likely you are to be able to say where it is you are going.

Still, it does look bloody glorious. All waving palm trees, azure seas, and well stocked mini bars. As I've just booked an all inclusive holiday our mini bar will be free for the whole week, so if my wallet is having a hard time with this purchase, then my liver will soon be joining it, and feeling even worse.

'Thank you baby,' Laura says as we get back into the car. She leans over and gives me a gentle kiss on the cheek. I smile and look in the rear view mirror at Poppy again.

'You can stop the teapot impression now Pops. The holiday is booked.'

My daughter relaxes and blows air out of her cheeks with palpable relief. 'Can we get McDonalds now, Mum?' she asks Laura, revealing the method of bribery with which my wife managed to convince her to take part in the Machiavellian Maldivian scheme.

I was somewhat annoyed that I had been so perfectly manipulated by the women in my life. The second I step off the sea plane and onto the Wimbufushi dock though, this annoyance melts away completely.

Hello, the island seems to say to you with a gentle caress of warm wind. **Welcome to the nicest place on Earth. Yes, the sun above your head does stay like that the entire time, and yes, it is as hot as you think it is. The sea really *is* that blue, and the sand really *is* that white. There's every chance that after spending a week here, everywhere else on Planet Earth will subsequently look like fried dog shit. And did I mention that the mini bar is stocked with enough Jack Daniels to drown yourself in?**

'Oh my,' Laura says from my side breathlessly. 'Oh my...'

Poppy is less subdued by the stunning scenery. 'Fish! Look at those big fish!' she screeches, pointing into the clear blue water at a passing shoal of bright pink parrotfish.

We are greeted, along with the dozen or so other holiday makers that flew in on the sea plane with us, by a collection of broadly smiling Maldivians, all dressed in pristine white linen. They supply us with cool towels to mop our brows, freshly made iced tea, and an assortment of sweetmeats to munch on. Our bags are whisked away by more of the smartly dressed Maldivians, and we are gently led down the dock and onto the island itself, which looks better than it did in the brochure. A sign greets you as you step off the dock that says 'no shoes beyond this point'.

Family Newman is led away from the main pack by a small Maldivian woman called Mimi, who takes us to our water bungalow. This is perched at the end of yet another long wooden dock that juts out into the turquoise ocean.

Inside is a huge apartment, tastefully decorated in various shades of cream and bamboo. The television is 50 inches if it's a foot, the bathroom gleams expansively, the beds are enormous, soft and inviting, and the mini bar... well, the mini bar is a thing of beauty as far as I'm concerned. It's stuffed to the gills with all manner of alcoholic beverages, and I intend to consume most of them in the coming seven days. Beyond the apartment itself is a wide expanse of decking, complete with sun loungers, that juts out over the glistening blue sea, a good six feet above the surface of the water. A set of steps off to one side takes you down there, should you wish to dip your toes in the warm Indian Ocean.

Frankly, the level of luxuriousness here is bordering on the idiotic.

Mimi gives us the guided tour, stopping every once in a while to let us ooh and aah for a few moments whenever we see something impressive. She then hands over the guest pack that details meal times, excursions, etc. Even this bloody thing is posh. I could swear the logo on the plush, padded front cover is stamped on in gold leaf.

We bid Mimi a pleasant goodbye once her job is done, and set about unpacking our suitcases, which of course have already been brought in by other smiling members of the Mildew Wibblefushi resort.

'None of them asked for a tip,' says Laura, as she begins to unpack about forty eight different bikinis. 'Muresh at The Dorchester wouldn't approve.'

'What?'

'Nothing, dear. Why don't you take Poppy onto the deck outside with the guest brochure while I unpack?'

I'm dumbfounded. 'Are you actually suggesting that I don't do any work?'

'Yes, Jamie. But only because if I allow you to unpack your own clothes, I will be spending the entire week with a walking crease.' She turns to where Poppy is already fiddling with the TV remote control. 'Poppy? Go and see the fish with Dad.'

Without questioning further, Pops and I make our way out through a set of pristine sliding doors onto the large wooden deck with the kind of view that immediately takes your breath away, and sells it on the black market in Hong Kong. Poppy immediately walks down the steps that lead to the ocean, while I park myself on one of the loungers and begin to read the brochure.

Considering these places are generally meant for people who just want to sit on their arses for a week, I'm surprised to see quite so many excursions and facilities on offer to occupy your time. There are snorkelling trips, diving adventures, and sailing days out. There's a gym, an outdoor cinema, and a snooker room. You can kayak, paddle board and even go out on a -

'Laura! Laura!'

'What?' my wife replies, hurrying out onto the deck with a concerned look on her face. 'What's the matter? Is it Poppy? Is she alright?'

'Yeah, yeah, I'm sure she's fine,' I say, without even bothering to check whether my daughter has been swept out to sea or not. 'They've got a *pedalo* here!'

'Excuse me?'

'A pedalo! It's a boat that you sit in and pedal, like you get on boating lakes back home.'

'Yes Jamie. I know what a pedalo is, thank you very much. Why on earth would you be excited about that?'

I go very quiet.

'What's the matter?' Laura asks.

'Never got to go on one,' I mumble.

'What do you mean?'

This might sound pathetic, but when I was a child on parental excursions to the seaside, my biggest desire was to have a go on a pedalo. Other children wanted to play in the arcades, build sandcastles on the beach, or eat chips until they burst, but all I wanted to do was sit in a large fibre glass boat with pedals and make my way around the whole boating lake until I was sick from over-exertion.

But it *never happened.*

You wouldn't imagine it possible, but on every single family day trip out during the formative years of my life, there were either no pedalos in the vicinity, or they were all being used by other holidaymakers. In fact, the only time I got close was on a visit to Canoe Lake in Southsea when I was ten. If it hadn't been my stupid sister bleating on about wanting to visit the nearby natural history museum, I would have had my go in a pedalo, *dammit.* But she couldn't stand to wait even ten minutes, so we had to go traipsing off to look at stuffed birds and fossils for an hour. I managed to hold my counsel until we reached the geology display, before I burst into tears and started stamping my feet. My mother, father, and the rather harassed young woman who ran the museum tried to calm me down, but to no avail. I was only mollified when I was allowed to leave the decrepit old building and return to the boating lake.

You can imagine my complete and total dismay when we discovered that the pedalo vendor had buggered off home for the day, and all the lovely big plastic red pedalos were chained up and no longer in use. I then proceeded to punch Sarah so hard on the arm that I believe the bruise has only just cleared up.

Not feeling the need to relay all this childhood misery to my wife, I elect to keep things simple. 'I've just never been on a pedalo before. Never had the chance.' I tell her.

Her brow crinkles. 'What, never?'

'No. Please don't make me talk about it.'

Laura sighs. 'Okay, my little boy. If you want a go on a pedalo, then who am I to argue?'

I beam at her happily.

'Mum! Dad! Look what I've got!' Poppy squeals with delight, coming straight at us both with a huge, pissed off looking blue crab clutched in her hands. All thoughts of pedalos and other waterborne entertainments are forgotten for the moment, as we try to wrestle the gigantic crustacean from Poppy's grip before it either dies or rips one of her ears off.

There's every chance a career in natural history is in my daughter's future, if she can just get past the poking phase, that is.

But of course, gentle reader, you already know that my pedalo based fantasy has not come true...

That no matter how hard I have tried over the past seven days, I have been unable to fulfill my childhood ambition.

You see, there is only *one* pedalo on the entire island. Ridiculous, yes?

There should be two, but one is broken, thanks to an over enthusiastic holiday maker crashing it into a reef and ripping a two foot hole in the fibre glass.

So, that's one pedalo to be shared between 364 guests.

How do I know exactly how many guests there are on Madwiddly Womblefishy? Because I've bloody counted them, that's why. I had to. I simply couldn't believe that one tiny insignificant pedalo could be in such high demand, so I had to know exactly how many people I'd been competing against all week for its usage.

Not that everyone has used the pedalo, of course. I've been keeping watch every time the sodding thing has come past me on yet another tour of the small island, being driven by some other bastard in a bathing suit, and it's plain that there are only a few people who actually use it.

There are at least two German couples who seem to have taken a great liking to the pedalo. I have counted them going past me on at least twenty occasions in the past week. I know they are German because I have engaged both in conversation at meal times. Know your enemy, as Winston Churchill would have probably said at some point.

Then there are the Chinese. Who knew that an entire nation of people whose country is two thirds landlocked, would enjoy a bit of aquatic pedalling action so much? It seems like every time I drag my family down to the end of the beach where the pedalo and kayaks are stored, we invariably see a group of Chinese people dragging the thing down to the shoreline, and jumping in with big smiles on their faces.

I then have to suffer the indignity of going out onto the water in a bloody kayak. There is no shortage of kayaks on Melbibbly Wimbewayfooshy. Not by a long shot.

But I've been kayaking *thousands* of times. The novelty wears off after a while, even if you are cruising over tropical reefs and exciting multi-coloured fish.

To compound my frustration, I would see other guests out on the pedalo while sat in one of the plentiful kayaks. This just rubbed salt into the wound.

It's got to the point where I have been making excuses to Laura just to go off on my own, to see if I can grab the pedalo while no-one is looking.

'Just, er, just going down to the cocktail bar to get a beer, baby,' I say to her yesterday, getting up from the sun lounger in as casual a manner as possible.

'There are loads of beers in the fridge, Jamie,' she replies from over her copy of Cosmopolitan.

'Um... I just fancied a different kind. Maybe something from Asia. I'm a bit bored with Corona.'

'Since when did you become such a beer aficionado? You've never - ' Her eyes widen. 'You're going to see if that bloody pedalo is free again, aren't you?'

'No!'

'Yes you bloody are!' Cosmo goes down onto her lap and she points a pointy finger in my direction. 'Just let it go Jamie! It's all you've gone on about all week!'

'No it isn't.'

'Yes it is! It's very hard to enjoy paradise when your significant other keeps making grumbling noises every time he sees a group of Chinese people float past in a big plastic dinghy.'

'It's a pedalo, not a dinghy,' I correct in a sullen voice.

'Whatever Jamie! Just drop it. It doesn't matter.'

But it *does* matter. At least to me!

And so here we are, on the last morning of our holiday.

And I have a *plan*.

It is a *good* plan. A *solid* plan. A plan that can only result in my successful acquisition of the pedalo, before we fly from the island later this afternoon.

From my detailed study of the pedalo's movements, I know that Richie, the guy who works in the boathouse, doesn't open until 10am; sometimes ten past if he's feeling lazy. I have tried on two occasions to be down there *at* 10am to get the pedalo before anybody else, but there has always been a queue.

To ensure that I would be the one to secure the pedalo on my last day, I had to do something to deter people of either German or Chinese extraction from getting down there before me and laying claim to the object of my unhealthy obsession.

This involved a pillow case, some chewing gum, Laura's eye liner, and a very early start...

At five this morning I was awoken by the vibrating of my iPhone from under my pillow. Without waking Laura I grabbed the pillow case and eye liner, and sneaked my way out of the water bungalow. Successfully managing to dodge the island's staff as they went about early morning jobs, I made my way stealthily to the boat house, where I stuck the pillow case onto the wall with the chewing gum, having written the legend 'PLEASE COME BACK AT 11AM' on it with the eye liner.

Genius!

Anyone who beat me down to the boat house before 10 o'clock would go away again, thinking lazy old Ritchie wasn't getting there until an hour later!

Fool proof!

The pedalo would be mine!

The second part of the plan involves convincing my wife that I really, really need a shit. I have to have a good reason why I need to leave her and Poppy at breakfast early, don't I?

'Oh dear,' I remark over my bacon and eggs. I also theatrically clutch my stomach and grimace.

'What's up?' Laura asks.

'My stomach feels funny,' I say, affecting a worried tone.

'Does it?'

'Yeah. It feels a bit... a bit *fajita-like*.'

Laura looks a little sick. 'Oh dear. Perhaps you should... you know?'

I nod vigorously. 'Yes. Perhaps I should.'

Assured that my ruse is working like a charm, I rise from the table and scuttle out through the palm tree fringed dining hall, making a direct bee-line for the boat house on the other side of the tiny island. A glance at my watch confirms that it is ten minutes to ten. By the time I reach Ritchie and his selection of fibre glass wonders, it should be ten o'clock, without the hint of another holiday maker in the vicinity.

I round a particularly thick cluster of palm trees, and the thatched roof of the boat house comes into sight.

...as does Ritchie and a small middle aged gentleman, who is picking up the end of the pedalo and moving towards the sea.

Aaarrgghh!

How can this be happening?

My sign was bloody fool proof!

My confident jog turns into a panicked scamper as I make my way across the white sand to my quarry... and my new enemy. As I get closer I can see that the man is easily in his late sixties, and is under five foot six. He's wearing bright blue long shorts and a white vest that exposes something of a pigeon chest. If it comes down to fisticuffs, I'm *fairly* sure I can take him. I recognise the old codger from somewhere, but can't quite put my finger on it. I must have seen him around the resort over the last week.

As I speed past the front of the boat house, I glance over to see my poor make-shift sign in a bedraggled heap on the decking, with a fat seagull on top of it, pecking away at one of the corners. It looks like he's after the chewing gum.

I hope you choke on it bird!

You can now truly see the depths of my irrationality here, can't you? I am actively wishing death on an innocent sea creature just because it's jeopardised my cunning plan to secure a ride in a rather shit plastic boat.

As I near Ritchie and the vest wearing pedalo stealer, I decide that the best way to handle this situation is with a display of Great British brashness.

'I say!' I bellow, one finger pointed aloft. 'I say there! I've booked that pedalo for myself today!'

You can't book the pedalo out - it's first come first served, but if I shout it loud enough I might sound convincing anyway.

Ritchie looks up at me, and his face drops with a look of familiar dread. 'Good morning, Mr Newman,' he says in clipped English. 'How are you today?'

I stop right in front of both men and put my hands on my hips. My nose goes in the air and I stare straight out into the ocean. 'Not happy Ritchie! Not happy at all!'

'And why is that Mr Newman?'

'You can plainly see why, Ritchie! I have asked you for usage of this pedalo all week, and not once have I been allowed to have it!'

Ritchie's shoulders slump. 'That's not true Mr Newman, you just keep coming over when somebody has already taken it out. If you had waited a little long - '

'I have a family to take care of Ritchie!' I exclaim imperiously. 'I can't just spend my entire time hanging out with you, waiting for Chinese people to return the pedalo, can I?'

'No, I suppose not, Mr Newman,' Ritchie agrees with a sigh.

'Excuse me?' says the small elderly gentleman. 'Can I take the pedalo out now please?'

Ritchie nods. 'Yes of course sir!' he says with a smile.

Oh god. This is getting away from me fast. I have to do something!

'No!' I bellow once more, and stamp my way around to the front of the pedalo, blocking its path to the sea. 'This pedalo is mine good sir, and I expect you to stand aside and wait your turn!'

The old man scowls at me in such a way that my sense of recollection gets even stronger. *Where have I seen that scowl before?*

'I will do no such thing!' he snaps. 'I got here first, laddie. Now you just stand aside and allow me to use it!'

That strident tone... Why do I recognise that strident tone?

In desperation, I try to appeal to their charitable side. 'I have cancer!'

'What?!' Ritchie and the old man say in unison.

'Yes! Cancer! You wouldn't deny a dying man his last ride in a pedalo, would you?'

My degree of insanity has now reached a level that not even Laura would believe.

'You look fine to me,' the old man says, giving me a suspicious look.

Where do I know him from?

'Well, I may look fine,' I begin, simultaneously trying to bolster my awful lie, and trying to remember why I recognise him so much. 'But the doctor says I may only have three months to... '

I trail off.

Doctor.

A doctor...

I mentally place a cream coloured pork pie hat on the old man's head, put a red, question mark shaped umbrella cane in his hand, and place a big blue Police box behind him.

'Are you Sylvester McCoy?' I ask in a hushed tone.

The old man draws himself up to his full five foot six inches. 'Yes, I am young man! Now kindly step aside!'

Well, this is excellent. I'm standing in thirty degree heat on the last day of a holiday that's been ruined by a childhood obsession, and I'm trying to steal a pedalo from Doctor Who by claiming I have a fatal disease.

I should just give up and fuck off back to the breakfast table, but even the prospect of offending the seventh Doctor won't stop me now. Nor will punching him in the face, if it comes down to it.

'Look Doctor... '

'That's not my name! It's Mister McCoy to you, laddie!'

At this moment Ritchie interrupts. 'Are you a doctor sir?' he asks McCoy. 'Perhaps you could help Mr Newman here with his illness?'

God bless you Ritchie. In the teeth of a brewing argument, you are trying your level best to bring both parties to the negotiating table.

'He's not *a* doctor Ritchie. He's *The* Doctor,' I try to explain. 'You know? Doctor Who?'

Ritchie looks puzzled. 'But he is much taller and thinner on the television. His chin is much larger too.'

'That's Matt Smith,' McCoy explains in a deflated voice.

'And you do not sound very Scottish!' Ritchie adds.

'That's Peter Capaldi,' McCoy adds in the same sad tone. You get the feeling he's been in this situation more than once in the past.

'He's the seventh Doctor,' I tell Ritchie. 'You know, the one that killed off the series back in the eighties? The unpopular one?'

Okay, so when trying to negotiate the usage of a pedalo, it's probably not best to deeply insult the other party.

'Why, you little sod!' McCoy exclaims.

There's nothing for it. Actions must speak louder than words.

I grab hold of the pedalo at the front end and yank it towards me. This will earn me a painfully torn shoulder muscle for the next few weeks, but I'm too het up right now to realise the damage I've done. 'It's mine Doctor!' I wail, sounding like I'm auditioning for the part of The Master. 'It's mine and I'm going to use it!'

I start to drag the pedalo towards the water. As I reach it, McCoy tries to pull the boat back in the other direction. Ritchie has wisely decided to stay the hell out of it.

Luckily for me, the momentum of the boat is with me as it dips into the sea, and McCoy is unable to stop it drifting in my direction. With a hop, skip and a jump, I am sat in the seat and starting to pedal furiously. McCoy comes alongside, now nearly waist deep in water. 'Give it back! Give it back this instant!'

'Or what? You'll hit me with your sonic screwdriver?' I sneer and push him away from the side of the pedalo, which makes him lose his footing and fall over with a big splash.

With a roar of triumph I start to pedal with even more gusto, and the boat picks up speed.

I ignore the roars of displeasure coming from the pensionable Time Lord and fix my glare on the horizon.

I have done it!

I have claimed the pedalo!

It is mine!

Mwaa haa haa haa!

My transition from successful novelist to capering pantomime villain is complete.

But no matter!

The pedalo *is* mine!

Nothing can stop me enjoying the endless aquatic fun I can have with it now!

Ten minutes later, I'm bored shitless.

It turns out that a pedalo is a right arse to operate, especially when you're on your own. It steers badly, you have to pedal like a madman just to get it to fart along at three miles an hour, and it wallows so much in the water that you're permanently being splashed by waves.

I should have stuck to kayaking.

I disconsolately stop and look around me. Despite my frantic pedalling I am no more than a hundred yards off shore. I can see McCoy stamping away in a rage, and Ritchie is walking back into the boat house, shaking his head back and forth.

All the adrenaline that kept me going through the argument on the beach leaves me in a rush, and I instantly feel dog tired. I have been awake since five o'clock this morning, so it's hardly surprising.

With a sigh of disappointment, I whip my t-shirt off in order to soak up a few last rays of Maldivian sun, rest my head back against the top of the warm pedalo seat and close my eyes. In a moment, I'll return the bloody thing with an apology to all concerned, but right now, I just want to float on the water for a bit, and feel relaxed for the first time in days...

My eyes spring open. They do this painfully. My whole face feels like it's on fire.

Sitting up, I look around to discover that I am surrounded by deep blue water. Gone is the gentle tranquility of the aquamarine beach water. Replacing it are the cold hard depths of the ocean proper.

With a whimper I sit up in the seat and whip my head around.

I can't see the island!

I'm adrift at sea!

I'm going to die!

I'm going to get eaten by sh -

Oh no, wait... there's the island. Right behind me.

But it looks so small! I'm miles away from it!

I look down at my arms. I'm also hideously sunburned. I must have fallen asleep for quite some time, to have drifted so far out and gotten so burned.

I look down into the scary depths and realise that a current is pulling me further away from the island every second.

With a louder, more desperate whimper, I yank on the pedalo's rudder and start to pump my legs feverishly.

As the boat slowly - oh so bloody *slowly* - begins to turn around, it dawns on me that I could be in a lot of trouble here. If the speed of the current below is stronger than the three mile an hour fart I am able to make the paddles below me turn at, I might be swept out to sea.

With a desperate gulp, I fix both the island and the faces of my family firmly in my mind, and start to pedal like Chris Hoy with the hosts of Hell right behind him.

Laura's Diary
Monday, March 29th

Dear Mum,

And so, a relaxing luxury holiday in the Indian Ocean turns into a frantic man hunt.

'Mum? Where's Dad gone?' Poppy asks from over her second bowl of Coco Pops.

I look at her from over the rather dog eared copy of Cosmo I've been lugging around for the past two days. What's the best way to break it to your seven year old that her dad has had an attack of the shits and can't be with us right now?

'Dad's fine sweetheart, he just had to go back to the room for a bit. I'm sure he'll be back soon.' I glance at my watch to see just how long Jamie has been suffering for, and note that over forty five minutes have passed. I frown. Even if he was caught a bit short, he would have been back by now. Maybe he's a lot worse off than I thought.

'C'mon sweetie. Let's go see what Dad's up to,' I tell Pops and rise from the table.

We then make our way back to the water bungalow. We're leaving this afternoon, so I make a point of soaking up every last detail of this gorgeous island as we go, a pang of regret already settling in my chest.

'Jamie!' I call as I open the front door. 'Are you alright?'

Expecting to hear the explosive sounds of one man's fight with a toilet bowl, I am surprised to be greeted with silence as I cross the room and go over to the bathroom. 'Jamie?' I ask tentatively by the door. Still no response. Where the hell is he?

His stomach issues must have resolved themselves, I suppose. But quite why he didn't come back to the table when he was finished baffles me.

'Dad's not here,' Poppy says in a quiet voice.

I give her a hug. 'I know, baby. But he must be back at the restaurant, eh? We must have just missed him.'

I lock up the bungalow again, and we traipse back across the island. This time I don't bother with the whimsical regret, my mind is on other things.

Over the course of the week, there is one waiter in the restaurant that we have befriended. A big smiling Maldivian called David, he's been our ever present congenial host for almost every meal. I see him standing by one of the breakfast buffet stations, and make my way over to talk to him.

'David?'

'Hello Mrs Newman! How is your last day on the island? Not feeling too sad about leaving I hope?'

'No... well, a little,' I reply with a nervous chuckle. 'Have you seen my husband, by any chance?'

'No Mrs Newman, I have not. I saw him leave about an hour ago, but have not seen him since.'

'Oh.'

David notices the look of worry now etched across my face. 'I'm sure he couldn't have gone far. Why don't I ask some of my colleagues if they've seen him?'

I give David an appreciative smile. 'Thank you. That would be nice.'

David takes himself off while Poppy and I stand a bit forlornly close to the buffet stations. I have to move away after a few moments as the smells are making me a bit sick. There's nothing wrong with the food, it's just that a little kernel of worry has planted itself in my stomach, and it's making me feel quite nauseous.

A good five minutes goes by before David returns. The look on his face doesn't indicate he's had much success. 'I'm sorry Mrs Newman. No-one has seen him.'

'Oh.'

'Where's Dad?' I hear a tremulous little voice say from below me.

I bend down to my concerned little daughter. 'It's okay Poppet. Dad probably just went for a walk. I'm sure he'll come back soon.'

I don't believe a word of it though. Jamie isn't the type to go wandering off without at least telling me what he's doing. It's completely out of character.

Oh God.

It's completely out of character.

That's what they always say about the missing people on Crimewatch isn't it?

My kernel of worry is instantly replaced by an entire bushel of dread. Jamie has suffered some kind of horrific attack of food poisoning, and is lying in a load of bushes somewhere on the island, his last, dying breath escaping his lips...

'David?' I whisper so Poppy can't hear. 'Could you put out some kind of alert for me? I think Jamie has gone missing. I have no idea where he can be.'

'Okay Mrs Newman. Are you sure there's nowhere else he might have gone?'

'No, I don't think so.'

'Maybe he went on a last tour of the island, and has sat himself down somewhere?'

I shake my head. 'That's not like him. Besides, we've been here a week, there's nothing left for him to do really - '

The image of a large plastic pedal driven boat fills my vision.

'Oh you little bastard!' I spit, loudly enough to be heard by some unfortunate nearby holiday makers trying to enjoy their eggs benedict and coffee.

'Mum!' Poppy gasps.

'I'm sorry honey.' I turn back to David. 'Cancel the alert, I know exactly where my idiot of a husband is.'

'Ah, so you do not think he is in any trouble then?' he replies.

'Oh, he's in trouble alright David,' I sneer. 'Thank you for your help and sorry to bother you.'

'No problem! It is what I am here for.'

'I'm sure. Let's hope you know some first aid too. You're likely to need it soon. Come on Poppy!'

I drag my daughter out of the restaurant, and make for the boat house. As I cross the island for the third time in ten minutes, I am neither filled by whimsy nor worry, but am instead powered by a towering rage that is singularly directed at the man whose penis I should never have allowed within fifty feet of me.

We reach the boat house to find a short man in his autumn years looking out to sea with a scowl on his face, and both hands planted firmly on his hips.

'Excuse me? Do you speak English?' I ask him, trying to contain my unholy rage for a second.

The old man sees us both and his expression instantly warms. 'Hello there. Yes, yes I do speak English,' he says.

'Could you possibly help me?'

'I would hope so, my dear.' The old man looks down at Poppy, and provides her with a warm, avuncular smile. 'Hello there, young lady,' he says, eyebrows wiggling up and down. This instantly makes Poppy giggle.

'I'm looking for an idiot,' I tell the man.

'Oh?'

'Yes. An idiot. Otherwise known as my husband Jamie. He's five ten, brown hair, wearing a blue t-shirt and grey board shorts?'

When the old man's face darkens I know I'm on the right track. 'Yes, I know who you're on about,' he replies.

I sigh heavily and cross my arms. 'What's he done this time?'

The man introduces himself as Sylvester and proceeds to spin me a tale of such unbelievable stupidity, it could only be Jamie Newman at the centre of it.

I start to issue profound apologies the moment Sylvester finishes his story.

'No matter, my dear, he says. 'The more important thing right now is the fact that your husband has been gone for quite some time. Over an hour I'd say. I've certainly been waiting here a while for his return.'

That kernel of worry replants itself in my gut. 'You've got a good point,' I say, looking back out to sea. In my anger, I'd glossed over the fact that Jamie has been gone far longer than he should. Even if he has taken the pedalo out, there's no way he would have actively stayed away from me this long. He's an idiot, but he's not completely inconsiderate. He'd never do anything to deliberately make me worry.

Poppy looks up at Sylvester, narrows her eyes a bit and pulls on one lip thoughtfully. 'Can you get my Dad back?' she asks him.

Sylvester takes her hand. 'I wish I could little one. But I'm sure your Dad is fine. He'll be back soon.'

'But you're a wizard,' Poppy says, which I find a little bizarre. 'You know Gandalf.'

Sylvester smiles a bit awkwardly. 'Aah. I see what you mean.'
I certainly don't.

'I'm an actor, Mrs Newman,' the old man says when he sees the expression on my face. 'Poppy here may have seen me in a film.'

I'm taken aback. 'Oh. Popular film was it?'

Sylvester smiles. 'Quite a bit, yes.'

I'm about to ask more when Ritchie the boat house guy turns up on the scene. 'Mrs Newman,' he says to me, 'when will your husband be back? No-one is supposed to take the pedalo out for more than an hour.'

'I know Ritchie, something's wrong. There's no way he'd be gone this long without telling me!'

Ritchie picks up on my fretful tone and puts a hand on my shoulder. 'Don't worry. This happens every once in a while. People just get out a little too deep. I'll jump on the jet ski and go find him. I'm sure he's fine.'

I thank Ritchie for his help, and stay next to Sylvester the actor as we watch the Maldivian jump onto the jet ski moored on the short pier thirty yards away and go speeding off across the water.

'Everything will be okay,' Sylvester says.

'I hope so,' I reply, nibbling one fingernail.

Thirty minutes later, everything is *not* okay. Ritchie has returned with no sight of my husband, and hurries off to the centre of the island to raise the alert proper.

I am now a bag of nerves, and am barely able to hold back the tears. My mind is awash with images of Jamie drowning, being eaten by sharks, or suffering a heat induced heart attack. Possibly all at once.

Ritchie returns, and lets me know that he's sent the balloon up, so to speak. Across the island, near the main dock where the plane comes in, I can see a lot of frantic action as various Wimbufushi staff members are taking to a variety of small boats in order to track down Jamie's corpse.

A flutter of panic threatens to escape from my throat.

'Perhaps you should go back to your bungalow, Mrs Newman,' Ritchie suggests. 'You might be more comfortable there.'

This is his attempt to get me out of the way so I don't have to see my husband's bloated body being dragged up onto the beach in half an hour.

'That sounds like it might be a good idea,' Sylvester agrees. He can't help but flick his eyes down at Poppy as he does so, indicating that he can read between the lines just as much as I can.

'Okay,' I agree reluctantly. 'But I want to know as soon as you know anything.'

'Of course Mrs Newman, of course!' Ritchie reassures me.

'Would you like some company?' Sylvester asks.

'Yes please,' I tell him. There's something ever so comforting about his presence, but I can't quite put my finger on why. He certainly seems to be good with children.

Sylvester accompanies Poppy and I back to the water bungalow. As we walk along the jetty towards it, I can see a small flotilla of boats fanning out in all directions, and my heart leaps with cold, clammy terror. I again picture a big bloated fish belly white version of Jamie Newman being extricated from the water, and not for the first time in my life, curse the fact that I have a very vivid imagination.

Inexplicably, the cool breath of air-conditioning that greets me when I open the bungalow door causes a sharp, horrible shiver to course its way down my spine, despite the thirty degree heat.

'Mum? I want to see Dad!' Poppy demands in a quivering tone.

'I know sweetheart. I'm sure he'll be back any minute.' I curse myself for saying such a stupid thing as soon as it's passed my lips. I don't know any such thing, and lying to Poppy is never something that sits well with me, especially when it's such a serious issue.

'Why don't we go and look for fishes and crabbies in the water outside Poppy?' Sylvester says in a light voice.

Poppy gives the old man a critical look. 'It's not fishes and crabbies,' she tells him.

Sylvester's face crumples in mock confusion. 'Isn't it?' he appears to think about it for a second. 'Maybe it's fishy wishys and crabbalors then?'

'No!' Poppy giggles, despite herself. 'It's fish and crabs.' She takes one of his hands. 'Let me show you them.'

This old man seems to have a supernatural ability to keep children amused - and distracted. If I thought he'd accept it, I'd pay him for his services. He takes Poppy's hand, leading her onto the decking outside, and down the steps to the water's edge. This leaves me standing alone and able to fully contemplate the disappearance and likely drowning of my husband. I wish Sylvester had a way of distracting me as easily as he has my daughter.

An hour passes, and I've move from the stage of cool, clammy fear, into the turmoil of sheer, outright, boiling hot terror.

I've had no less than *three* separate visitors from Wimbufushi's staff - each more important than the last - culminating in the soft features and smooth tones of Mr Kadesh, the resort manager.

'I assure you Mrs Newman, we are doing everything in our power to find your husband.'

'Then where the hell is he?!' I rage. 'We're on an island in the middle of bloody nowhere! It's not like he can go and hide behind another island!' My eyes narrow. 'Unless you let him go out there on a faulty pedalo! Did you? Did you let my poor stupid husband out on to the open ocean on a malfunctioning pedalo, Mr Kadesh? Because if you did, you can be the one to explain to my poor daughter that her father has been killed thanks to your pedalo based negligence!' I'm obviously being crushingly unfair to Mr Kadesh, but I'm scared, tired and angry, so I have to lash out at someone.

'Now, now my dear. Try to stay calm,' says my new friend Sylvester from my side. He came back into the bungalow when Mr Kadesh arrived, leaving Poppy happily prodding a defenceless crab with a pencil.

'I don't want to stay calm! I want my husband back!'

'We have all our available boats out looking for him,' Mr Kadesh continues. 'I have also alerted the authorities in Malé, who are preparing a search and rescue team as we speak.'

The word 'search and rescue team' sends another gut-wrenching shiver down my spine.

I slump onto the bed and put my head in my hands. I'm trying very hard not to cry, but I'm failing miserably. Sylvester sits down next to me and puts an arm around my shaking shoulders. Mr Kadesh, a man evidently not used to this kind of thing, stands awkwardly in front of us both, looking into the middle distance.

'Mum!' I hear Poppy exclaim from the decking outside. 'Come and look!'

I wipe tears away and look at my daughter, who is standing up and holding a small and abused aquamarine crab in one hand. Bless her, she has no idea that our lives are about to be shattered. All she wants to do is show me her crab. I can't bear to break her childhood innocence, but I know the moment will come - right after I've identified Jamie's bloated corpse, I should imagine.

I need to compose myself before going out to her. 'I'll be there in a second sweetie, I promise,' I tell her, wiping my face again.

'No Mum! You need to come and look *now*!' Poppy insists, and whips her head around to look down over the railing that runs around the decking. She must have spotted an even bigger crab down there in the water.

'Okay Poppy, I'll be there in a second.' The last thing I need now is my daughter to go off into a tantrum because I'm not paying enough attention to her crustacean discoveries.

'Come here now Mum!' she demands, even louder.

'Poppy!' I snap. 'Just wait!'

She plonks the small crab down on the decking, stands upright, points one imperious finger over the railing and looks at me in no uncertain terms. 'It's Dad! Dad's here!'

Oh!

My poor sweet child!

Here I am snapping at her because I think all she cares about is a stupid bunch of crabs, and she's actually started to imagine that her father has returned! She must be so terrified!

I am the worst mother in the world!

I stride out onto the decking and gather her up in my arms. 'I'm so sorry Pops! I wish your Dad was here too!'

'He is Mum!' she says, squirming to and fro to get free.

'No Poppy... he's lost at sea! I'm so sorry! But there are plenty of people out looking for him, I promise you!'

The look of exasperation I am greeted with should not be possible for a seven year old. They simply haven't had enough life experience. Nevertheless, Poppy pulls it off with startling aplomb.

'No Mum! Dad isn't lost. He's down here!' She once again points a dainty finger down over the railing. If this is all in her imagination, it's doing a very good job of convincing her it's real.

I join her at the edge of the deck, and look down.

My heart skips ninety three beats in the space of a quarter of a second - which I realise is impossible, but it happens anyway.

Below me, bumping gently against one of the concrete pillars the decking is propped up with, is a pedalo. Slumped in one seat of the ridiculous contraption, with his head lolled back on his shoulders, is the pinkest Jamie Newman I have ever seen.

Pink, and very much alive, I am pleased to say.

'Hey baby,' he says in an exhausted and pained voice, as his eyes focus on me. 'I may have got a little bit sunburned. Do you think you could get me a drink and some aloe vera?'

'Jamie!' I cry in shock. 'You're not pale and bloated!'

He gives me a confused look. 'Er... thanks?'

'I mean... you're alive!'

'Dad!' Poppy exclaims happily. 'Do you want to see my new crab?'

Jamie gulps and blinks several times. 'I'd love to Pops, but first I think I might need some help. Laura, can you go and see if you can find me a doctor? I don't feel right.'

It is at this moment that Sylvester joins me and pokes his head over the railing. Jamie sees the helpful old man, and his face immediately darkens. 'Not that kind of fucking Doctor!' he wails, before promptly fainting into unconsciousness.

Luckily, Jamie's injuries appear to be confined to the kind of sunburn they warn you about on public information films, and a degree of dehydration that is solved by the consumption of two litres of water. By the time half an hour has passed, my husband is looking a lot better. So much so that the island's doctor has left us alone, as has poor old Sylvester and the rest of the Wimbufushi staff. Ample opportunity then, for me to enter into scolding mode.

'You absolute twat.'

'Yes, dear. I know.'

'You selfish, irresponsible idiot.'

'Yes, that's me.'

'You thoughtless moron.'

'Thoughtless moron... yes, I am indeed one of those.'

'You could have left me a widow and your daughter fatherless, just so you could have a go on a child's toy.'

'Hey, hey, hey! Steady on. It's not a child's toy.'

'Be quiet Jamie! I am the one speaking here, not you!'

'Yes dear.'

And so on, and so forth, for a good fifteen minutes, until Mr Kadesh knocks politely at the bungalow door. I open it and provide him with my best apologetic facial expression. It's one I'm well practiced at making, so it's very convincing.

'Hello Mrs Newman. How is the patient?'

I roll my eyes. 'He's fine. Sporting one hell of a sunburn and extremely embarrassed, but apart from that he'll be okay.'

'Excellent,' Kadesh beams, probably out of relief that his resort island hasn't been the site of a tourist death today. 'Do you think you will be able to make your plane back to Malé at three o'clock?'

I glance up at the clock on the wall of the bungalow, and am stunned to see that it's only just after half one in the afternoon. There's nothing like a heightened sense of panic to make you lose track of time. I could have sworn the search for Jamie went on for a good ten hours, but here we are, a mere three hours later and all has been resolved. 'Yes, definitely. He's fine to travel - as long as I cover him in enough cream. You'll probably want to lay down some plastic sheeting on the plane's seat.'

Mr Kadesh stares at me with mixed confusion and revulsion.

'Just kidding. We will all be fine to travel.' I bring out the apologetic smile again, because at this point, it really can't hurt.

'Mr Kadesh!' I hear Jamie call from behind me, and look round to see him coming towards us. Given that he is more sunburned than the Sahara, Jamie is walking with a strange, stiff gait that makes him look like C3PO with troublesome bowels. 'Thank you for all your help,' he says to the other man, offering a hand with a wince of pain.

Mr Kadesh warily reaches his own hand out. I can tell he's debating on whether it's a good idea to shake my husband's hand, for fear of some of the stupid rubbing off on him. Eventually good customer service wins out over understandable trepidation, and he pumps Jamie's hand up and down a couple of times, before letting go. 'No problem, Mr Newman. I'm just glad you are well.'

'Oh yes! Nothing that a bucket of Sudocrem and a visit to a skin specialist won't cure!'

The poor resort manager doesn't really know how to respond to this, so he simply bids us both good day, and scuttles off back to the island, no doubt to hand in his resignation and look for a job on the nearest fishing boat.

'Come on tomato boy, we'd best make sure we're packed properly if we're going to get off this island on time,' I tell Jamie and wander back across the bungalow to get my suitcase.

It's just as well we have a good hour and a half before the sea plane leaves, as it takes almost that long for Jamie to get dressed.

Picture, if you will, a man in moderate pain asked to accomplish a simple task on his own.

It's not a pretty sight, is it?

What should be the easiest thing in the world for a fully grown adult to do - get dressed - becomes a Herculean task for a man, when you introduce a bit of discomfort into the equation. You would think that given how violent and aggressive the buggers can be given the right motivation, they would power through pain in a very macho, Michael Bay movie kind of way, but nothing could be further from the truth.

I watch in dismay as my husband becomes a dainty little girl in front of my very eyes, wincing coquettishly every time he slides an item of soft material over his reddened skin. The painful enterprise is conducted at a snail's pace. Tectonic plates shift faster than a sunburned Jamie Newman putting a t-shirt on over his head.

I look over to where Poppy is happily packing her suitcase and evil, evil thoughts fill my head.

'Pops?' I call to her.

'Yes Mum!' she replies enthusiastically.

'Why don't you help Dad pull his t-shirt down for him?'

It's cruel, I know. But so is putting your family's future well being at risk because you want a go in a bloody pedalo.

'Okay Mum!'

Poppy skips over to where Jamie has the t-shirt just over his head and is contemplating the next tortuous move. She reaches up, grabs the hem and in a triumphant voice says 'let me help you Dad!'

'No, no, wait Poppy!' Jamie screeches, but to no avail.

With a mighty tug Poppy yanks the t-shirt down, scraping it over Jamie's lobster red belly.

You can tell he wants to scream at the very top of his lungs, but Jamie is a good father and he wouldn't want to scare his daughter that way. I am instead treated to the sight of his eyes bulging out of their sockets as he tries to contain the agony.

'Thank you sweetheart,' he tells Poppy in a high pitched, strangled whine, before shooting me a look of disgust.

I suppress the broad, smug grin that is threatening to envelop my head. 'Perhaps Poppy can help you with the rest of your clothes, Jamie? It might help you get packed a bit quicker?'

'No no! I can manage!' he moans and starts to awkwardly gather up his clothes. There are many ways to get a man to do what you want, but I can't think of a better one than aiming a well meaning seven year old in his direction.

Sadly, what I can't get Poppy to do is make Jamie walk any faster, so my daughter and I have to accompany C3PO and his bad bowels as he makes his turgid way back to the island and over to the jetty where the plane is due to take off. Still, at least I know what it'll be like to go for a walk with Jamie when we're both in our eighties.

As we shuffle our way towards the open plane door, I spy something out of the corner of one eye in the water about thirty yards away to my left.

With a grin of pure delight, friendly old Sylvester is paddling towards us on the pedalo. He looks to be in the absolute lap of luxury as he expertly steers the contraption around a couple of rocks and out around the plane.

I hear Jamie start to growl.

'Are you alright?' I ask him.

'That little bastard...' he hisses.

'What?'

'That little time travelling bastard. He's just rubbing it in!'

'You mean Sylvester? Be nice! He was very kind to Poppy and I while we thought you were fish food!'

Jamie growls again as Sylvester reappears from behind the tail fin of the plane, looking directly at Jamie with the most self-satisfied smile I've ever seen.

'Sod off Doctor!' Jamie shouts at him. 'I hope the bloody Daleks get you!'

In response, Sylvester simply laughs and pokes out his tongue at my irate husband.

With another growl, Jamie puts one foot up into the plane and moves painfully inside. But at the last minute he sticks his head back out and fixes the old man with another glare of pure malevolence. 'You know what?! I always preferred Colin Baker to you anyway! Everyone did!'

'Jamie! Get on the bloody plane!' I snap. For what feels like the umpteenth time that day I effect the apologetic smile and throw it in Sylvester's direction.

'Bye bye Mr Wizard!' Poppy shouts at the old man and gives him a wave.

Doctor? Wizard? What the hell are these two going on about?

It's just as well we're leaving the Maldives, as I think the sun has well and truly got to the two other members of my family and boiled their brains.

You can imagine how much fun the ten hour flight back to the UK is, can't you Mum?

The pained shuffling through the airport is bad, the constant hisses and moans coming from the seat next to me is far worse. You'd think Jamie was sitting on a giant cheese grater, rather than a plane seat, the way he keeps going on. He's also radiating an uncomfortable amount of heat from the sunburn. It's rather like being sat next to a malfunctioning boiler.

It is with some considerable relief that we start our descent into Gatwick. If nothing else, the cold March drizzle outside should sooth Jamie's injuries somewhat and give us all a bit of peace and quiet.

'Good to be home,' he says to me as we shuffle through customs.

'Yes, it is,' I say in a distracted voice. I'm slightly afraid that Jamie's odd gait will look deeply suspicious, and at any moment we're going to get pulled over by a customs officer, so he can check what my husband has got stuffed up his arse to make him walk in such a funny manner.

Luckily, no such thing occurs and before you know it we're out of the airport and making our way back to the car.

I hadn't planned on driving home, but I'd rather put up with that than listen to more malfunctioning boiler, so I tell Jamie to lie down on the back seat for a rest, and have Pops up front with me.

Jamie doesn't protest, and is fast asleep by the time we hit the M3. This suits me fine, as it gives me a bit of peace, and allows me to concentrate fully on the road, which is no easy thing at nine thirty in the morning when you've had about an hour's sleep and are jet lagged to the eyeballs.

I breathe a sigh of relief as we turn into our road, and breathe and even bigger one as I pull into the drive. All I can see in my future is a nice hot bath and some crisp white bed sheets. I'm going to sleep for a fort -

There's a man outside the house, huddled in the porchway to stay out of the drizzling rain.

As I pull into the drive, he walks towards the car. The hood of his battered old black coat is up so I can't quite see who it is.

I switch the engine off, open the car door and climb out.

'Hello there,' I say to the man with tired curiosity. 'Can I help you?'

'Well, you can start by giving me a hug!' he says in a cheerful voice as he whips back the hood.

The blood drains from my face.

My knees go weak.

The world starts to swim away.

'Dad?' I say in a faraway voice.

Bet you didn't see that one coming, did you Mum?
No, neither did I.

Love you, miss you, and want you around right now more than ever.

Your tired and shocked daughter Laura.

XX

Jamie's Blog
Saturday 8 May

Things have been a tad fraught in the Newman household over the past few weeks.

This sentence makes me a master of understatement to the extent that I believe I should be allowed to wear a shiny golden hat with the words 'Master Of Understatement' emblazoned across it.

The reasons for the complete lack of tranquility, peace, or sanity, are twofold.

Number one: Laura's father Terry has turned up out of the blue after thirty years of absence.

Now, a long lost relative appearing on your doorstep the minute you get home from a disastrous luxury holiday is enough to send anyone into a state of shock, but when said long lost relative is the only parent you have left on the planet, the shock and surprise are magnified beyond all comprehension.

Given the fact that Laura has not seen her father in three decades, and given the fact that he's only returned after she's come into some money, you can understand that her levels of suspicion were absolutely stratospheric once she'd got over the initial shock of seeing the old bastard.

'What do you want?' Laura asks him in a thin, growling tone, holding one hand out to ward him off from attempting to hug her. As she does this, I open the rear door of the car and slowly get out, trying not to rub any more sunburned skin off on my clothes.

Terry shakes his head in apparent dismay. His long, grey thinning hair sways around his head as the drizzle continues to come down. 'Wow. I knew you'd be surprised to see me, but I was really hoping you wouldn't be mad.'

'Wouldn't... wouldn't *be mad*?' Laura responds in flinty fashion.

'Mum? Who is this?' Poppy asks her mother as she clambers out of the car.

'Nobody,' Laura tells her in a flat tone. This makes Terry wince.

From the looks of the straggly long hair and badly maintained beard, it appears Terry's hippy tendencies haven't deserted him as he enters his old age. I'm fairly convinced that at any moment he's going to start talking about bad vibes and dark auras. I can't say I see much of Laura in his features - she really does take after her mother. There's a hangdog quality to Terry's looks that Laura has thankfully avoided.

'I'm your Grandad, little 'un,' Terry tells Poppy softly. 'Your long lost Grandad.'

Laura takes Poppy's hand. 'You are no such thing,' she snaps. 'Now I think you should leave.'

Terry looks disheartened. 'But I came to talk to you sweetheart! To see if I can, you know, mend things between us.'

'*Mend things*? There's nothing *to* mend! You left me when I wasn't much older than my daughter here. You're not part of my life! You never have been! You elected to leave me all those years ago, now I want you to do the same.' Laura walks Poppy around Terry across the front garden, giving the old man a wide berth.

It occurs to me that sunburn or not, I'm going to have to order this man to go away in as manly a tone as I possibly can. 'I think you'd better get out of here, Terry,' I tell him, lowering the octave of my voice slightly.

He points a finger at me and smiles. 'You're Jamie, right? Love your books, mate.'

'Do you?' I reply suspiciously.

'Yeah! They're great.' Terry's eyes go wide as he realises the implications of what he's saying. 'But Laura! That's not why I'm here! Your books I mean!'

She turns back to him. 'Really?' she says in disbelief. 'You mean that you haven't just turned up here after all this time because you've found out that my husband and I have done alright for ourselves writing books?'

'No!' he rubs his eyes. 'Well, of course that's how I heard about you and found you... but I'm not here for anything!' He puts out his hands, palms up. 'I don't want your money, Laura! I don't want anything from either of you.' He sighs. 'I just... I just saw your face in a magazine, and even though I haven't seen you since you were a little girl, I recognised it instantly, even before I read the article. And I just felt so bad that I didn't know you any better than anyone else who could pick up that mag and read it.' He walks toward Laura, arms still open. 'I've been a stupid, selfish, awful man. All these years. All I wanted to do was come see you. Come and apologise. To tell you that I am so, so sorry for everything I've done... and not done over the years.'

It's heartfelt, it's convincing, it's eloquent, it's raw.

And I don't believe a fucking word of it.

However, this is something I must sit back and watch. If I jump in now (sunburn notwithstanding) and get in the middle of this, I will come to regret it. I have to trust that Laura will make the right decision here.

My wife swallows hard, blinks away what I'm sure is a combination of rain water and tears, and fixes Terry with a hard stare. 'I have just got off a plane. I am tired, dirty and fed up. I do not need to be standing here having this conversation with *you*.'

'But - '

'You need to leave Da - *Terry*,' she tells him. 'I can't deal with this right now.'

Well done, I think. *Give the old bastard his marching orders.*

'But you can come back tomorrow morning.'

What?

'I'll be in a better frame of mind then... and maybe I'll listen to what you have to say.'

I'm somewhat flabbergasted by this turn of events, but age has brought me wisdom, so I keep my thoughts to myself - for the minute at least.

Terry seems very pleased at this last minute reprieve. But then he would, wouldn't he?

'Okay sweetheart,' he says, backing away with his hands still out. 'That's fine, that's fine. I'll come back tomorrow and we'll talk then.' As he moves away, he comes closer to where I'm still standing by the car door.

'Watch it, pal,' I say in a dark tone as he almost backs right into me.

Terry looks around. 'Sorry mate!'

'I'm not your mate, Terry. I suggest you go away now - *quickly*.'

The old hippy doesn't need telling twice. He hurries off down the driveway and out into the street, turning back for a final time to give Laura a wave. 'I'll see you tomorrow!' he calls to her, before he flips the hood of his old coat up again, and wanders back towards the main road.

I carefully approach my wife where she stands watching him go. She catches sight of my expression. 'Don't say it, tomato boy.'

'Don't say what?'

'What I know you're thinking.'

I sigh. 'I don't think this is a good idea, baby. But he's your father. I'll go with whatever you say.'

Her eyes turn flinty again. 'He's not my father Jamie... at least not yet.'

Terry does indeed turn up the next day, bright and early. Discretion being the better part of valour, I decide to take Poppy down to the park for a few hours so Laura can bash things out with her father in private. Besides, I'm not that keen on Poppy hanging around the old codger, and getting her away from him suits me just fine.

By the time we get back home, Terry is thankfully gone, and I find Laura standing in the kitchen with a coffee in her hand looking deeply contemplative.

'How did it go?' I ask cautiously.

'I'm not sure. He certainly says all the right things. I don't think I've ever spent so long in the company of someone who felt the need to apologise to me over and over.'

'Blimey, and this is coming from a woman married to me,' I respond, trying to add a little levity to the situation.

'Quite,' she says with a half smile. 'I'm going to see him again,' she adds.

'Okay,' I reply, keeping things nice and neutral.

One eyebrow arches. 'I thought you'd be mad.'

'Oh, I'm mad, Laura. Just not at you. If you want to give him a chance, then I'm not going to stop you. Just understand that I'm not going to embrace the old sod as my father-in-law any time soon either.'

'Fair enough.'

So begins an extremely tentative campaign of father/daughter reconciliation.

Over the next few weeks Laura starts to see Terry more and more. They go for coffee together in town, she visits him in the flat he's renting a few miles away. He continues to apologise profusely for all the wrongs he's done her, she continues to listen and evaluate how honest he's being. I continue to not trust him as far as I can throw him - which of course starts to cause tension between Laura and I.

This tension only grows when, after a month, things between them have thawed to the point that she asks me if she can bring him along to my 40th birthday party on Friday.

Which, my friendly, happy reader, brings me to the second reason for why the Newman household has been so fraught recently.

I am turning 40.

Let me just repeat that in bold capital letters for added effect: I AM TURNING FORTY.

How the fuck have I allowed this to happen?

How the hell can it have come to pass that Jamie Newman has reached the fourth decade of his life on this little blue planet?

It's inconceivable.

What's made the whole thing ten times worse is that I didn't realise it was happening until about four weeks ago.

Oh, of course I knew *intellectually* that I was going to turn forty very soon, I'm not that forgetful. But on an emotional, visceral level, I'd managed to block the horror of the whole thing out, right up until the point my mother tells me she's arranged for a fortieth birthday party at her house one afternoon over coffee.

'What?' I splutter at her, looking up from my task of intently picking off a small bit of peeling skin from my arm. The sunburn had gone down nicely by this point, but I did resemble a snake in the middle of an annual shed, unfortunately.

'A birthday party, Jamie. It's your fortieth. You can't let that go by without a party.'

'My fortieth,' I repeat in a stunned voice. 'I'm going to be forty.'

'Yes son, you are. And I thought it might be nice if I arranged things for you, instead of Laura. The poor girl sounds like she's got her hands full with her father returning out of the blue like that, so I'm sure she'd appreciate it.'

88

'Yes. Yes, she probably would,' I say in a light, sing song voice. For some reason the world has gone a bit grey around the edges.

'Are you alright?' Mum asks.

'Oh, oh, I'm fine mother. Absolutely fine.'

She rolls her eyes. 'You're turning forty Jamie, not dying.'

'Yes, yes. Turning forty. Not dying.' I sit there slack jawed for a moment. 'It's just a little... a little bit of a shock, that's all.'

'A shock? It's not like it's a surprising turn of events, Jamie.'

'No. I'll concede that. But, there's been a lot going on. What with the books, and Terry, and sunburn, and... ' I can't actually think of another 'and' off the top of my head, but surely those three things are enough to distract anyone from their slide into old age, aren't they?

'Well, it's coming. And we should celebrate it properly.'

'Okay. Can we all wear black and play the funeral march?' I ask, only half joking.

Mum snorts and slaps me gently on one arm. 'Oh, you think turning forty is bad, do you? You wait until you get to my age!'

I wisely choose not to respond to that.

'It'll be fun, Jamie,' she continues. 'We'll make sure your brother and sister are here. You can invite some of your friends too, if you like.'

'Just family is fine!' I hurriedly respond. Mum might want to make an event of this, but I'd rather keep it as low key as possible, with the minimum number of people present. Frankly, the ideal number of people present would be zero, but I know better than to argue with my mother when she's planning something, so I just smile and nod as she starts to list what wonderful methods we can employ to mark my descent into frail dotage.

I'm happy with her suggestion of a nice meal and a bit of cake, but draw the line at the outdoor bunting and over-sized gazebo.

Mum inevitably looks upset. If there's one thing she loves to do, it's organise a party. 'Okay Jamie. Whatever you want,' she says, in something of a huff.

When I return home and tell Laura that Mum has volunteered to organise the party, I expect fireworks. Laura has never been keen on my mother stepping into roles that she thinks are fixed firmly in her domain as my wife. It's a testament to how preoccupied Laura is with her father's return that she doesn't put up any kind of protest whatsoever. 'That's very nice of her, baby. I'll look forward to it.'

'So, you're fine with this, are you?' I ask warily.

'Yep. Why wouldn't I be?'

'Oh. Okay.' I have to confess I am both surprised, and I'll admit, a little hurt.

I know Terry's reappearance has been a huge deal for my wife, but I can't pretend that it doesn't sting when Laura displays a complete lack of interest in my birthday celebrations. I just have to hope things settle down in the not too distant future and I can go back to being the centre of Laura's attention, as is my right as a complete and utter selfish bastard.

There's tension to be had in spades as we get closer to the day of my birth, and the day of the party.

As the days, hours and minutes go by, I get increasingly waspish and irritated with just about everyone. I snap at Laura, I'm dismissive of Poppy, I have at least two arguments on the phone with our agent Craig, and complete strangers in cars are treated to my middle finger being thrust at them every time they so much as dare to drive in a way I do not find one hundred percent acceptable.

'Jamie,' Laura says to me on the couch two days before the main event, 'just tell me this. After your birthday has passed, is there any chance you're going to stop acting like a complete arsehole? Only, if you think this personality swing is more permanent I'm going to have to consult our solicitors, and get papers drawn up that you really aren't going to want to sign.'

I sigh. 'I'm sorry sweetheart. I'm sure I'll be fine afterwards. I'm just not having a particularly good time dealing with this. I just see this horrible thing coming towards me that I can't avoid.'

'You're turning forty. You haven't been diagnosed with a terminal disease.'

I shake my head ruefully. 'My mother told me much the same thing.'

'Well, you should listen to us both and stop being such a mope. Look forward to the party.'

I look horrified. 'You do remember that my *mother* is organising it, don't you?'

'What's that supposed to mean?'

'It means that Mum is not one for the small, subtle gestures Laura. I dread to think what she's got in store for me.'

And before I know it, the terrible, terrible day dawns.

Disappointingly, it turns out to be warm and sunny. I was rather hoping for a hurricane, or the type of electrical storm that causes wild animals to leave the area six hours beforehand; either would have felt more appropriate. Having to wade your way through such a horrendous occasion should not be accompanied by twenty three degree warmth, with the sound of happy birdsong in the background.

It's 11.30am before I manage to get off the couch. As I rise, I make a grunting sound that I swear I didn't make this time yesterday - when I was still thirty nine and young.

Laura suggests a walk for the three of us in the nearby forest, which I half heartedly agree to. It's very hard to spend your time sighing and feeling sorry for yourself when you're walking through sun dappled woods under a bright blue sky.

Poppy seems extremely keen on the idea though. Mind you, she's a seven-year-old girl, so the chance to go outside and play is always met with huge enthusiasm, even if it took place during the aforementioned hurricane.

Twenty minutes into the walk and I'm feeling a little better - and a little more philosophical - about the aging process.

'It's not so bad, I suppose,' I tell Laura, as we both watch Poppy picking up pine cones.

'What isn't?'

'Turning forty.'

'Why the change of heart?'

'Well, it's better than the alternative, isn't it?'

'Which is?'

'Not turning forty.'

'Eh?'

'It's either keep getting older, or go six feet under. There are no other choices available.'

'I see.'

'In a way, every birthday should be greeted with a degree of relief. It means you've managed to avoid getting yourself killed for another year.'

'Which for you is something of a miracle, of course.'

'Very funny.'

We continue to walk in silence for a few metres, gazing on in parental satisfaction as our only child cartwheels her way along the path, giggling every time she does one full rotation.

'Jamie?' Laura says.

'Yes, sweet?'

'Do you mind if my father comes to your birthday party?'

I stop dead in my tracks. 'What? You *want* him to come?'

'Yes... well, at least I think so. We're getting along far better than I ever thought we would. And your whole family will be there, and I just thought... I just wanted... '

'To have your own family there too, for a change?' I finish for her in a soft voice.

Damn it. I was all ready to be angry at her for suggesting that Terry the grey hippy attends what should be a family occasion, but the catch in her voice and the look of sadness in her eyes are just too much for me.

Laura grabs my hand. 'Please don't misunderstand, Jamie. You and Poppy are my family, and you're both all I'll ever need, but I haven't had a parent by my side for most of my life. And even though I'm still not convinced my father isn't a complete idiot, I do want to keep trying. He's the only dad I've got.'

I lean forward and give my wife a gentle kiss. 'Of course he can come, baby.'

I'm not happy about it. *You're* not happy about it. But what else am I supposed to do?

Sometimes you just have to bite the bullet and put somebody else's feelings first.

'Evening Terry,' I say as cheerfully as I can when the old man gets into the back seat of the car.

'Hi Jamie!' he replies, and passes me a rather battered looking envelope. 'Happy birthday!'

'Thanks.'

'Hello Terrygrandad,' Poppy exclaims from her booster seat beside him. This is the name she's settled on for her grandfather. You get the feeling that she's as unsure about the man's intentions as I am, and wants to keep her options open on the naming front.

'Hello Poppy!' Terry replies. 'Doesn't your mum look beautiful this evening?'

For once I can agree with the old hippy. Laura does indeed look stunning in her new blue evening dress. I also got a glimpse of the lingerie set she's wearing underneath it earlier - which my forty-year-old penis was delighted about, let me tell you.

'Thank you Dad,' Laura responds. 'You look nice too.'

If you can call a faded black and red tie dyed shirt, and twenty year old chinos *nice*, I suppose.

I immediately feel disgusted with myself. I sound like a bitchy drag queen. The sooner we get this evening over and done with, the sooner I can return to being the happy go lucky, carefree Jamie Newman that everyone knows and loves.

Hmmm.

It is with a mounting sense of terror that I park in Mum and Dad's driveway. While I can see no gigantic gazebo peeking out from the back garden, or hoards of unlikely well wishers crowded around the front windows, I can't quite shake the feeling that my mother has got something planned that I don't know about.

The feeling goes away a little as we enter the house to be greeted by members of my extended family - and *nobody else*. Okay, I could have done without Uncle Fred and Auntie Kathy being invited, given that I haven't seen hide nor hair of them for seven years, and pulling my poor old 92 year old grandmother Enid out of her nursing home for the night is cruel and unusual punishment for one so frail - especially given that it's bridge night. Apart from that though, Mum has stuck to her word. She's managed to resist the urge to invite everyone I've ever met, and pack the house to the rafters. This party might not actually be as bad as I was fearing.

In fact, once we've got all the birthday kisses and present fondling out of the way, I'm feeling decidedly good about myself. The large Jack Daniels and Coke I have gripped in one hand is no doubt helping matters. I'm not even mad that Terry appears to be going down a storm with my family. The old sod may be the worst father in the world, but he's a charming bugger, and no mistake. Fred and Kathy seem delighted by every word he says, and even my cynical and world weary sister Sarah seems to approve of him.

'He's very funny,' she tells me as she sips her Bacardi. 'You should ask him about living in Goa. It sounds like he had a wonderful time.'

'The wonderful time he was having when he should have been a father to Laura, you mean?'

Sarah lays her hand on my shoulder. 'You're having a hard time with this, aren't you?'

'Do you blame me?'

'No. But Laura seems happy.'

I sigh. 'Yes. She does, doesn't she? I guess if she can get over it, I can as well.'

Sarah blinks a few times in surprise. 'Bloody hell! You actually sounded like a mature adult for a second there, bruv. You want to be careful!'

'Piss off.'

'Attention everyone!' I hear my mother's voice call from across the broad expanse of the country kitchen. 'It's time for the cake!'

On cue, my father appears from the walk-in pantry, carrying what looks like a giant copy of Love From Both Sides on a silver platter. As he draws closer though, I can see that the book is actually a cake. The cartoon versions of Laura and I have been replaced by real pictures of us both, and the title has been changed to read 'Happy Birthday Jamie'. In every other respect though, it looks identical to the book that has changed our lives so much in the past couple of years.

I actually feel a little choked up. The time, effort and thought my mother must have put into getting this made is unbelievable.

'Wow,' is all I manage to say.

'Happy birthday, my son,' Dad says to me as he puts down the cake.

My mother joins him, and places a single candle in the middle of the intricate icing. She lights it and stands back. 'Time to sing everyone!' she says. 'One, two, three... *happy birthday to you,*'

And so everyone joins in with the time honoured - and very expensive to use in a book, if you include more than one line of the lyrics - theme of a million birthdays throughout history.

It's all jolly nice. Even my sainted old grandmother Enid is singing along, though there's every possibility she thinks she's singing happy birthday to Winston Churchill.

There's even a spontaneous round of applause at the end. It's all enough to give me a warm fuzzy, forty year old glow. Though that may also be the Jack Daniels.

'Blow the candle out!' Sarah demands with a laugh. I duly oblige, which grants me another round of applause. Birthdays are very strange things. In no other circumstance in normal human social interaction would a group of people clap the simple task of puffing out a candle. It's rather like everyone giving you a cheer every time you sneeze into a hankie, or walk through an open doorway without tripping up and falling on your arse.

'Thank you, Mum,' I say, like the indulged child that I am. 'Thank you everyone. You've made the horror of turning forty just that bit more beara - '

DING DONG!

Mum and Dad's comically loud doorbell interrupts my impromptu birthday speech.

'Aha!' Mum cries in excitement. 'That'll be my special treat for you, Jamie!'

Special treat?

Special *treat*?

But I already have a cake in the shape of my book, and am already surrounded by my loving family (and Terry). What on Earth else could I want right now?

'Come on everyone, out into the hallway! Chris!' My mother points a finger at my older brother. 'You wheel Enid out!'

Chris rolls his eyes, but accepts his job as designated Enid carer, and grabs the handles of her wheelchair.

Nervously, I shuffle out into the broad expanse of Mum and Dad's entrance hall, along with everyone else. Mum is already at the front door, and is swinging it open to reveal four men dressed in waiter's outfits. They each have a fake twirly moustache, slicked black hair, and neat black waistcoats over their pristine white shirts. They also all wear large, floppy bowties and have the shiniest shoes I've ever seen.

...actually, they don't look like waiters, they look more like -

Oh good lord.

Mum has ordered me a barbershop quartet for my birthday.

She claps her hands excitedly and turns to look at me. 'Isn't it brilliant Jamie!'

'Er... '
'They come highly recommended!'
'Okay... '
'They've got a special birthday song for you!'
'Right... '

The four men file into the hall, and fan out in front of us. One produces what looks like a kazoo from his back pocket and plays a single note.

Then the song begins.

All four men burst into harmonious singing - and boy, the lyrics are something else.

'Hello Jamie, that's your namie,'
'It's your birthday today, and you're looking rather gay,'

Terrible start. Let's hope it improves as it goes along.

'You're turning forty, but you're not warty,'
'Your skin still looks clean, and it has a healthy sheen,'

Getting worse.

'You're getting older, but not much bolder,'
'As the years ebb away, you'll get wrinkled and grey,'

Oh, well that's charming. Where did Mum find this lot?

'You'll get a bad cough, your cock will drop off,'
'Your teeth will fall out. You'll look horrid, there's no doubt,'

I stare at them in amazement. Am I actually hearing this right? From the look on Mum's face, it appears that I am. She has gone from sheer delight during the first verse, to horrified dismay as the song has gone on. The rest of my family are looking equally shocked. The Newmans are not an attractive bunch when we're all standing open mouthed, looking like a bunch of guppies at feeding time.

'You'll have a huge stroke, it will be no joke,'

'They'll have to feed you with a spoon. Your sad death is coming soon,'

What makes this awful song even worse, is that all four men are singing in happy, light tones, with the broadest shit eating grins I've ever seen across their faces. It's like all my worst enemies have clubbed together and hired the barbershop quartet from Hell to serenade me into an early grave.

If we weren't all quite so fucking British, one of us would surely have stopped the harmonious character assassination by now, but as it is, the singing lunatics are allowed to do another verse.

'Your corpse will bloat up, so let's raise one last cup,'
'As they throw you in the ground, you won't make a bloody sound!'

I feel like crying.

'Woah, woah, woah!' Laura shouts and waves her arms angrily about in front of her. She steps forward and moves towards the quartet - who thankfully stop singing, before they can launch into another verse about how my loved ones will cry... and then go and eat some Thai.

The broad smiles have been replaced by a mixture of fear and confusion. This is obviously the first time somebody with an angry look on their face has interrupted them mid-flow, which, given the content of their lyrics, astounds me.

'What the hell are you doing?' Laura says to them incredulously.

'We're... we're singing our birthday song,' one of them replies in a doubtful voice.

'But it's horrible!'

'Well, yes. We know. But... but that's the point.'

'What do you mean, *that's the point?*'

'We're The Black Barbershop Quartet, aren't we.'

'Are you?'

'Yeah!'

'Is that supposed to mean something to me?' Laura demands.

I think I'm beginning to grasp what's going on here. I figure I'd better step forward before my wife chins one of these poor buggers. I have the feeling that the blame does not lie with them for this.

'Mum?' I ask. 'Where did you find these guys?'

'I looked them up online, Jamie,' she replies in a faraway voice. She's obviously having trouble getting past the idea of me having a stroke and being fed with a spoon. 'They were one of the closest and one of the cheapest, so I thought they would be good.'

'And I guess you didn't read much about their actual act?'

'They're a barbershop quartet. Everyone knows what a barbershop quartet does, don't they?' She gives me an imploring look.

'Oh my God!' I hear Sarah exclaim from behind me. She's holding out her iPhone to me. 'I've just looked them up! It says they specialise in blackly humorous four part harmony. It looks like Mum ordered the 'We'll Sing You Into Your Grave' package.'

'Yep, that's the one,' the guy replies. 'Only forty quid, very reasonable.'

Mum continues to look aghast. 'But... but, I didn't know Jamie! I honestly didn't!'

Time for some careful reassurance, I feel. I put one arm around her shoulder. 'It's okay Mum. You weren't to know. Laura? Could you see the gentlemen out please?'

'Sure.'

I give them all a smile. 'Thank you for coming. You, er, you rhyme very well, and have lovely singing voices.'

Laura ushers The Black Barbershop Quartet out of the door, and I gently coax Mum back to the kitchen.

'I wanted to hear more!' pipes up Enid from her wheelchair. 'Haven't heard a good barbershop quartet since Pearl's wedding. Very handsome they were.'

'I'll ask them for a CD, Mum,' Dad says, taking over from Chris in the wheelchair guiding department.

It takes me a good ten minutes to calm my poor mother down to the point that I've managed to convince her she isn't the worst parent in the history of the world. I'm half tempted to point at Terry to underline my point, but manage to resist the urge.

The rest of the party goes off more or less without a hitch. Enid spends most of it telling Terry about how dishy the barbershop quartet at Pearl's wedding looked. To be fair to him, he fakes his interest very well. Mum is fine after a couple of Baileys over ice, which gives me a chance to detach from her and speak to my two siblings - something which I don't have much opportunity to do these days. Uncle Fred and Auntie Kathy are being completely captivated by Poppy and her fascinating stories about how many small, defenceless creatures she's poked in the past couple of weeks. This leaves Laura talking to my father. Or rather, trying to keep a smile on her face as my father's eyes inevitably wander down to get a quick look at her tits every thirty seconds or so.

By 10.30 Poppy is yawning her head off. 'Can I put her in the spare room, Jane?' Laura asks Mum.

'Of course, my dear. It's all set up for the night, as we agreed.'

What's this? I didn't know Laura had arranged for Mum to babysit tonight.

I say as much to my wife as we go to get our tired daughter from where she's flaked out on Uncle Fred's lap.

'Well, I haven't given you your birthday present yet, Jamie,' she tells me softly, as I carry Pops out of the room and up the stairs. This'll have to stop soon. Poppy is getting far too big to be carried, but it's hard to let go of the fact that your little girl is growing up - and is not actually so little anymore.

'I thought we agreed the holiday was my early birthday present this year?' I say to Laura. 'Given how much it was? I told you I didn't want anything else.'

'I know, but the whole pedalo debacle put the dampeners on it a bit, so I thought I might give you a little something extra.' Laura arches one eyebrow suggestively. 'Your birthday present this year is going to be one word.'

'One word? What do you mean?'

'You'll find out later,' she says cryptically and pats me on the cheek. 'Now let's put Poppy in bed for the night. She knows she's staying with her Grandma, so she'll be fine.'

We both coo for a few moments over our gorgeous sleeping offspring, and then wend our way back to the party, which, I'm grateful to note given what Laura has just told me, has reached the point where people are checking their watches and flicking their eyes occasionally at the door.

Uncle Fred and Auntie Kathy lead the grand exodus, offering to drop Enid back at the care home, before the staff send out a search party. Enid doesn't seem happy about it, given that she's moved on from telling Terry about Pearl's wedding, and is now regaling him with the time she seduced the local postman in a pair of French nylons that Pearl gave her for her twenty fifth. Terry looks relieved when Fred wheels Enid away. The green complexion really doesn't go well with the straggly grey beard.

Mum is once again highly apologetic at the front door as we leave. Sarah is still humming the tune The Black Barbershop Quartet used to inadvertently humiliate me, while Chris is now on his phone trying to book them for his mate's wedding in a month.

'Don't worry, Mum. I really enjoyed myself. The cake was fantastic,' I tell her.

'Thank you, son. I do feel so embarrassed. It's like something from one of your books!' Her eyes go wide. '*Please* don't put this in one of your books!

'Of course I won't!' I lie expansively. I'm already formulating a suitable plotline.

Laura, who kindly offered to be designated driver for the evening, then takes us away and back towards Terry's flat in the city. We drop him off and head home, blissfully on our own for the first time all day.

By the time we're indoors, I've started panting like a dog.

'Calm down boy,' Laura says in a husky voice. 'Just enjoy the anticipation for a moment. I want a nice big glass of wine before we get down to any funny business.'

I pour us both a glass and we settle down to drink it at the dining room table. It doesn't take either of us long to down the wine. It's rare these days that we get time alone in the house without Poppy, and both of us are eager to make the most of it.

'So, what's my one word birthday present then?' I ask, trying not to salivate too much.

'Come upstairs with me,' Laura replies and moves towards the stairs.

My mind is racing. What one word could she possibly say that would be a birthday present? There are plenty of great words in the world. *Kumquat*, for instance. Or *verisimilitude*. *Azure* is lovely, as is *coruscate*. I always like to use *defenestrate* in conversation wherever possible, and get a thrill every time I hear somebody else say *intransigent*.

All great words, but none that I would consider worthy of giving to somebody else as a gift.

We reach the bedroom.

'So? What's the word, baby?'

Laura backs away from me slowly. She stands to one side of the bed and slowly starts to unzip her dress, her eyes not leaving me for a second. The dress is shrugged off to reveal her stunning lingerie set.

She takes a deep breath, licks her lips slightly and runs her hands over her breasts.

In a soft, husky voice, she says one solitary word to me. And it's all my birthdays and Christmases come at once.

'Anal.'

My penis, no stranger to the metaphorical victory lap, is now circumnavigating the entire globe at five thousand miles an hour, while blowing loudly on a three headed trumpet. As he reaches the African continent, he sets off several million pounds worth of fireworks and high fives at least sixty percent of the population, before performing a victory moonwalk over the North pole while curing cancer.

I can't fucking *wait* to turn fifty!

Laura's Diary
Wednesday, May 19th

Dear Mum,

One thing I wasn't prepared for when Jamie and I embarked on our joint career as authors was how much interaction with the public we'd have.

Now, don't get me wrong, I like to talk to new people as much as the next person, but when that conversation is held in a crowd of well meaning fans - and the conversation topic is usually about what continuity errors you've made between chapters four and five - it can get a bit disconcerting.

I'd always had a romantic vision of what being a writer was about in my head. You know the one. It features an expansive study lined with bookshelves, an antique desk in gorgeous stained cedar wood, a comfy, plush Chesterfield chair, and a polished, vintage typewriter sat next to a pile of crisp, clean paper. There's always a shaft of warm morning sunlight filtering in between the curtains, and the smell of freshly made coffee is in the air.

All utter bollocks, of course. I write at a two hundred quid flat pack desk from Staples, sat on a blue office chair that squeaks every time you so much as move it half a millimetre, and I type on a bluetooth keyboard connected to an iMac that is at least two years out of date.

Also utter bollocks is the notion that you get to write in splendid isolation, safe in the knowledge that all you have to do is hand your completed book off to a publisher, and sit back while they sell the bugger to the public.

Aha ha. *Nope.*

That may have been the case back in Hemingway's day, but in the 21st century, being an author is as much about being a master of self promotion as it is sitting at a computer and knocking out eighty thousand words of prose every six months.

I have a Twitter account.

Me. Laura Newman.

A woman whose attitude to the internet has always been one of annoyed tolerance. I know it's there, I know it can be useful, and I'll use it when absolutely necessary, but other than that, it can just stay over in the corner where I can't see it. Jamie's different of course. He's been writing that bloody blog for a decade now, so he's well versed in the vagaries of social media. I therefore let him handle all the comings and goings that occur via the Twitter handle @NewmanWriters.

I might occasionally dip in and see what people are talking about, but once my well-meaning husband starts going on about hashtags and trending topics I tend to lose interest.

Along with creating an 'online presence', I am also required to be available offline for public appearances - designed to give the fans chance to say hello, and for our publishers to ram our newest project down their throats.

These appearances generally take place in bookstores, involve Jamie and I signing copies of our books, and are about as well received as genital herpes.

That's the impression I've take away from the two signings we've done, anyway. During the first, we had two people show up for a signed copy of Love From Both Sides. I say two - one of them was an elderly lady who quite clearly suffered from Alzheimer's and thought I was Ethel Merman. The other was my best friend Mel, who had only come out to show us a bit of solidarity. It transpires that success in the book charts does not necessarily square with the public's desire to turn out and meet you in person.

The second signing had more people - approximately a dozen - but half of them had only come in to get out of the driving rain outside, and the other half looked decidedly disappointed to meet the real Jamie and Laura Newman, after having read about the far more exciting and better looking versions they'd encountered in our semi-autobiographical comedies.

Given these previous experiences, you can imagine my joy when Watermill's bouncing publicist Tori Brightling arranges a third book signing for Love Under Different Skies. The book has been faring quite well online, and in high street retailers, so Tori has decided on a third bite of the cherry.

'You're bound to get more people out this time!' she tells me excitedly down the phone. Tori does everything with excitement, up to and including urination, so I'm taking her optimism with a pinch of salt. 'I've booked you and Jamie in at Morninghouse Books on Tuesday May 17th. Do you know it?'

I gulp. Oh yes. I know Morninghouse Books very well, thank you Tori. It's the oldest bookstore in a hundred mile radius, and has squatted in the middle of the old Victorian terraces just off the High Street for the past century. Run by a succession of stern faced Morninghouse men, its cramped three stories of bookshelves are famous for both their musty smell, and their collection of rare books you'd struggle to find anywhere else. If it could, Morninghouse Books would give the nearest Waterstones a clip round the ear and tell it to bugger off home to its mother.

I haven't been into the store for over twenty years. Not since I got caught by a stern Morninghouse in the cookery section with Dan Sanderson's hand halfway down my bra.

You remember Dan, don't you Mum? Nice boy, bit of a squint.

I feel that all these decades later, I can admit to the fact I used to let him put his hand down my bra - if he'd been nice to me and we were in a suitably private place, that is. On that particular day, we'd only popped into the store so Dan could pick up a birthday present for his Gran, and one thing had led to another, so to speak.

I've never been thrown out of a shop before, and haven't since, so the prospect of returning to the scene of my mild teenage crime is not one that fills me with pleasure.

Still, Tori has gone to all the trouble of arranging this signing, and I'm contractually obligated to do at least one of these things when a book comes out, so it's time to swallow any fears or doubts I might have... and warn Jamie that he won't be getting to repeat any of Dan's antics.

I know my husband well.

'Spoilsport,' he says, when I tell him of both the signing and my previous experience in Morninghouse Books. 'I feel as your husband that I should be allowed to place my hand down your bra at every given opportunity.'

'And I feel as your wife that I should be allowed to ignore everything that comes out of your mouth at every given opportunity,' I reply in a withering voice, and turn to write the date for the signing on the kitchen calendar.

A date that comes around altogether too bloody quickly. I do find these public events something of a trial.

It's not an issue Jamie Newman has, however. He's positively vibrating back and forth in his seat as we park in the multi-story car park close to the shop.

'I bet there will be more people at this one!' he crows triumphantly. 'After all, we've got a few books out now. We must have built up a fairly decent fan base. Certainly enough to fill up a tiny independent book shop, anyway.'

I give him a look. 'You've never been in Morninghouse Books, have you?' I point out.

'What makes you say that?'

'Morninghouse Books is *enormous*. Not in that open plan layout, modern way that you get in Waterstones. It's a three story monstrosity, with more shelves than you can shake several sticks at. The place is crammed to the rafters with books, but there's still enough room for a few hundred people, if needs be. There's every chance there's a doorway to Narnia somewhere in there, or possibly the corpse of Lord Lucan.'

Jamie's face falls. 'Damn. I was hoping it'd be titchy so it looks like we can fill up the place.'

I roll my eyes. My husband has developed slight delusions of grandeur over the past few months. The successful author thing has gone to his head. Sadly, even with authorial success, there are levels to your popularity. Stephen King might be able to pack out a bookstore for a signing, but Jamie and Laura Newman are nowhere near that famous - or rich, unfortunately.

I'll just be pleased if I don't get mistaken for Vera Lynn, to be honest.

Jamie tries to avoid looking disappointed as we round the corner, and Morninghouse Books homes into view. I bet in his mind's eye he saw a queue of people outside, all eagerly clutching a copy of Love Under Different Skies. In the real world however, no such thing has occurred. There is one chap stood outside the store, but he is wearing a fluorescent green council jacket and has a broom in his hand, so I think we can safely say he's not here to speak to a couple of romantic comedy authors.

A funny feeling washes over me as we walk up to the shop's entrance. It's part nostalgia, and part the lingering sensation of broad teenage embarrassment. The large shop window doesn't seem to have changed much in twenty years. 'Morninghouse Books' is still emblazoned across it in serif gold writing, and the wooden display stands are still dark stained oak. Before I even open the door, I know that once I do that musty smell will assail my nostrils again.

'Cor, smells a bit in here. They need to get some air fresheners in,' Jamie comments as I lead us into the store.

Before I get a chance to reply, Tori Brightling bounces her way over to us. 'Morning Jamie and Laura!'

'Hello Tori,' I reply and try to shake her hand. This proves difficult because the girl can't seem to stay in one place for a nanosecond.

'Morning Tori,' Jamie adds.

'Would you both like to meet Mr Morninghouse?' Tori asks us.

'Sure!' Jamie says.

I am *not* so sure.

Could this be the same Mr Morninghouse who so unceremoniously threw me and Dan Sanderson out all those years ago for a bit of heavy petting? He of the stern gaze, frazzled grey hair and tobacco stained cardigan? And if it is him, will he recognise me? There's every chance he may have caught a quick glimpse of my teenage boob, which is something that an old man might well remember well into his dotage.

My fears are not borne out however, as from behind a long bookshelf containing various atlases of the world comes a plain looking man in his mid forties. He is bespectacled, and dressed in a grey suit that has seen better days.

'Good morning Mr and Mrs Newman,' he says in a pleasant voice. 'I'm so pleased you chose our store for your signing today.'

'It's a pleasure,' I tell him, knowing full well that we had nothing to do with the arrangements, but happy to take credit it for it, because these small victories are few and far between at the best of times.

'Mmmm,' Jamie adds absently as he looks around the room. I know what he's thinking: if we'd only agreed to do this in Waterstones or Blackwell's, the joint would be heaving with Newman fans.

He's completely wrong of course, but I have to admire his optimism.

Tori and Morninghouse guide us over to where they have set up a table and two chairs, surrounded by bookshelves heaving with copies of our books. Somebody in the Watermill Publishing warehouse must have put their back out bringing this lot over here. 'It's a while before we're due to officially kick off,' Morninghouse says. 'Would you both like a cup of coffee while we wait?'

'Oh, thanks very much mate. That'd be fantastic,' Jamie says, parking himself on one of the chairs, and regarding the pile of our three paperbacks set out in front of him.

'Yes please,' I add and join him. I look at my own watch to see that it's coming up to eleven, and crane my head to look out of the window. Still no-one in sight. I look at Jamie's limp expression, and resign myself to the fact that I'll probably be massaging his ego for the rest of the day.

But colour me surprised when, at just gone eleven o'clock, some people do start to trickle in.

It's only when they do that I remember how excruciatingly embarrassing this whole enterprise is. Jamie and I are sat together in plain sight of the entrance, so that every time a new punter walks in, they get to see us gurning at them from the corner, with our pens poised and ready. This wouldn't be so bad, but just because a customer has come into the store, it doesn't necessarily follow that they are here to get an autographed copy of a book by the Newmans.

Can you imagine popping into your local bookshop to pick up the latest Jodi Picoult, only to find yourself confronted by two complete strangers sat at a table and surrounded by books you've never heard of, both with expectant looks on their faces? You'd be tempted to think that the local mental home had chucked out a couple of its patients for the day; ones who like to scrawl on innocent passers-by with a biro.

Alternatively, you might realise that there *is* a book signing going on for two people you've never heard of, and then you'd have the exquisitely awkward experience of trying to purchase the latest Jodi Picoult without looking like a complete and total bastard for not going over and picking up a copy of their less popular hardback.

Over the next hour or so, I figure that at least ten percent of the customers who walk into the store are in this very camp. Most manage to buy whatever it is they were after and leave quickly without making eye contact, but there are a couple of punters whose British guilt gets the better of them, and they end up buying a copy of Love From Both Sides each. I almost want to tell them both that they don't have to buy our book, but then stop myself, because every copy sold puts a few pence in my back pocket, and economics beats social niceties every time.

Fortunately, the luckless sods who have just stumbled unwittingly into our book signing are few and far between. Most of the people who turn out *are* actually here to see Jamie and I. In fact, by lunchtime, we've had such a healthy trickle of people through that my wrist is already starting to hurt from all the signature writing.

Jamie is of course as happy as a pig in shit. My ego massaging can be put on hold for another day. By the time we've got through the first twenty people, he's in his element, chatting away to all and sundry with a never ending supply of enthusiasm.

I am more than happy for him to take the lead. Of the two of us, I have always been less comfortable with being in the public eye, and am therefore happy just to provide back-up to Jamie's witty repartee.

This also gives me a chance to evaluate the kind of people who read our work, which is always a valuable exercise. The better you know your audience, the easier it is to write the type of books they want to keep reading.

By and large, I'm pleased to say our fans are a healthy, normal bunch. Not a raving psychopath or obsessive stalker in sight. Okay, a few might need a bit more sun, and there's one odd lady in a top hat who asks us to sign her breasts, but other than that, they all seem well adjusted and without criminal convictions. I have to confess, I'm a little surprised. Given our combined track record of attracting unhinged people, I really did think that we might get at least one person who -

'Where are they!?' a voice screams from behind the small crowd stood in front of the table. 'Where are those minty bastards!?'

Spoke to soon, didn't I?

'I wish to speak to them, post haste!!'

The crowd parts to reveal Sherlock Holmes.

Nope, not kidding. It's a guy dressed as Sherlock Holmes. And not the Cumberbatch variety. This is full on Rathbone. He's wearing a tweed cape, tweed trousers, a white button-down shirt, and a deerstalker hat.

Sherlock fucking Holmes.

The effect is only somewhat ruined by the fact he is also wearing a moth-eaten cable knit cardigan in a delightful shade of vomit green underneath the cape.

As it's not Halloween for another five months, I slump down in my chair and look around for heavy objects I can fight him off with.

Sherlock strides purposefully up to the table, pushing past everyone even slightly in his way. As he arrives, he slams down a book onto the table and regards Jamie and I with such a look of sheer animal loathing that I start to blindly dial 999 on the phone that's still in my pocket.

He points one tremulous, bony finger at us. 'You!'

'Er, can we help you?' Jamie asks.

'Can you help me!? Can you help me!?' the man wails in a voice as tremulous as his finger. 'I very much doubt that you scabrous, loathsome popinjays could supply me with any kind of practicable succour in this time of extreme existential crisis!'

'Come again?' Jamie says, the lack of comprehension writ large across his face.

Tori steps in to try and calm the situation. 'Excuse me? Can I help you with something? I'm the Newman's publicist. Maybe it would be a good idea if we stepped back from the table?' she suggests, attempting to take one of the man's thin arms.

He twists away from her with a high pitched shriek. 'Do not attempt to lay your vile protuberances on my person, oh painted jezebel!' he spits at her. This is a tad unfair. Tori may go a little overboard with the foundation and eyeliner, but she hardly comes across as a jezebel, painted or otherwise.

Jamie stands up. I do like it when he snaps into manly mode.

'Have you got a problem, mate? Only we're trying to have a nice book signing here for all these lovely people, and you're ruining it.'

The lunatic regards Jamie with acid contempt and presses one thin hand to his chest. 'Do I have a problem, sir? Do *I have a problem*?'

Jamie looks highly confused. 'I don't know, do you?'

Cardigan Holmes reaches inside his thick woolly undergarment. My mouth goes letterbox shaped as I imagine him producing a handgun and shooting everyone within point blank range. Instead - and inexplicably worse - he pulls out a book. Not one of ours either. And definitely not the latest Jodi Picoult.

He slams the hardback down onto the table and stands back, pointing that tremulous finger down at it.

'Look! Look I tell you, you ravening charlatans! Look at the misery you have wrought upon me!'

The book is a hardback of average size. It looks quite old, with a rather tatty jacket and some definite wear along the edges. On it, in one corner, is a picture of what appears to be a muscular gent in a strongman outfit, playing a trombone and standing on the corpse of a large African lion. In the opposite corner is a blonde woman barely dressed in a floaty negligee, lying across the back of what looks like a very grumpy elephant. She has her head back and her hand to her forehead in the classic 'swoon' position.

The title for this book, writ large and diagonally across the cover, so as to separate the two melodramatic images, is 'Taming The African Love Goddess: A story of love divided by the veldt'.

Being divided by the veldt sounds extremely painful, but the title and cover suggest that this is some kind of love story, possibly told from both male and female perspec - *oh shit*.

I look up at Jamie, who has obviously reached the same conclusion as me, as he looks like he's just licked a goat's bum.

This isn't the first time we've been accused of plagiarism. It's just the first time it's been in person, and wearing a vomit green cardigan and Holmesian cape.

Being a writer invites this kind of thing, especially when you write commercial fiction. There are millions of books out there in the wild, and every so often a few are bound to have similarities to your own work. It's a total coincidence of course - after all, there are only so many different stories to be told - but you try convincing the author of a book that came out before yours that you haven't deliberately plagiarised their writing for your own personal gain.

'Thieves!' Cardigan Holmes roars. 'Defalcators of dialogue! Purloiners of prose!'

Jamie groans and sits back down. We both look over at Tori with imploring eyes.

'I'm sure Mr and Mrs Newman are none of those things, sir,' she says in her best 'trying to keep calm, but rapidly losing the plot' tone of voice.

This only causes Cardigan Holmes to turn his unholy rage back on her. 'And what would you know, oh foul and pestilent purveyor of propaganda?!'

You've got to give the bloke something, he certainly has a wide and varied vocabulary.

'Look, Mister...? ' Tori pauses, aware that the lunatic has, as yet, not divulged his name to any of us.

I look at the book's spine and am delighted to discover that the man's name is Hedley Mislington. You'd have to wear a cape and cable knit cardigan if you had a name like that, wouldn't you? It's my turn to stand up, with open hands raised, and what I hope is a United Nations kind of expression on my face. 'Mister Mislington...'

'It's pronounced Misserlingertun!'

Of course it is. 'Mister Misserlingertun, I gather that you feel our work may in some way be similar to yours?'

'Similar? *Similar*!?' Hedley Mislington bellows to the rafters. 'The rancid effluence that you call Love From Both Sides copies my searing indictment of one man's love for one woman on the plains of Africa almost to the very letter!'

'Does it really,' I reply, resisting the urge to chew on a knuckle.

'Yes, woman! Yes it does!'

'Why don't you read a bit?' a voice pipes up from the small crowd surrounding this little pantomime. I turn to look at a cheerful hipster in a bobble hat, and wish I could set his beard on fire.

Unfortunately, the idea seems to appeal to Hedley Mislington immensely. 'Yes indeed! A fine suggestion from the hirsute manchild in the corner! Let us read from both books, and the crowd shall see your evil thievery in all its contemptuous glory!'

I groan out loud.

'Fair enough,' Jamie says from beside me.

What?

I shoot him daggers.

He shrugs his shoulders. 'Well, why not? Let's hear what Mister Misserlingerpingertun's book is all about, shall we?' There's distinct mirth now playing around my husband's eyes. The situation has evidently developed into one of much amusement for him.

'Fine!' I thrown my hands up, and sit back down on my seat with a huff. 'Why don't you go first, Mister Misserlingertun?'

This concept is greeted by a look of such unbridled horror that I fear the man is about to suffer a massive cardiac episode. 'I cannot read my own writings aloud, you scabies ridden pensmith!'

'Fine! I'll read a bit of Both Sides then,' I snap, and grab up the nearest copy. I turn to Jamie and narrow my eyes, 'then my husband here can read *your* book.' Jamie starts to protest. 'After all,' I cut across him, 'he thought it was a good idea, *didn't he?*'

Cardigan Holmes crosses two thin arms across his chest. 'That is acceptable to me,' he intones with a sniff.

'Excellent!' says the hipster, and the rest of the crowd nod in agreement. A book signing is one thing, but two sets of authors at each other's throats is entirely another. I'm sure Morninghouse is kicking himself that he doesn't have any popcorn to sell.

Trying to resist the urge to tell the universe to fuck off, I crack open the copy of Love From Both Sides I have in my hand and start to read.

For the next few minutes I read the first chapter of the book aloud. Everyone is silent as I do so, apart from a few titters from the crowd when I read a funny bit, and many huffs, sniffs and tuts of disgust from Mislington whenever I read something he doesn't like the sound of - which seems to be every other word.

I finish my recitation just at the point where Jamie is taken back to Isobel's house for some humiliating sex. It's not my favourite part of the book, to be honest. There's something about the idea of Jamie's semen sliding down a picture of Jesus that gives me the heebie jeebies.

I get a small round of applause for my efforts, which I take with as much good grace as possible.

'Right then!' Jamie exclaims with glee and picks up Taming The African Love Goddess. With a grin of delight he opens to the first page and starts to read.

'*It was, as ever, a thunderous morning to be sailing a camel on the incandescent plains,*' Jamie begins. '*But I was not overtly concerned, for I had my trusty Dromedarian ally betwixt my thighs, and my rambunctious trombone slung native-like across my back.*'

Jamie stops for a second and looks up, giving everyone a chance to process what they'd just heard. It takes a few moments, but confusion slowly gives way to unsteady comprehension as they realise what those mangled sentences were actually about. A couple of the slower ones need the answer whispered to them, but by the time Jamie continues, everyone seems up to speed.

'*Oh, how the temperate bosom of the veldt did clutch me in its unyielding embrace, as I traversed its oatmeal coloured peaks on my way to new undertakings of grave import.*'

I can't be a hundred percent sure, but I think this story is about a bloke on a camel. He may, or may not be, in love with said camel, but I'll have to wait for more details before reaching a definite conclusion.

'*My breast beat with the excitement of my incipient adventures, and my loins grew engorged at the prospect of the dark and hairy maidens I would encounter amongst the sundrenched flora and malnourished fauna of this most intransigent geography.*'

Yep, he's definitely going to have sex with that camel at some point.

Thus far, what Jamie has read is... well, the nicest thing I can say is that it's not boring in any way shape or form. It's also barely comprehensible, and written with a contempt for narrative structure that borders on the psychopathic.

What it definitely is *not*, is anything like Love From Both Sides.

I choose to point this out before Jamie can get any further. This earns me a look of unconcealed malice from Cardigan Holmes. 'Skip to page 39!' he orders Jamie. 'Read the second chapter from the perspective of my glorious heroine Revagina!'

'Sorry, *who?*' Jamie asks.

'Revagina!' Mislington repeats. 'The ravishing beauty who steals the heart of the brave Captain Hambernought!'

At this point, Jamie is barely able to conceal his mirth. I must admit I'm close to joining him. A man who has sex with a camel is one thing, giving your heroin a name that sounds like an operation to reverse a sex change is quite another.

Jamie obediently takes up the story from page 39.

'*My day begun as much as all others have began in this harsh desert realm,*' Revagina starts, mangling the English language for all she's worth. '*The feel of the silky smooth satin underwear fills me with delight as it slides over my womanhood.*'

I have a womanhood somewhere. It keeps me nice and dry when it's raining.

Jamie keeps reading, and as he does so, it becomes apparent that Revagina is one giant wank fantasy for poor old Hedley Mislington. In the half chapter that Jamie gets through, she manages to take a bath with two dusky African maidens, and has some kind of awkward orgasm while riding a camel. She also spends an inordinate amount of time pining for a large white man to come and save her from the harem of Goodnight N'Tungu - the local African warlord that captured her three years ago, from what I can just about gather was some kind of expedition to look for a one-eyed, giant chimpanzee called Horace.

Now, my memory may not be what it once was, but I'm fairly sure that there is no giant, one-eyed chimpanzee called Horace in any of our books.

Jamie closes the hardback slowly, as if it might explode in his hand at any moment if he makes any sudden movements.

The crowd are stunned into silence. There are just no words. I think most of them were okay until the one-eyed chimp, but after that, it was downhill all the way.

In fact, the only person in the shop who is not stupefied by the whole experience is Hedley Mislington. 'There!' he shrieks triumphantly. 'Now you all see it! Now you all see that my brilliant usage of both male and female perspective has been roundly plagiarised by these two mountebanks!'

Jamie sits forward and addresses the crowd. 'What do you reckon guys? Do you think we've ripped off Mister Misserlingerwingertun's book?'

This is greeted with a lot of shaking heads and exclamations in the negative. Even the beardy hipster, who is apparently recording this entire debacle on his phone, pipes up with a heartfelt 'No!'

All this manages to do is turn Cardigan Holmes's towering resentment on them. 'You! All of you! Pudding-brained lemmings to a man!'

'Steady on, these are my customers,' Morninghouse says in a hurt tone from where he's been hiding by the front door.

Mislington spins back to me and Jamie, obviously feeling he's on firmer ground insulting us. 'You have ruined my life!' he utters with loathing. 'Destroyed my art! Embezzled my talent for your own nefarious purposes!'

'Have we?' Jamie replies, putting a hand over his face.

'Yes! And for it, I shall now have to soundly beat you with my truncheon!'

Without another word, Mislington reaches into the green cardigan and produces a long black rubber implement, brandishing it above his head like an enraged Masai warrior.

'What's that?' I ask.

'It is my truncheon, foul woman!'

'That's a dildo.'

'Nonsense! It is a truncheon! A weapon of ill device that I shall use to beat a confession from you both!'

'Nope, it's definitely a dildo,' Jamie adds, leaning back and crossing his arms. 'You can tell by the veins and helmet.'

Mislington regards his weapon with not a little doubt. 'It is a *truncheon*. I know it is, because I took it from my late mother's wardrobes. She once told me she used it to beat off a burglar who entered her bungalow one night.'

'I'm sure she did,' Jamie replies with a smirk.

From the crowd, a few voices pipe up to point out to Mislington that he is in fact holding a sex toy, and not a weapon with which he can exact his revenge.

In the face of such overwhelming public opinion, the writer's shoulders start to sag and the rage that burns within his soul is diminished.

For the first time since he entered the shop, Hedley Mislington looks confused... and not a little vulnerable. 'I, uh... I don't quite know what to say,' he utters in a quiet voice.

I instantly feel a wave of guilt pass through me. While it's never pleasant to be insulted by a man dressed as Sherlock Holmes and waving a dildo at you, it's also obvious that this is someone with a rather tenuous grip on reality, and should probably be treated with a degree of kindness.

...once someone takes that dildo off him anyway.

I move round the table. 'Mister Misserlingertun? How would you like a nice cup of tea?' I say in a soft voice. 'Maybe you can tell us all a bit more about how you came up with your story?'

'A cup of tea?' he replies.

'Yes. With two sugars, I'd say.' I look over at Morninghouse. 'Can you sort that out for Mister Misserlingertun, please?'

'Certainly!' Morninghouse agrees with delight, obviously pleased that the situation has been defused somewhat.

Jamie also gets up from the table, and taking his cue from me, he approaches the unstable writer slowly. 'How about you give me your dildo?' he asks.

'Truncheon,' Mislington corrects.

'Yeah... *truncheon.*' Jamie gently takes the enormous sex toy from the man's hand and passes it to the hipster, who takes it a little too enthusiastically.

'I know, why don't you come and sit at the table?' I suggest to Mislington.

'Um. Very well,' he agrees and allows me to lead him to the chair.

Everyone in the shop is now on tender hooks, waiting to see if there will be any more verbal explosions forthcoming. I get the impression though that the wind has been taken out of Hedley Mislington's sails, and that the worst may be over.

Morninghouse brings over a steaming hot cup of tea and plonks it in front of Mislington, who takes a sip and looks up at all of us with a slightly lost look on his face.

'Hey, Hedley?' Jamie asks.

'Yes, young man?'

'Can I have this copy of your book?'

The man looks stunned. 'Why yes, you can indeed.'

'Thank you! And would you sign it for me?'

Oh well done, Jamie. Very well done indeed.

For the first time since he strode into the bookshop and started spouting accusations of fraud, Hedley Mislington smiles and gathers up my pen.

I look around the shop and a wry smile crosses my face. The crowd is now ignoring Jamie and I completely. All their attention is focused on the eccentric writer. I have no problem with this whatsoever.

'When was that published?' our bearded hipster friend says, pointing at Jamie's newly signed copy of Taming The African Love Goddess.

'Ah... ' Mislington pauses, mulling the question over for a moment. 'I published it in 1984 originally. Back in the good old days when publishers still took a chance on a new writer.'

Boy, did they take a chance. I'm tempted to ask if the publisher is still in existence, but manage to bite my tongue. I don't want to rile him up again.

The hipster then says something totally unexpected. 'Where can I buy a copy?'

'What?' Mislington asks in disbelief.

'What?' Jamie and I echo.

The hipster shrugs his shoulders. 'Well, you know. I'll probably put this video on YouTube, and wouldn't mind a copy of the book to go along with it, so I can show it to people.'

I look over at Morninghouse. 'Can you order a few copies in?'

The bookshop owner looks stunned. 'I don't know. I'll go and have a look on the computer.'

Miraculously, Taming The African Love Goddess is still available. When Morninghouse announces this, and asks if anyone's interested in buying it, six hands immediately shoot up - a testament to the power of YouTube, if ever there was one.

I turn back to Mislington. 'So Hedley, why did you write a book about Africa?'

He gives me a look of such heartfelt gratitude that it nearly brings a tear to my eye. All this man wanted was a little attention. His book may be awful, his clothing may be worse, but neither makes him any less of a human being - one who just wants people to hear his voice.

I'm forced to reflect that all writers probably feel the same way.

Jamie and I have been lucky enough to have our voices heard by thousands of people. It gives us both a great deal of pleasure to step aside today, and let this man's voice be heard instead.

The next hour is a fascinating - if rambling - monologue conducted by Hedley Mislington that holds his audience rapt. If the guy could only write as well as he spins a verbal anecdote, Taming The African Love Goddess would be a best seller.

Jamie and I collectively decide it's time to leave while Hedley is regaling the crowd with the tale of how he once got lost in a Moroccan souk for three days. I very much doubt we'll be missed, and there's no way we could compete with such a stirring tale - not even with another retelling of the fajita incident.

As we back out of the store with Tori in tow, I can't help but feel I've learned a valuable lesson today.

Be kind to somebody who needs it, and it'll help them do wonders.

The hipster did indeed upload the video to YouTube Mum. He melodramatically called it 'The Newmans Vs The Cardigan God.'

At last count it's had over one hundred and seventy thousand hits, and Taming The African Love Goddess is at number 26 in the Amazon store - seven places above Love Under Different Skies.

I couldn't be happier.

Love you and miss you, Mum.

Your 33rd placed daughter, Laura.

XX

Jamie's Blog
Monday 14 June

Oh God, why did I ever think joining social media was a good idea?

Jamie and Laura @NewmanWriters Jul 6
Hey everyone! Jamie here, out walking with the family. It's a lovely day! Sunny for once! #walking #sunnyday #summer

Dan Jones @DannyTwoTone Jul 6
Makes a nice change, doesn't it?

PiddlePops @Piddlepops12 Jul 6
Love your books Jamie! When's the next one out?

Jamie and Laura @NewmanWriters Jul 6
Thx @PiddlePops! We're working hard on the next book now! More info soon!

Rudyard Stripling @Rudyardbutgentle Jul 6
For a writer, you use way too many exclamation marks.

Jamie and Laura @NewmanWriters Jul 6
@Rudyardbutgentle Sorry Rudyard! I will try to do better!!!!!!! :)

Rudyard Stripling @Rudyardbutgentle Jul 6
Very funny.

***

Jamie and Laura @NewmanWriters Jul 7
Back to the grindstone today! Two thousand words done by lunchtime! #amwriting

Carla @Snoopydrawers Jul 7
Excellent! Write quicker! Have run out of Newman books to read :)

Minch @MinchieMoo92 Jul 7
Are you writing another book about yourselves? Or is this a new idea?

Jamie and Laura @NewmanWriters Jul 7
@MinchieMoo92 A new idea for us! Hope it's one that you will enjoy!

Minch @MinchieMoo92 Jul 7
Great! Will look forward to it :) What's it about?

Jamie and Laura @NewmanWriters Jul 7
@MinchieMoo92 It's about how I love to masturbate geese in the park at 3am. I always wear rubber pants & stick a finger up my arse.

Minch @MinchieMoo92 Jul 7
Lol! What?

Carla @Snoopydrawers Jul 7
ARE YOU SERIOUS???!!!

Jamie and Laura @NewmanWriters Jul 7
Oh God. I didn't write that! What's going on?

Jamie and Laura @NewmanWriters Jul 7
Yes I did. I did write that. I love sexy geese. All feathers and beaks. Dirty avian whores. I love them.

Dan Jones @DannyTwoTone Jul 7
I think you've been hacked Jamie. Happened to me last year!

Jamie and Laura @NewmanWriters Jul 7
@DannyTwoTone Thanks Danny! You're probably right. I'll change my password now!

Dan Jones @DannyTwoTone Jul 7
Good idea!

Jamie and Laura @NewmanWriters Jul 7
All done! Password changed. Phew!

***

Jamie and Laura @NewmanWriters Jul 8
Hi everyone! Today, I'm going to stick my penis into a frozen turkey and pump it like a flat tyre! #birdsmakemehorny

Tom @Thunderbratz Jul 8
Dude. You're weird. My wife said read your book. Don't think I will now.

Beaky @Beaksandwings_xxx Jul 8
#birdsmakemehorny too Jamie. Maybe you could write about them? I'd love that. That'd be really sexy. #fantasy

Jamie and Laura @NewmanWriters Jul 8
@Beaksandwings_xxx That wasn't me! Sorry! My account's been hacked again! I didn't write that!

Beaky @Beaksandwings_xxx Jul 8
Oh. :(

Jamie and Laura @NewmanWriters Jul 8
@Beaksandwings_xxx Just kidding. I love me some poultry. Want to swap pics? the_newman_family@hotmail.co.uk. #dirtierthebetter

Beaky @Beaksandwings_xxx Jul 8
:) I'll send you some of my best. You'll love me in my crotchless emu costume.

Jamie and Laura @NewmanWriters Jul 8
@Beaksandwings_xxx Mmmmm. I'm getting hard just thinking about it.

121

Jamie and Laura @NewmanWriters Jul 8
Who the f*ck are you?! Stop hacking my account!! I'm changing passwords again! Please leave me alone!

***

Jamie and Laura @NewmanWriters Jul 10
It's been a couple of days, and no sign on being hacked again. Phew! #bigrelief

Dan Jones @DannyTwoTone Jul 10
Good for you. It's horrible when that happens. Glad you don't actually find birds sexy!

Jamie and Laura @NewmanWriters Jul 10
@DannyTwoTone Only the human kind! :)

Dan Jones @DannyTwoTone Jul 10
Lol. Now get back to writing that new book!

Jamie and Laura @NewmanWriters Jul 10
@DannyTwoTone Will do! Got to go fuck an albatross first though! I have him pinned down in the back garden. Where's that Swarfega?

Dan Jones @DannyTwoTone Jul 10
Oh dear...

***

Jamie and Laura @NewmanWriters Jul 11
Hi all. This really is Jamie this time. I'm sorry about all the bird stuff. Damn hackers.

Minch @MinchieMoo92 Jul 11
Have you got it fixed now?

Jamie and Laura @NewmanWriters Jul 11

@MinchieMoo92 Yeah. Had to redo everything though. Took hours :(On the phone to them and everything :(

Minch @MinchieMoo92 Jul 11
Never mind! At least it's all sorted now :)

Jamie and Laura @NewmanWriters Jul 11
@MinchieMoo92 Hopefully! I don't know what I did to deserve it though.

Rudyard Stripling @Rudyardbutgentle Jul 11
Maybe you shouldn't be so rude when someone points out your overuse of exclamation marks. #revengeissweet

Jamie and Laura @NewmanWriters Jul 11
@Rudyardbutgentle What? It was you?

Jamie and Laura @NewmanWriters Jul 11
@Rudyardbutgentle Are you still there?

Rudyard Stripling @Rudyardbutgentle Jul 11
Yep.

Jamie and Laura @NewmanWriters Jul 11
Gimme some big hard cock. A big hard cock's cock. Mmmmm. Finger licking good. #flightlessissexiest

Jamie and Laura @NewmanWriters Jul 11
@Rudyardbutgentle Sod off!!!

Rudyard Stripling @Rudyardbutgentle Jul 11
That's two more exclamation marks than you need there, Jamie. I can start posting pictures any time I like...

Jamie and Laura @NewmanWriters Jul 11
@Rudyardbutgentle Okay, okay. I'm sorry, you win. I'm very sorry for being rude to you.

Rudyard Stripling @Rudyardbutgentle Jul 11

Alright then. Apology accepted. No more saying you like to have sex with birds.

Jamie and Laura @NewmanWriters Jul 11
@Rudyardbutgentle Thank you very much.

Rudyard Stripling @Rudyardbutgentle Jul 11
No problem. Now, how do you feel about fellating leprechauns?

Jamie and Laura @NewmanWriters Jul 11
@Rudyardbutgentle Leprechauns? Oh God, they are so sexy! I'll chug down a leprechaun's length to get at his pot of gold! #suckmyluckycharms

Jamie and Laura @NewmanWriters Jul 11
You utter bastard!

Tom @Thunderbratz Jul 11
Dude. You have some serious issues. I'm reporting you.

***

Jamie and Laura @NewmanWriters Jul 12
I'm a tiny leprechaun, all dressed in green. I am the smallest man that you've ever seen.

Jamie and Laura @NewmanWriters Jul 12
If you rub my belly, I'll laugh all the day. If you go down on me, then you're probably gay.

Jamie and Laura @NewmanWriters Jul 12
@Rudyardbutgentle You're back then Rudyard...

Rudyard Stripling @Rudyardbutgentle Jul 12
Yeah baby! What'cho you gonna do about it?

Jamie and Laura @NewmanWriters Jul 12
@Rudyardbutgentle Not much. I'm no expert at this stuff.

Rudyard Stripling @Rudyardbutgentle Jul 12
Nope. That'd be me! Hee hee hee! Blow any dwarves today Jamie?

Jamie and Laura @NewmanWriters Jul 12
Not yet... I don't have many tech skills, but you know what I do have?

Rudyard Stripling @Rudyardbutgentle Jul 12
What's that, you midget molesting maniac?

Jamie and Laura @NewmanWriters Jul 12
Fans.

Rudyard Stripling @Rudyardbutgentle Jul 12
So fucking what?

Jamie and Laura @NewmanWriters Jul 12
A lot of them DO have tech skills Rudyard. Way more than me... or you. And so now I have something else.

Rudyard Stripling @Rudyardbutgentle Jul 12
What?

Jamie and Laura @NewmanWriters Jul 12
Your IP address.

Rudyard Stripling @Rudyardbutgentle Jul 12
No you fucking don't!!!

Jamie and Laura @NewmanWriters Jul 12
Is that THREE exclamation marks I see there, Rudyard? ...Or should I say, Dave Pinder from Cleethorpes???!!!!!!!!!!!!!!!!!!!!!

Rudyard Stripling @Rudyardbutgentle Jul 12
Oh shit! Please don't tell my mum!

Dan Jones @DannyTwoTone Jul 12
@Rudyardbutgentle Ha! Fucking owned!

Minch @MinchieMoo92 Jul 12
Woo hoo! Well done Jamie!! :)

Jamie and Laura @NewmanWriters Jul 12
#revengeissweet

When venturing into the thorny world of social media, it's vital to have one thing.
Back up.

Laura's Diary
Wednesday, July 21st

Dear Mum,

I fear I may have created a monster. Said monster is in the shape of a seven-year-old girl, but is a monster nonetheless.

Last night was the occasion of Middle Park Infant School's annual summer play, which shall hereafter be known as 'the night of the Newman creature'. If I was embarrassed when I had to fish my sunburned husband out of the Indian Ocean, then I felt triple the degree of shamefacedness by the end of yesterday evening, thanks to my lovely daughter Poppy, and her newfound aspirations towards stardom.

You would imagine that a school play is an innocuous thing at the best of times. An event trotted out by the weary teaching staff on an annual basis, to provide them with something to entertain the children with in the run up to the school holidays - and an opportunity for proud parents to come to school and see where all those hard earned taxes are going.

In Middle Park Infant School's case, those tax pounds are going into a slavish recreation of the story of Noah And His Ark. It's the ideal play to stage for seven year olds, given that it features a large amount of colourful animal costumes that they can be stuffed into, and is a story everyone knows - and is therefore easy to follow - even when the stars of the show inevitably forget their lines, or pee themselves before the end of the first act.

For most children, being a part of Noah And His Ark would just be a chance to run around making farmyard noises in front of two hundred adults, but for Poppy Helen Newman, it represents the opportunity for her to firmly set out her store as a future star of stage and screen.

At least it would be if she hadn't been cast as a chicken.

This news of dreadful import was delivered to me with a scowl about two weeks ago, upon Poppy's return from school with her father.

'I don't want to be a chicken!' she snaps, throwing her backpack down onto one of the kitchen chairs in disgust.

'But that's the part Mrs Carmoody has given you Pops,' Jamie tells her, sitting himself down at the breakfast bar.

Poppy crosses her arms and twists her perfect little mouth. 'Mrs Carmoody is a poo head,' she declares in tones that brook no argument.

I gasp in horror. 'Poppy Helen Newman! You do not say that kind of thing about your teacher!'

'No Poppy, Mum is right,' Jamie agrees, but you can quite clearly see he's not that bothered about his daughter's choice of words, given that there's a distinct smile playing across his lips, and a twinkle of veiled parental approval in his eyes.

'But I should have been Noah's wife!' Poppy counters. 'I was the best at her, and I looked the best in the sheet thing, and I made Briony Peters laugh so much that she snotted a bit.'

Not being a Christian, I don't know whether Noah's better half displayed the ability to make snot come out of people's noses in The Bible, but I'm going to go out on a limb and say probably not.

'Well Mrs Carmoody obviously decided that you were also very good at being a chicken,' I say, trying my hardest to make her feel better. I doubt that anyone since the beginning of time has comforted somebody effectively by comparing them to a chicken, so I'm not all that surprised when Poppy's eyes start to well up.

'Mrs Carmoody doesn't like me,' Poppy intones.

'What makes you say that, sweetheart?' Jamie asks.

'Coz I trod on her foot at playtime two weeks ago. The one she always has in that funny bandage thing.'

Now, I've met Mrs Carmoody a couple of times, and while she does look a trifle stern and authoritative, she doesn't come across as the kind of person who'd hold a grudge based on a little girl's clumsiness. 'Did you say sorry?' I ask Poppy.

'Yes.'

'Well I'm sure it played no part in your casting as a chicken then.'

To be honest, I can well believe that Mrs Carmoody put Poppy in such a lowly role to teach her a bit of humility. My daughter is not one for being humble or self-deprecating. She tears through the world like a whirlwind in a Hello Kitty t-shirt, and tends to get what she wants 99% of the time.

In fact, there's every chance she might be an entitled brat.

I have no-one to blame for this but myself - and Jamie, of course. Though mostly me, because at no point have I wanted to go through the misery of pregnancy again to grant Poppy a little brother or sister. Some may see this is selfish, but they can quite clearly fuck off. I love my daughter unreservedly, but am happy with just one child, and don't see how there's anything wrong with that. Besides, there's every chance that by now Poppy would have engineered an 'accident' for her younger sibling, to make sure that they weren't getting more attention than she was. Possibly something involving a fork and the nearest electrical socket.

No, it's been best for us all that family Newman has remained a three part harmony - rather than a four or five part cacophony.

That's not to say I don't feel horrible for not supplying Poppy with a playmate. That would be far too sensible, and not at all in keeping with the uncanny ability that my brain has to completely contradict itself. I feel *incredibly* guilty sometimes that Poppy is an only child, even though I'm happy with my decision not to have another baby.

Now, parents who feel this way tend to do one of two things. They either feed their single child so much food that they find themselves raising a barrel with arms and legs, or they lavish money and presents on them.

This second choice requires money, of course.

I have no doubt that if I were still working in a chocolate shop and Jamie were still in a lowly marketing job, then Poppy would now be a good eight stone, and unable to see her own feet. As it stands, Pops is kept whip-thin by all that swirling around like a miniature hurricane, and has now reached the point where her levels of entitlement are becoming something of a problem.

What Poppy wants, Poppy rather inevitably gets.

Her bedroom is awash with Disney merchandise - in every colour as long as it's pink.

I could quite cheerfully open the room up to strangers and make a tidy profit flogging all the hideously expensive plastic crap we've accumulated in there in the past couple of years.

To give you some idea of how bad it is, Poppy has no less than *four* Nemos. Finding the little sod would present absolutely no issue for Dory, should the little fish find herself in Poppy's bedroom. In fact, the only danger she'd be in is being crushed by the largest of the four - Poppy's enormous two foot high night light that we bought her for Christmas this year. This is what happens when you buy a present off the internet without looking properly at the measurements.

If it's not Finding Nemo stuff, it's Frozen merchandise. If it's not Frozen, it's The Lion King. Graven images of Simba, Nemo and Elsa fight for supremacy on almost every surface. I have to confess I occasionally get the creeps when I put Poppy to bed, as they all look at me with that dull eyed expression stuffed toys seem to suffer from.

The spoiling of Poppy Newman doesn't end there.

We generally end up cooking her something she likes every night for tea, with one of us taking on the task of preparing our own meal, while the other devotes themselves to making sure that Poppy gets her turkey dinosaurs and potato waffles just the way she likes them. Thankfully her child's palette does like to take in some vegetables alongside all the brown crap, which is a saving grace. I don't have the strength to put up with the tantrums I would have to endure should it prove necessary to force feed her broccoli or peas.

Poppy also watches what she wants on the TV. Until 8pm, it's pretty much exclusively her domain, with Jamie and I forced onto our iPads, while she stares endlessly at the Disney channel.

Pathetic, isn't it? Poppy receives little to no discipline from either of us most of the time, if I'm being honest. Jamie and I dote on her to a level that completely negates our ability to punish her for anything she does wrong - and boy is that lack of parental control coming back to bite us on the arse now.

'But I don't want to be a chicken!' she screeches and literally stamps her feet on the floor.

'Why don't you show Mum the costume Pops? Maybe if she likes it, you won't mind being a chicken quite so much?' Jamie ventures and looks at me. 'They let her bring it home to show us, as long as *she takes care of it.*' I get Jamie's meaning straight away. The costume will be kept away from Poppy under lock and key, so she doesn't get the chance to attack it with her plastic craft scissors.

Poppy turns slowly to regard her father with a look of distain. 'She won't Dad.'

'I might Pops!' I say, trying to sound enthusiastic. 'Let's have a look at it, shall we?'

Poppy thinks about this for a second. Her desire to continue the tantrum is weighed against her love of showing off for her parents. The showing off wins.

'Come on sweetheart, I'll help you with it,' Jamie says, and gets up from his seat. 'We'll go upstairs and Mum can wait down here.' Jamie gives me a hopeful look. 'She could make a nice cup of tea while she waits.'

I roll my eyes and pick the kettle up.

I hear Poppy's loud, stamping footsteps coming down the stairs about ten minutes later. They are the sound of pure, distilled, and unadulterated anger.

She appears in the kitchen doorway, a sullen look on her face. Jamie stands behind her with a broad grin.

'Doesn't she look fantastic!?' he says in excited joy.

This is a masterpiece of amateur dramatics, as poor old Poppy does *not* look fantastic. It's not her fault of course, my daughter is gorgeous; but not even her elfin good looks can make up for the fact that the costume she is jammed into is utter shit.

It consists of what looks like a faded yellow bath mat with a hole cut in the middle for Poppy to stick her head through. Somebody has attempted to draw a red chicken's wattle coming from the hole in thick marker pen. Sadly, what they have actually managed to draw is two big hanging red testicles. It doesn't help that what remains of the bathroom mat's thick shag pile looks like pubes.

On Poppy's head is a second bath mat (I can only assume somebody really liked yellow bathroom accessories in the seventies) that has been awkwardly cut and stitched into a hood shape. Protruding from the top of the hood is the end of an orange sock that I presume is meant to be the beak. There are a couple of those plastic googly eyes stuck on either side of the hood above the sock, and more red marker has been employed to colour in something of an irregular mohawk down the middle of the sewn together bathmat.

All efforts to resemble a chicken sadly stop at waist level, as Poppy has also been forced into a pair of bright yellow jogging pants that are at least four sizes too big for her.

The overall effect is not a convincing representation of barnyard fowl. Unless it had been run over by the tractor, and had a set of testicles glued to it afterwards.

'Wow Poppy!' I over compensate. 'You look brilliant!'

'Doesn't she?!' Jamie agrees, nodding his head vociferously.

Poppy is having *none* of it.

'I look really silly Mum!' she wails and pulls at the bathmat poncho. 'It smells funny, and it itches!'

'Don't worry! I'll give it a wash,' I assure her, intending to do no such thing. If I introduce the costume to a wash cycle, there's every chance that at the end I'll have a few tattered pieces of yellow bathmat and half an orange sock. This would suit Poppy down to the ground, but wouldn't go down well with Mrs Carmoody one little bit.

'Why don't you go take it off again and I'll make sure it gets a nice clean?' I shamefacedly lie.

Once Poppy is back out of the costume, her mood lightens... a little.

'I have to stand on stage with Jake Potter,' she tells us. 'He's the other chicken.'

'Well that doesn't sound so bad,' I say.

Poppy shakes her head slowly back and forth, regarding me with a look of black doom. 'Jake Potter picks his nose and smells of wee.'

I have to confess that I'm starting to have some sympathy for Poppy's plight. I wouldn't want to spend forty five minutes stood on a stage in a moth eaten chicken costume, while a smelly boy stands next to me picking his nose.

There's every chance that Mrs Carmoody might actually be a poo head.

Still, a seven year old's ego and temperament are very fragile, so we must do our best to put on a brave face, and show Poppy how proud we are of her.

This starts with letting her eat all the turkey dinosaurs and potato waffles she can manage for tea. I don't even complain too much when she only eats half her broccoli. Frozen goes on the TV for the seventy millionth time, and I spend an unconstructive half an hour on EBay looking for chicken costumes.

The day of the Middle Park Infant School Summer Play rolls around quickly. Poppy's mood has grown more waspish as the days have gone by, so by the morning of the show, she is so bad tempered and thoroughly pissed off with the universe that it's rather like having a miniature, fair haired Basil Fawlty in the house.

'Eat your porridge Pops,' I tell her.

She jams a spoonful of the beige gunk into her mouth and mumbles something just on the edge of my hearing. The only words I can make out around her mouthful of porridge oats are 'chicken' and 'wee'.

She remains in this black temper for the rest of breakfast, despite all our efforts to pull her out of it.

'Come on Pops!' Jamie cries cheerfully up the stairs from the front doorway. 'You don't want to be late for school!' This is greeted with more heavy and loud footsteps from Poppy's bedroom, indicating that nothing would suit her more than being late for school today.

Eventually, I manage to pack the two of them off. Jamie is visiting his mother this morning before coming back at lunchtime to pick me up, so I have a couple of hours of blissful peace to get a bit of writing done.

I'm just hitting a purple patch of prose when Jamie walks in through the front door.

'How's it going?' he asks from the doorway to the spare bedroom we've converted into a study.

'Oh, fine. Got a good two thousand more words done. This chapter is finished.'

'Brilliant! I'll get on with the next one tomorrow.'

This is generally how we like to work - taking turns to write from the two different perspectives. I do the woman's side, Jamie does the man's. So far, it's proved to be very productive, and we can motor through an entire book in two months if we've got the bit between our teeth.

'How was Poppy when you dropped her off?' I ask him.

'A little ray of bright summer sunshine.'

'Really?'

'Hell no. I had to resist the urge to sketch the sign of the cross as I opened the car door to let her out.'

'Did she take the costume?'

'Reluctantly. I had to make her swear she wouldn't 'lose it' in the nearest dustbin.'

I stand up and go over to give Jamie a hug and kiss.

'Well that's very nice,' he says with a smile.

'Yes it is. I just thought we could both do with a bit of happy time, before we have to enter the lion's den.' I think for a second. 'Or should that be chicken's den?'

Jamie laughs. 'I'm sure it won't be that bad, baby.'

For a moment we both fall into silence as we consider how factually accurate that statement is likely to be.

Jamie then breaks the rather contemplative mood with an idea I find myself one hundred percent in agreement with. 'We don't have to leave for a couple of hours. How about we have some *proper* happy time?' he says, waggling his eyebrows.

My eyes light up. I hadn't even thought about that when I decided to give my hubbie a kiss and cuddle a moment ago, but now he's put the notion in my head...

An hour later we're in the car and on our way to Middle Park School. My left leg is still slightly trembling, so I'm glad Jamie offered to drive.

The play is due to begin at 4pm, so by the time we reach the school's car park at twenty to, it's packed with cars. There will be plenty of doting parents at today's play, it seems. Jamie manages to find us a space next to a massive 4x4.

We park up and walk over to the school's entrance, which has something of a queue outside it, as the parents pay for tickets and shuffle their way in. Half the reason for putting this play on is to raise funds for the new gym roof, and I'm sure they'll have no problem reaching their target, given that each ticket costs £10.

'Ten bloody quid?' Jamie remarks. 'For a forty minute play involving a load of seven year olds?'

'Yep. Just grin and bear it,' I whisper, so as not to be overheard by anyone else in the queue. Being in the financial position we are these days, we are no longer allowed to complain when something seems too expensive. It's not British, and would be unseemly.

Jamie forks over a £20 note. 'What? No programme?' he says, when the girl behind the temporary kiosk hands him two badly cut paper tickets. She gives him a blank look.

'Just go in, Jamie,' I say with a slight tone of exasperation.

He does as he's told, mumbling 'rip off' under his breath as he does so.

We walk through the school, following the signs leading to the assembly hall, where the epic tale of Noah's fight against the elements will take place. The red curtains are drawn, hiding the stage beyond, and rows of plastic school seats are laid out in a rather haphazard fashion all the way along the hall itself.

We sit down a few rows from the front and settle ourselves in. I can't help but try to listen for the sound of Poppy's raised voice over the hubbub of parental chatter. You wouldn't think that a seven year old's voice could carry through thick curtains, and over the combined speech of a hundred adults, but when Poppy loses her temper, she'd give the lead singer of Iron Maiden a run for his money.

At precisely 4pm, old Mrs Carmoody the poo head emerges from one wing of the stage and shuffles her way over to where a microphone stand has been placed in the centre.

'Good afternoon parents,' she says in clipped, enunciated tones. If this woman wasn't teaching young gels how to walk with deportment and grace with a book on their head thirty years ago, I'd be flabbergasted. 'Welcome to our annual school play, involving the children of years one and two. I do hope you will all sit back and enjoy our retelling of the classic, wonderful Biblical story of Noah And His Ark.' Mrs Carmoody supplies us all with an indulgent smile. You can tell this is a pet project of hers. Not least due to the large crucifix hanging on a chain around her neck. 'So without further ado, let the curtains open and the entertainment begin!'

Carmoody flourishes one hand in the general direction of the wing she emerged from, before shuffling her way back towards it. As she does, the heavy red curtains starts to open with a protesting squeal from the runners hidden in the architrave.

Revealed is what looks to be a rather idyllic scene. Evidently some money has been spent on this production. There is a large, hand drawn backdrop of beige mountains and hills, set below a bright blue sky and blazing yellow sun. In front of this are four small huts arranged in a semi circle, all on rollers so they can be removed from the stage when required. Standing on the stage, and ready to go, are several small, scared children dressed in distinctly Middle Eastern clothing. One boy, taller than the rest, actually *is* Middle Eastern, and the poor sod looks more uncomfortable in the heavy rolled headdress he's been forced into than any of the others. The big bushy white beard stuck on his face isn't helping I'm sure. This, I presume, is our titular main character.

Standing next to him is the girl who got the part of Noah's wife over Poppy. At least I assume it is from the way she's awkwardly holding Noah's hand. For an irrational moment I want to leap out of my seat and go kick her in the arse, but I suppress my natural instinct to defend my child's honour, and pull a small bag of mints out of my handbag.

As I'm offering one to Jamie, more children appear on stage, all dressed as animals of one type or another. The costume quality of each is roughly on a par with that of the one my daughter has to endure for this production.

My jaw clenches around my mint imperial. This probably means we're about to see Poppy for the first time in all her bathmat glory.

Sure enough, a small person dressed as a chicken emerges from stage left, all flapping arms and bobbing head. It's not Poppy however. This must be the legendary nose picker Jake Potter. Behind him, not attempting to flap arms or head bob in the slightest is Poppy Helen Newman.

Can chickens scowl?

Can they stare at the world around them with barely concealed loathing?

Can they convey, through their stiff and unyielding body language, that the universe is a harsh and unforgiving place?

If the answer to these questions is yes, then my daughter is providing the most accurate interpretation of natural chicken behaviour in history.

'Oh good grief,' Jamie says in a quiet voice.

We both sink slowly in our seats.

From the right side of the stage a tiny boy appears in a white sheet with a gold halo parked on his head. He's carrying a scroll, which he holds up and reads out loud. *Very* out loud.

'Noah and his wife lived in a village!' the boy screams, as if he's the town crier letting everyone know the windmill's on fire. 'One day he was visited by God!' The boy pauses and looks across the stage expectantly. 'One day he was visited by God!' he repeats, even louder.

Another small boy is shoved onstage from the wings. He's wearing a big blue sheet, another badly stuck on white beard, and is carrying a silver lightning bolt made out of cardboard. It looks like Mrs Carmoody is a big fan of the old fashioned fire and brimstone type of creator, as favoured in the old testament.

'Noah, you will build an ark,' God mumbles into his beard. I very much doubt anyone past the fourth row can hear him. The atheist in me pipes up to remark that it's still more people than can hear the actual God, but I ignore it, as this really isn't the time or place for that kind of thing. 'There will be a flood, and everything will die,' mumbly God carries on, 'except the animals you take onto the ark with you, along with your family.'

As a storyteller myself I wholeheartedly approve of Mrs Carmoody's decision to get to the meat of the story as quickly as possible. Who needs all that tedious preamble?

Noah steps forward. 'Yes God. I will build an ark and take the animals and my family on it so we don't all die.'

This really is the most astute rendering of the story I think I've ever seen. I might hire Carmoody as our new editor.

'Wife!' Noah orders the terrified looking girl stood next to him. 'Gather all the animals for me and I will go to find some wood for the ark!'

Noah then buggers off as quickly as he can into the wings. The wife steps forward. 'Come on animals! You will come with me and we will go to where Noah is making the ark!' With that she starts to make shooing motions to the gathered farmyard animals. The two cows obediently trot off stage, as do the two sheep, two pigs, and two dogs. However, only one chicken obeys her orders. The other gives her a look of disgust. Noah's wife tries to shoo the recalcitrant chicken off the stage again, having about as much success as King Canute did with the tide.

'Get off the stage Poppy!' the little girl hisses loud enough for the whole hall to hear. There are a few chuckles from the crowd around us as they realise things have gone off book.

The chicken folds its arms.

Noah's wife then gently pushes the chicken. The chicken does not respond well to this and pushes Noah's wife back. It's apparent that this is not a chicken comfortable with the idea of being cooped up on an ark with a load of other smelly animals. Now Noah's wife seeks to reassert her authority by kicking the chicken on one ankle. This is a chicken not to be trifled with however. It growls in a way that shouldn't be possible, given how a chicken's larynx is constructed, and smartly punches Noah's wife on the shoulder. This causes Noah's wife to start crying and run off stage. The chicken, at last happy to have got rid of all those pesky humans, looks out at the crowd, gives us all a wave and starts to flap her arms about. This triumphant scene is made all the more sinister by the continuing sounds of distress emanating from off stage.

This is the first time I've ever watched a version of Noah And His Ark where thus far the over-riding moral of the story has been 'don't fuck with poultry, or you see what you get'.

Proud as the chicken is of its victory over womankind, the celebrations are short-lived when the scowling visage of Mrs Carmoody appears from the wing. 'Poppy! Leave the stage please!' she whisper shouts at the chicken, who scowls again in response, but does start to back away to the other wing, eventually disappearing like a yellow doom cloud behind the tabs.

And so, a definite tone is set for the rest of the performance. One that ensures Jamie and I will need extensive treatment for a very nasty case of cringitis.

By the time the actual flood arrives (in the shape of a group of extremely tiny year ones holding long blue bits of netting) we are both so low in our chairs, there's every chance we're about to fall off and break a coccyx or two.

Poppy has continued to protest about her role throughout proceedings. In one particularly cutesy scene, all the animals are meant to 'speak' to Noah. I rather feel Carmoody is ripping off Doctor Dolittle here, but I'll give her a pass, as it's a very efficient way of making sure as many children as possible get speaking parts. The horses neigh, the pigs grunt, the sheep baa. The chickens resolutely do not squawk, or even go 'buck buck buck'. One certainly makes a jolly good go of it, but the other? Well, let's just say the other is not putting a hundred percent into the performance. While Jake Potter is making an attempt to sound like a chicken, Poppy just stands there and goes 'Squawk'. Literally, she says the word *squawk*. 'Buck buck buck,' she also intones in a flat deadpan, looking completely disinterested. It's a horrendous spectacle to behold.

Then we come to the actual entrance to the ark - which comprises of a wooden slope, and the side of the boat, all on wheels. Quite how they managed to maneuver this monstrosity onto the stage is a testament to Mrs Carmoody's dedication to the theatre.

Not that Poppy Newman gives a flying fuck about that. Noah stands at the bottom of the ramp, naming each animal as it comes past him.

'And now, the chickens!' he says as loudly as possible. Jake chicken starts his ascent, but Poppy chicken merely stands there and growls at him. I'm sure when Noah in The Bible bid the animals board the ark in standard two by two formation, he would have expected the wolves or the tigers to growl at him, not the bloody chickens.

Poppy gives Noah a look that would kill him stone dead if looks could indeed kill, and stamps her way up the wooden slope, the hollow, booming noise of her feet echoing around the assembly hall.

Am I allowed to drink a bottle of vodka while sat in the audience of a children's play? If so, I'm sending Jamie to the nearest off license while they change the scenery.

After twenty more minutes of good, well behaved children acting their little socks off, and one very badly behaved child acting like a sociopath, we get to the grand finale of Noah And His Ark, where land has once again been discovered by the bearded ship builder, and everyone onboard is saved the fate of all those heathens who have just drowned in hideous agony thanks to the will of their god. There's every chance Mrs Carmoody could have recreated Saving Private Ryan up on stage today and it would have been less traumatic.

The stage is set as a tropical island for some reason. I'm assuming this is for the sake of variety, but I'm not sure the polar bears are going to appreciate it. Nevertheless, against a backdrop of palm trees and a white sandy beach, Noah walks back down the ark's ramp, leading his wife and all the animals behind him. Inevitably, Poppy reluctantly appears last, with that look of contempt still plastered across her face.

All the other parents are cooing and aahing over their children. About the only thing I'm doing is trying to decide which of her toys I'm confiscating for the next five years in response to this afternoon's shenanigans.

The animals line up in a semi-circle around Noah. Poppy and Jake are stood on one end right by the left wing, with Jake closest to it. He has started picking his nose again, given that he is required to do little else other than stand there while Noah and God have another conversation centre stage.

'I have brought your animals to dry land!' Noah bellows at God.

'Thank you, my son. You have done well and I am pleased with your obedience,' God mumbles back to him.

'Will the waters go away now God?'

'Yes. And there will be room for all the animals of my creation.'

As the two chat back and forth for a while about how great it is that several billion people have just been murdered, and how wonderful it is that 95% of all the species on Earth have just been eradicated thanks to the fact they couldn't fit on the bloody ark, I notice Poppy becoming more and more disgusted by Jake's nose pickery.

She stands aghast, staring at his finger as it disappears up to the second knuckle. Aghastness is replaced by sheer, unbridled revulsion as Jake removes the finger and a bogey the size of a golf ball with it. He then makes a terrible, terrible error. One that almost brings this play to a swift and tragic conclusion.

I do feel slightly sorry for Jake. He has had to put up with my moody daughter throughout the entire play. It can't be much fun to be the one making all the effort, while your partner makes none.

However, this does not excuse him waving the golf ball sized bogey under Poppy's nose, before attempting to wipe it on her face.

Poppy realises what the little bastard is doing and moves her head back with a scream of horror. 'Stop it Jake!' she wails.

Noah and God cease their discussion about how pious it is to systematically wipe out nearly all life on Earth, and turn to see what's going on.

Jake, all that pent up frustration bubbling to the surface, comes at Poppy again, his bogie covered finger waving at her. Pops then takes a drastic but understandable course of action - she pushes Jake Potter away as hard as she can. The nose picker stumbles backwards and falls off stage with a loud clatter. The scream of an elderly teacher having her bad foot crushed beneath the weight of a seven-year-old boy is heard from backstage, followed by the sound of expensive electronic equipment hitting the floor.

Instantly, the stage is plunged into darkness, save for a single spotlight in the centre. Noah hesitantly moves into this and starts to frantically turn his head between the audience and the wings. 'Do I do my speech now?' he whisper shouts.

'We haven't done the song yet!' God tells him from the gloom.

Noah looks confused. Obviously the spotlight is meant for him, but it's come on too early, thanks to Jake Potter's tumble. Noah's lip trembles. 'I don't know what to do.'

We're all waiting for Mrs Carmoody to bring some order to the chaos, but she does not appear.

Noah continues to stand still in the harsh glare of the spotlight, not knowing what to do. Some children are just not meant to be under such pressure, alone in front of a hundred expectant audience members.

Others however, are more than willing to step up and bask in the glow of the spotlight.

Poppy, seeing her opportunity, leaps forward and approaches the stage struck boy. 'Noah!' she shouts. 'I am a chicken, and I will sing you a song of thanks for bringing me and the other chicken here to this island. I really love coconuts!'

Noah looks totally confused.

'You go and stand with Briony - sorry, Mrs Noah, and I will sing for you!' Poppy continues, pushing Noah out of the spotlight.

As soon as he's gone, Poppy turns to the crowd with a gleaming smile spread across her face. Off comes the ridiculous bathmat chicken head, and at the top of her voice Poppy starts to sing.

I'm dumbstruck.

I feel Jamie's hand tightening around mine in terror.

Things only get worse when we realise what song our chicken daughter has chosen to serenade Noah and his wife with. She could have chosen something from a Disney movie, she could have gone with a nice hymn, she could have decided to sing a children's nursery rhyme.

She chooses none of these though. Instead, Poppy starts to sing Umbrella by Rihanna.

Why, I have no idea. Quite what an umbrella has to do with being a chicken on a tropical island is unclear, but this is the song Poppy has chosen, so we're just going to have to accept it.

'Now it's raining it's not clever!' she sings. *'I'll be your best friend forever! You can stand with me and my umbrella! You can stand with me and my umbrella!'*

These aren't the correct words to the song, not by a long shot. But I'm less concerned with Poppy's lyrical accuracy, and more concerned with the fact she's started gyrating around in a manner completely inappropriate for a seven-year-old.

Given that Poppy only knows the chorus to Umbrella, she then switches the song up and starts to belt out Wrecking Ball by Miley Cyrus.

'I came in with a wrecking ball! A really big heavy wrecking ball!'

Of course, when singing Miley Cyrus, there must be twerking involved.

Yep, in front of a hundred parents, and proving what *terrible* parents Jamie and I are, Poppy starts to wobble her bottom up and down awkwardly as she sings. I knew I should have cancelled our subscription to MTV. I *knew* it!

'Oh Jesus Christ,' Jamie utters in dismay.

Poppy's twerking is greeted with a mixture of laughter and horrified gasps from the crowd. I look behind her to see all the other children standing slack jawed in amazement.

Where the hell is Carmoody? She needs to stop this!

But there is still no sign of the old woman. I can hear a load of kerfuffle going on backstage though. I hear a man's voice asking for a first aid kit, and somebody else asking if they should dial 999.

And all the while, Poppy Newman continues a medley of popular hits by today's female singers, while waving her extremities around in an inappropriate fashion. She's now moved onto Roar by Katy Perry.

Oh God, I'm going to have to stop her before she gets to Gaga.

Slowly, I rise from my seat.

'What are you doing?' Jamie asks in a hoarse whisper.

'Stopping our daughter getting expelled from infant school,' I reply, and walk down the aisle towards the stage. Poppy notices me coming and thankfully stops dancing. From the look on her face, she knows that Mum is *not* happy. In an attempt to deflect my parental ire, she tries to dazzle me with the cutest smile she can construct in such a short space of time.

I look up at her, my lips pursed.

'Hello Mum,' she says.

'Poppy. Go and stand over there with the other children,' I tell her.

'But I'm dancing and singing,' she replies in a small voice.

'Yes, I know. But you shouldn't be, should you?'

'But Noah didn't know what to do.'

'Well, it's not up to you to interrupt him,' I reply, acutely aware that everyone in the room is now staring at the back of my head.

Poppy pouts.

I'm about to order her to move away from the spotlight again, when all the lights suddenly come back up. Mrs Carmoody, being held up by a couple of other teachers, shuffles painfully onto the stage and looks daggers at me.

This is my queue to fuck off back to my seat as quickly as my legs will carry me. I point to Poppy and gesture for her to move backwards, before turning smartly on one foot and scampering back to Jamie. As I reach him and sit back down, he leans over. 'You're paying for the therapy sessions,' he says in a low voice.

'Apologies to everyone!' Mrs Carmoody says to us all. 'A slight technical hitch!' She can't help but quickly glance at Poppy as she says this. 'We will now continue with the show... *as it is meant to be performed.*' Another look at Poppy, this time more obvious. She then stares at Noah. 'Go on Mahir! Get on with it!'

Mahir Noah doesn't need to be told twice. You can see he's just as eager to end this living hell as we are. He steps forward again. 'Praise be to God for bringing us to this place! We will sing you a song of thanks for your help!'

So, it turns out that Poppy had a better grasp of the storyline than I thought. She managed to pre-empt the finale all by herself. That's my girl.

To be honest, I think I preferred her twerking to the droning rendition of He's Got The Whole World In His Hands we get delivered to us now by a group of hot, tired and frazzled infant school children.

Except Poppy of course, she's looking at Jake Potter with deep suspicion and isn't even trying to sing.

The song comes to a weary close and the God of Mumbles steps forward into the spotlight that has now reappeared. 'And so the righteous have been saved.' He is joined by Noah. 'Now let us feast and be merry!'

Really?

After all that, Noah thinks it's a good idea to kick back, open up a few brewskis and slap some steaks on the barbecue? If he does, he'll drive at least one farmyard animal extinct before they've had so much as a chance to eat the nearest palm tree.

All the children (except Poppy) bow, and the curtain squeaks its way closed again, mercifully ending the story of Noah And His Ark, and Poppy And Her Entitlement.

'I'm going to sit in the car, you go and collect Poppy,' Jamie says.

'No fucking chance, sunshine. You're just as much at fault for this as I am.'

Jamie effects a pained expression. 'But I've got a headache.'

'I don't care if your head is about to fall off, you're still collecting our daughter with me,' I order, and we move towards the stage. I'm making a point of not having eye contact with any of the other parents as we do so.

As we stand there for the next five minutes waiting for Poppy to come out, we are forced to endure a lot of comments about how awful that chicken girl was. One particularly loud Northern man is the most critical. 'She bloody well tripped him up on purpose!' he says.

'Our Jake's a lovely lad. Wouldn't say boo to a goose,' a woman standing next to him adds. These are obviously Jake Potter's parents.

This is, of course, the perfect moment for Poppy to emerge from behind the stage curtain, her face like thunder. I feel a hundred sets of eyes swivel to greet her arrival. 'I want to go home, Mum,' she says, lip trembling.

I grab her from down off the stage. As I turn with her in my arms, I see Potter's parents sneer at me. 'Maybe if you'd raised a son who could resist the urge to pick his fuc – *fudging* nose in public so much, my daughter wouldn't have had to trip him up,' I tell them. 'Come on Jamie, we're leaving.' I sound imperious, and I storm off in an imperious manner. If any of the crowd were in any doubt as to 'where she gets it from' then I have now provided them with all the evidence they need.

I frankly don't care. I get to admonish Poppy for her behaviour tonight. *Nobody else does.*

The car ride home is mainly conducted in silence.

The silence ends later that evening when I confiscate Poppy's TV and blu ray player. I also put a parental lock on the Sky box so she can't watch MTV anymore.

The ensuing tantrum is apocalyptic.

'When she's older,' I say to Jamie in an exhausted voice, having finally put her to bed. 'Old enough to get married, I mean. I'm going to pull the poor boy to one side and say one thing to him.'

'What's that?'

'*Run.*'

I do hope I wasn't quite that bad when I was seven, Mum. If I was, I apologise, and can almost understand why Dad buggered off.

Love you and miss you,
Your newly disciplinary daughter, Laura.

XX

Jamie's Diary
Friday 13 August

So now I've got a fucking dog.

Oh no, I'm sorry, did I say dog? That's not an accurate description in the slightest. When you think of the word 'dog' you tend to picture a furry animal of between a foot and four feet high that likes to run after balls and bark at the postman when he comes past in the morning. You do not think of a bulgy eyed rat creature that shivers ninety five percent of the time and, despite its miniature proportions, seems to take up more room in your house than a pack of Great Danes.

Interesting fact: the word 'Chihuahua', when translated from its native Mexican, means 'Go on, kick me, I fucking dare you.'

I could have cheerfully throttled Terry when he turned up at the door with his present for my moody daughter. Just because your first night treading the boards ends in total disaster, it doesn't necessarily follow that you should be given a small yapping twat as a consolation prize.

And yet, here it is. All twelve inches of it. A small, shaking, bad tempered monstrosity that Poppy has decided to name Winklehoven.

Yes.

Winklehoven.

Not Choco, Chico, Chippy, Chappy - or other such suitable names for a dog of its type. No, my daughter has chosen to give her new best friend the name *Winklehoven*.

Where the hell she got Winklehoven from, I have no idea.

I even asked her.

'I don't know Dad, it just sounds nice,' she replied, with a twinkle in her eye.

Oh, nice to *you*, young lady, but you're not the one who will have to take this idiot for a walk every day are you? You're not the one that will have to call its name in public, *are you*?

If Terry was in my bad books for leaving my wife when she was a young girl, then he now has multiple entries in bold writing for giving Poppy this dog thing.

Laura should *never* have told him about Poppy's dismal performance at the school play. Nor should she have told him how miserable our daughter had been for the two weeks afterwards. This is exactly the kind of situation a man of Terry's stripe can take advantage of - and with one swift stroke he manages to ingratiate himself on Poppy forever.

'I don't think she should have that,' I warn Laura's father, as he produces the Chihuahua pup and hands it over to Poppy. I have to shout to make my voice carry over her loud squeals of delight.

'Where did you get it Dad?' Laura asks in some distress, as she watches Poppy instantly bond with the twitchy mutt.

'An old friend of mine. His daughter breeds them. She had a new litter, and offered me one for free.'

'And you thought the best thing to do would be to give it to Poppy without consulting us first?' I say to him, trying my best to keep out of the way of child and pup as they bound around the living room together.

Terry blinks a couple of times in surprise. 'I just thought she'd love it, and it would cheer her up.'

Laura grits her teeth. 'Well, if you had told us you were going to do this, we'd have asked you not to,' she says. 'Poppy is still being punished for her behaviour.'

'Yes,' I agree. 'And we wouldn't have wanted a dog anyway, would we Laura?' I look at my wife. '*Would we Laura?*' I repeat, seeing the way she's looking down at the stupid little rat creature with misty eyes.

'I'll just take it back then,' Terry says with a sigh.

'No!' Laura stops him. 'You can't do that now, can you? Look at them! It'd break her heart.'

'Er... he could you know, Laura,' I say cautiously. 'I mean, Poppy would get over it eventually.'

Laura bends down and picks up the tiny dog, which wriggles uncontrollably in her hands. 'No she wouldn't, Jamie. It would be too cruel to them both,' she tells me, and laughs out loud with delight as the toothy pipsqueak licks the end of her nose.

I put my head in my hands for a moment and try to hold back the tears, before looking up and giving Terry a look of unconcealed loathing.

So now I've got a fucking dog.

And boy, is it a turd factory. It may be little, but the bloody animal seems to shit every thirty eight seconds.

Half the time this takes place wherever I'm likely to put my feet five minutes later.

Do you know what the worst experience of my life has been?

No, it's not getting food poisoning from a Mexican snack.

No, it's not nearly being eaten by a crocodile.

No, it's not nearly dying of exposure in The Maldives.

The worst thing that has ever happened to me was treading my bare foot into the lump of shit that Winklehoven left on the kitchen lino this morning.

It was *squishy.*

So very, very *squishy.*

One second I'm yawning my way past the dishwasher to make a nice hot cup of tea, the next I'm screaming in horror as the brown nastiness sinks its way between my toes.

'Aaaargggh!'

'What's the matter Jamie?!' Laura demands from where she's sat at the breakfast bar.

'Fucking poo!' I holler.

'What?!'

'Fucking dog poo!' I repeat, holding up my foot and pointing at the mess on the end of it.

'Jesus Christ!' Laura wails and covers her mouth. 'I'm eating bran flakes here, you psychopath!'

'Oh, I'm so *sorry*, Laura. Are you distressed by the sight of Winklehoven's shit on my bare, naked foot? Well, maybe you *shouldn't have agreed to keep the trembling arsehole then!*'

'Just go and clean it off!' she orders.

'Where? Where exactly would you like me to scrape these animal faeces from my body part, Laura? The bathroom perhaps? I could tread some into the hallway carpet as I go, to add to the stain the little skipping twat left there last night!'

'Use the hose outside!'

So, there you have it.

We've had the dog less than two weeks, and I'm already out in the garden hosing myself down like an animal. By the time the crapping monstrosity reaches adulthood I'll be washing myself down in the local creek, shouting at strangers as they go past.

I *hate* that dog!

Sadly, both Poppy and Laura love it to pieces. Not a day goes by without me having to resist the urge to upchuck the contents of my stomach every time they ooh and aah over something cute the big-eared pillock does.

The day Poppy got it to give her its paw to receive a treat, the volume of female squealing reached such a crescendo that I had to get my hearing checked the next day.

If I hate Winklehoven, then Winklehoven absolutely *detests* me.

It's almost as if it knows I'm not happy about its presence in my house, and it intends to make sure that presence is as uncomfortable for me as is doggedly possible. First we have the aforementioned shitting where I'm about to step.

By the time I limped back into the house this morning, one foot dripping wet, I could see the little shitbag sat next to Laura's leg, grinning at me.

Yes, you heard me right! The dog was *grinning at me.*

I am *not* insane.

Winklehoven also likes to bite me. Those Chihuahua teeth may be small, but they are razor sharp. I only went to move it off the couch last week so I could sit down and watch the Grand Prix, and the tiny bastard nearly had my middle finger off.

'Oww! You little sod!' I exclaimed at the time, putting the finger in my mouth and tasting blood.

'You have to do it nicely, Dad!' Poppy informs me in a disapproving tone.

'I was doing it nicely!' I snap back at her. 'Shoo!' I order the dog, waving my copy of this month's GQ at it. This finally gets it to move, but not without a growl, and a look that tells me I'm going to get my face ripped off at about 3am.

Even when the dog is not directly trying to injure me, the little blighter is making my life a misery in other inventive ways. I used to very much enjoy sitting out in the garden with my Kindle, reading whatever the latest bestseller is that I'm insanely jealous of. Ours is a nice, secluded back garden, with high walls covered in ivy that block out the sights and sounds of the surrounding suburban area. It's like a small oasis. At least it was until Winklehoven happened. These days, no sooner have I plonked myself down in the warm summer sun, than out trots the pesky creature to cause havoc. It then proceeds to stand at the back wall of the garden and bark at everything it hears. It doesn't matter if it's a car going past in the distance, or a small inoffensive bug minding its own business near the busy lizzies, Winklehoven will fucking bark at it until it's happy the offender is gone. Poppy usually runs out into the garden to see what all the fuss is about, which just sends Winklehoven off into an excited doggy fit that, if anything, is even more annoying. I end up having to go back in the house and sit upstairs just to get a bit of peace and quiet.

If reading is bad with the yapping gobshite around, then writing is a thousand times worse.

It's very hard to write broad comedy when there's a small bug-eyed dog squinting at you permanently from the study doorway. One minute I'll be happily composing a sentence of such witty genius that I have to wonder where I get it from, the next I'll feel the gaze from those bulgy eyes resting on the back of my neck, and the hairs on it will start to rise. I'll try to ignore the dog for a good ten minutes and concentrate on what I'm doing, but I suddenly find it very hard to even string a sentence together.

'Fuck off Winklehoven,' I'll mutter under my breath, in the hopes that it will do the trick. It never does though. The dog is implacable.

It now becomes a battle between man and beast. I try my level best to ignore its presence and get on with my work, in an attempt to prove that it has no effect on me whatsoever. Winklehoven is intent on proving the exact opposite.

There are times when I think I've won. A good half an hour will pass, and I'll be convinced that the stupid mutt has fucked off to annoy Laura, or gone to bark at the traffic again. But just at that moment, the sodding thing will yawn, or move slightly, just to let me know that it's still there - watching me and planning the best way to run up the back of the chair and plunge its little Chihuahua teeth into the back of my defenceless head.

'Poppy! Come and get Winklehoven!' I'll eventually scream downstairs, signalling the dog's complete victory over me.

Ha! You're so pathetic that you have to get a seven-year-old to come save you, the dog is no doubt thinking in the vaults of its tiny canine brain. I'm in your head bitch, and it's some mighty fine real estate I'm taking up in here. Why don't you just accept your fate, and admit I am the boss of you? Once you do, I'll leave you alone to your wretched scrawlings. Maybe you can write a book about me? It'll be better than that crap you churn out.

And here I am! Writing all about bloody Winklehoven!
The dog has won.
Pity me.

If I seem a little overboard with my Chihuahua prejudice, and you're not behind all this Winklehoven hate, allow me to regale a story to you that will firmly put you in my camp, and assure you that we are in fact dealing with a creature spat from the very depths of the underworld.

It is Saturday morning. One of the really good ones you get now and again in August. The air is calm, the sun is shining, the temperature is five degrees above the average.

It is 8.45am and I am lying in bed, dozing lightly, and contemplating a day of doing not very much in particular. I might give the old car a nice wash in the gentle summer sun this morning. Maybe a trip to the local garden centre is in order for later in the afternoon - and maybe, just maybe - there's potential for a Chinese takeaway around seven o'clock, if Laura thinks my waistline will take it, while we all watch Doctor Who and I try not to think about pedalos.

All in all, it sounds like a fabulous Saturday in the Newman household.

'The dog needs a walk,' Laura mumbles from beside me.
Damn!

For a brief, shining moment I'd forgotten that Winklehoven was now part of our lives. In my doze, my brain had gratefully removed the shivering bell end from existence.

I groan out loud. Then Laura says something even worse, if that were possible. 'It's your turn to do the walk, remember? We agreed you would if I did the answers to that questionnaire Woman's Own sent us.'

I groan again. She's right. I detest completing the email questionnaires we often get from journalists. Not because they ask anything annoying, but just because I've done so many of them, and the questions are always pretty much the same. If I have to write another paragraph about how it felt to get a publishing deal, I might have to commit messy suicide.

Last night then, I agreed with Laura that she would write the email, and I would take Winklehoven for its morning trot around the leafier sections of our immediate suburban area. This would mark the first time that I would be walking the dog on my own, as getting Poppy out of bed before 9am on a Saturday is roughly akin to trying to remove a King Cobra from its basket.

Last night the idea of a nice sunny walk sounded preferable to being hunched over a keyboard, writing about how it felt to write a best seller for the umpteenth time.

What a fucking idiot I truly am.

'You want to swap jobs?' I gamble, hoping that Laura would enjoy the prospect of a sunny walk just as much as I stupidly thought I would twelve hours ago.

'Not a chance,' she replies. 'I'm warm, comfy and don't intend to get dressed until at least midday. Get your arse out of bed and go make sure Winky doesn't crap in the kitchen again.'

I sigh. She's an awful, cruel woman sometimes. But she also makes a good point. If I don't get up and take the twat for a walk now, I will inevitably be stepping in its warm faeces at some point during the day - probably as I'm walking through the kitchen holding my plate of chicken chow mein and sweet and sour pork balls.

I reluctantly get out of bed, throw on my dressing gown and make my way downstairs. I open the kitchen door to be greeted with a growl coming from Winklehoven's cage. When it's Poppy or Laura, the dog sits up expectantly and wags its tail. With me, it's always the growl.

'Morning rat,' I say as I pass it to put the kettle on, which gets me another growl. The sodding thing can stay in its cage until I've had a bowl of cereal and my morning shit. Then I might just be in a good enough mood to take it out.

An idea occurs as I'm munching my way through my All Bran. Instead of just taking Winklebastard around the local streets, I'll jump in the car and march the little sod around the walking track at Langtree Lakes - all three miles of it. With any luck, the longer walk will tire it out more, and I can get some peace and quiet later to sit and have a nice read.

Genius!

With this thought in mind, I finish my cereal, have the aforementioned bowel movement, and get dressed.

By the time I hear Poppy and Laura stirring upstairs, I am slipping on my trainers by the front door. The dog is sat watching me with its new lead and collar on. These cost an arm and a leg, given that they are branded - rather inexplicably - with the Hello Kitty logo. Surely a Hello Doggy equivalent would be a better idea, but sadly no such thing exists. The only solace I can take is that I doubt Winklebastard is any happier about my daughter's choice of bright pink cat-branded dog walking accessory than I am.

'I'm off! I'll be back in about an hour!' I shout upstairs. 'C'mon twatface, let's go,' I tell the dog, and yank it out through the doorway into the bright morning sunlight.

If there's one saving grace of Chihuahuas, it's that they're too small to be much of a bother when it comes to transport. A decent sized dog needs to be stuck in the back of the car, usually accompanied by several blankets, toys and a couple of air fresheners. With Winklebastard, I just have to wrap its lead around the seatbelt clasp a few times, and it can sit safely in the passenger seat next to me.

Oh, don't get me wrong, I'd like nothing more than to 'accidentally' have to brake hard on a roundabout and send the dog into the foot well headfirst, but returning home with its corpse in a brown paper bag wouldn't go down too well, now would it?

The drive to the Lakes only takes about ten minutes, giving Winklehoven ample time to bark at the passing cars, and for me to develop a tension headache above one eye because of the noise. Once we're out of the car though, the headache starts to clear again, thanks to the park's wonderful clean air and tranquil atmosphere. Not even Winklehoven's inherent Winklehovenness can wipe the dumb grin off my face as I walk down the sun dappled pathway. If only the UK had this kind of weather all year round, it would be the most magnificent country on Earth, and I would never want to leave.

I'm fine and dandy until we start to come across other dog walkers. It's one thing to walk a twelve inch long Chihuahua on a pink Hello Kitty lead when you're on your own and not in sight of another human being, it's quite another when other people start to see you coming.

It's not the women. They're generally fine. They find dogs like Winklebastard quite cute most of the time, and are able to look past how ridiculous I look walking it.

The men, on the other hand, are completely different.

I am judged at every turn.

They see me coming towards them, and each and every one has to suppress a mirthful grin.

Look! Here comes a man who must have had his testicles removed on the day of his wedding! they all think. *See how he holds limply on to the lead of the tiny rat creature. I bet my ten-year-old could beat him in an arm wrestle blindfolded. Why, this man's penis must be like the surface of the Moon - hard to see with the naked eye.*

For my part, I tend to return their unspoken condemnation with a look of anguished resignation.

Yes, I know how wretched I look, my expression says. *See how I gaze upon your proper dog with seething jealousy, and try to hurry past you as quickly as I can, before the emasculation takes my legs out from under me.*

Not only do I have the judging of my masculinity to deal with, I also have to watch out for any signs from the other dog that it's about to eat Winklebastard. Anything larger than a Springer Spaniel sends shivers down my spine. Dogs get hungry when out on walks, and I'm sure most of them wouldn't be above a little light inter-species cannibalism if the opportunity presented itself. You couldn't get much meat off those tiny little bones, but it might keep you going until your lunchtime bowl of kibble, if nothing else.

On this particular morning I have been in luck. Thus far, I've only had my masculinity questioned non verbally once, and the dog he had with him may have been a large Labrador, but it looked on its last legs, and probably couldn't have managed much more than a light suck of Winklehoven's head.

The only other dog walker I can see in my vicinity is a brown haired woman in a black t-shirt and blue jeans, coming towards me with a Border Terrier. Luckily, it's a small one, so there shouldn't be any cannibalistic tendencies in evidence, and she looks like a pleasant kind of person, one who wouldn't judge me for walking such an effeminate dog. Not out loud at least.

Usually, I find the prospect of communication with a complete stranger to be exquisitely awkward. If you're out on a nice walk by yourself, and you see someone coming the other way, you have a hard decision to make. On the one hand, do you greet the fellow walker with a cheery smile and a heartfelt good morning? Or do you scurry by and make no acknowledgement of their presence, just in case they're a raving lunatic, who likes to tear the ears off people who speak to them in public?

Mind you, the idea of being eaten alive by a mentalist is a breeze compared to the absolute worst thing that can happen when you wish someone a good day.

They could ignore you completely.

Aaaarggh! Think of the shame! The cold, cold British shame! To be rebuffed by a total stranger when attempting to be polite in Great Britain is like being slapped in the face and spat upon in any other civilised country.

Happily, all of these horrid considerations go out the window once both parties have a dog. There seems to be some kind of solidarity between dog owners that breaks down the social walls, and allows for some bright chit chat in the middle of the path, while the animals get to know each other better.

Also, it's a bit difficult to retain any British aloofness when your dogs suffer from no such awkwardness. While you're still getting used to the idea of having a conversation with somebody you've never met before, they're already sniffing each other's behinds and arguing over who gets to play with the stick.

I've decided, in my lack of infinite wisdom, that this is the primary reason why so many people in this country have a dog. It's not so much that we're a nation of dog lovers because they're cute and friendly, it's because they allow *us* to be more friendly to one another, without all the inherent stress.

As if to prove my point, the woman with the Border Terrier gets within ten feet of me and issues a cheery hello.

'Morning!' I say back with enthusiasm.

'Isn't that a gorgeous little dog!' she says, as Winklehoven trots over on the end of its retractable Hello Kitty lead to say hello to the small Border, which is off the lead and looking very happy about it. I say *small*, it still towers over Winklebastard - and looks quite amazed by the whole experience. There can't be many occasions in a small Border Terrier's life that this occurs.

'I like your Border,' I reply, loudly enough for Winklebastard's bat ears to pick up on. 'What's her name?' I'm guessing the sex of the dog due to its size.

Correctly, it transpires. 'Bluebell. Yours?'

Shit. I was having such a nice time.

'Winklehoven,' I mutter in a low tone. 'This is Winklehoven. Winklehoven the Chihuahua.' The desolation in my voice is palpable.

'Oh, that's an... interesting name for such a small dog.'

'Yes, it is, isn't it?'

The woman delves into a pocket and produces a large treat, which she passes down to Bluebell. I have neglected to bring treats with me for Winklehoven, because, as I think we've firmly established by now, I can't stand the cunt.

Bluebell starts to chew on the treat as Winklehoven looks on in what I can only assume is supreme doggy jealousy. This warms my heart, and goes some way to making up for the painful bite marks on my finger that still haven't healed properly.

'Lovely morning, isn't it?' the woman says, entering into the requisite small talk that we are forced into while our dogs bond.

'Yep, makes a nice change.'

This is a stupid thing to say, as it's been like this for the past week. I just say it out of habit, given how changeable the British weather usually is. The woman then squints slightly, and a curious look crosses her face. I think I'm about to get recognised again.

We really have to stop going on the telly, or agreeing to be in articles in the newspaper. It's getting silly now.

'Don't I know you from somewhere?' she says.

'Well, yes, I guess you might,' I reply, trying to keep the smugness out of my voice, and failing completely.

'Yeah, I definitely know you!'

I chuckle self indulgently. 'I get this quite a lot.'

'Do you?' she looks amazed.

'Of course! I'm lucky enough to be quite popular.'

'What? Just because you used to work at the paper?'

Oh.

I appear to have read this a bit wrong. She obviously recognises me from my previous life as a poor, downtrodden copywriter for our local news rag.

'Um... yeah! Lots of people knew me there!' I say, trying to cover my mistake, but still sounding like an egomaniac. 'Where did you work?' I add.

Her face clouds. 'About three offices down from yours. We'd see each other in the kitchen most days.'

Oh, for fuck's sake.

Quick Newman! Use the dogs to get you out of this!

I look down. 'Aaah. Isn't that sweet? The way they're getting on with each other.'

Actually, they don't look like they're getting on with each other at all. Bluebell is still chewing away on her big treat, her eyes occasionally darting to Winklehoven. My dog is sat on its haunches, growling gently under its breath.

I recognise the signs. This is the noise Winklebastard makes when it's about to have a go at you for daring to not share your food. The amount of times it's sat staring at me from the arm of the sofa, growling like that until I give it a chip, doesn't bear thinking about. If I don't service it with some free food off my plate, it will be down off the arm and thieving my pork chop quicker than you can say severe behavioural problems. The blame for this lies squarely at my wife and daughter's combined feet. They can't resist the stupid little dog's cutesy face, and spoil it rotten at every opportunity.

Bluebell knows none of this, and is therefore about to get a nasty surprise.

'Yes, they do... do look sweet,' the woman, who now dislikes me intensely, says, watching both dogs. She sounds quite unsure of herself. I can't blame her, as Winklehoven's growl has grown louder.

In an instant, the little dog ducks its head in, and tries to grab the treat from under the Border's nose. Bluebell is having none of this, and goes from being a well-mannered little doggie, to a gnashing ball of furry terror in a nanosecond. She goes for Winklehoven , slamming into the Chihuahua and sending it sprawling. In a split second she's on top of it, teeth bared and issuing a high pitched snarl that wouldn't sound out of place coming out of the gob of Cerberus, the three headed hellhound from Greek mythology.

I am paralysed.

While I might fantasise about harm coming to Winklebastard thanks to its attitude, to see it actually happening in front of me is quite another thing. What am I supposed to do if Bluebell isn't stopped? Squish Winklehoven's body back through our letterbox and run for the hills when I hear it plop wetly onto the welcome mat?

'Oh no!' the woman yells, bending down to pull Bluebell away. The Border is having none of it though, as she is quite happy treading on Winklehoven's head right about now, and doesn't want anyone to spoil the fun.

My paralysis breaks as I see her lunge for Winklebastard's throat. I reach forward, batting the Border away with one hand, and scoop the Chihuahua up with the other, attempting to get it out of danger. This only terrifies Winklehoven even more, causing a fountain of piss to erupt from its nether regions and RIGHT INTO MY MOUTH.

'Oh fuck!' I scream in disgust, holding the dog away from me. This only changes the direction of the piss fountain, so now Winklehoven is panic urinating all over the poor woman, soaking the front of her t-shirt.

She screams as well, skipping backwards to get out of range. Bluebell, seeing this (quite rightly) as an attack on her owner, runs over to me and sinks her teeth into my canvas trainer.

'Ow! Fuck!' I screech, pain immediately replacing disgust.

So now I have one dog attached to my foot, its needle teeth puncturing at least one of my toes, while another sits in my hand, wriggling like mad and spraying urine all over the place.

'Bluebell! Leave him alone!' the now urine soaked woman commands her dog. The Border does so, much to my surprise. She must have it well trained.

I figure trying the same tactic can't hurt. I point a finger at the Chihuahua. 'Winklehoven! Stop pissing!' This doesn't work, of course. Even an obedient dog would have trouble obeying an order like that.

I take hold of Winklebastard with both hands and attempt to control its wriggling a bit, in a valiant attempt to stop the piss fountain from spraying the entire area. I can't put the dog down, for fear of it being attacked again by Bluebell. Imploringly, I look back up at the woman, who obviously has a better grasp of dog training than me. 'Can you make it stop pissing? Why won't it stop pissing?' I wail in combined disgust and horror, as the little sod continues to void its bladder all over my hands.

'I, er, I... ' she replies, completely and understandably lost for words. She only came out this morning to give her lovely little Border Terrier a nice walk in the sun, and now she's being asked to give dog training tips to a piss soaked madman holding an epileptic Chihuahua.

'Why won't it stop?' I moan in a high pitched howl, looking at the golden stream the dog is still producing. 'Where's it all coming from?' I add, my face scrunching in revulsion.

'I don't know! Are you squeezing it?' she replies.

'I don't think so,' I tell her, loosening my grip anyway, just to be on the safe side. 'Can you squeeze piss out of a dog?' I ask over the never-ending spray. Even if this woman were the late, great Barbara Woodhouse, I think she'd have trouble answering that question.

'Put it down? That might stop it,' she suggests.

'But what about Bluebell?'

The woman looks down at her dog, who is now sat by her legs watching events unfold.

Have you ever seen a slack jawed dog?

Well, I fucking have, and it's a sight to behold, let me tell you.

'Bluebell won't attack again, don't worry!' the woman assures me. She still takes hold of Bluebell's collar as a precautionary measure though.

I lower Winklehoven to the ground, making sure to keep the genital region pointing away from me. It lies on its back for a moment, still urinating and wriggling, like the ugliest newborn you've ever seen. Then it realises that the only creature it's still pissing on is itself, and decides enough is enough. The stream of golden nastiness diminishes and Winklebastard rolls over and stands up again.

I look for signs of damage, but there don't appear to be any. All legs are pointing the right way, and no bloodstains are apparent. I breathe a sigh of relief.

Then I remember I am now covered in fresh dog urine.

'I'm covered in piss,' the poor woman says to me, echoing my thoughts.

'I'm so sorry about that,' I tell her. 'Can I wipe you down?'

A hand shoots up. 'No! I think I'll just go back to the car and make my way home. I can clean up there! Come on Bluebell!'

And with that, my poor dog walking chum is off back in the direction she came in, no doubt hurrying away as quickly as she can, just in case I decide to chase after her so I can squeeze some poo out of the stupid Chihuahua that I can then fling at her.

I look down at the offending article, which looks back up at me, trembling slightly.

'You've only got yourself to blame, you know,' I tell it. 'You really shouldn't have gone for her treat like that. You've learned a valuable lesson here today... Stop looking at me like that... I said *stop it*. I've got no sympathy with you at all. Absolutely none, so you can stop looking all vulnerable and scared, because it won't work. I am immune to your doggy manipulations... There, there Winklehoven, never mind.'

I reach down to give the little dog a pat on the head. The little fucker bites me on the finger.

'Oh, you utter cunt!' I shout, just as a tall, thickset man in a red chequered shirt walks round the corner with a large Staffordshire Bull Terrier. His eyes go wide as he realises what he's witnessing.

Look! Here is a man so utterly worthless and without manly virtue that not only does he own a small, teacup sized handbag dog, he feels the need to swear at it in public, in some pathetic attempt to exert what little remains of his natural authority over it. And does he smell of piss? Why yes, he does smell of piss. Have I ever seen such a god-awful display of humanity before? No, I don't think I have.

The man walks past and avoids me as best he can, given that we're standing on a narrow path next to a lake. Luckily, Winklehoven smells as much of piss as I do, so the Staffy also gives us a wide berth, figuring that breakfast should never be urine flavoured, unless you're absolutely desperate.

In shame and misery I walk us back to the car, trying to breathe through my mouth and not look down at the new stain rapidly drying on my shirt.

Back home, I walk in through the front door to be greeted by Laura coming down the stairs in her dressing gown. She looks at my hangdog expression, the drying streaks of piss on my clothing, the cut on my finger, and the trembling dog at my feet. 'Went well then, did it?' she asks.

'I don't want to talk about it,' I tell her, and drop the dog lead. 'I don't ever want to talk about it,' I add, moving past her and up the stairs. 'I'm going to have a shower,' I say, yanking my shirt off.

'What about the dog?' Laura calls up to me.

I swivel in an instant and look down at her, brow furrowed in impotent fury. 'I do not *care* about the dog, Laura. Unless your next request of me is *'Jamie, could you find the nearest mincer and put Winklehoven through it head first?'* I do not wish to hear another thing about the dog for the rest of the day... if not the week, month, year, or millennium.'

'Dad! That's horrible!' I hear Poppy shout from behind me.

I hold my bloody, painful finger up. 'So is this Poppy! So is this!'

Giving my daughter a look that suggests it would be best for her continued well-being that she gets out of my way, I stride across the landing and into the bathroom, locking the door behind me so I can't hear the inevitable sounds of dog mollycoddling going on downstairs. With a shiver of revulsion, I remove the rest of my clothing, turn on the shower, and step into the cubicle.

My foot comes down on a squishy lump of Winklehoven shit.

'Oh, for fuck's sake!' I scream in horror.

Still, at least I won't have to wash it off with a bloody hose this time.

Today, I sat and ordered two things on Amazon. One is a small book entitled 'Buying The Right Cat'. I intend to leave it strategically around the house so Winklebastard sees it as much as possible. The other is a life sized cardboard cut out of a Border Terrier. This I intend to park outside Winklehoven's cage every night, until the little sod starts treating me with a bit more respect. If this doesn't work, my next purchase will be a book entitled 'Buying The Right Border Terrier' - and a fucking mincer.

Oh, and one more thing - you may have noted that throughout this rambling anecdote I haven't referred to Winklehoven's gender. This has been entirely deliberate. The second I start calling it 'he' or 'she' is the moment you might start identifying with it more, and that's the last thing I want. Everyone around me has fallen for the little bastard's dubious charms, and I need to keep you onside as much as possible. So, no taking a sneaky peak between its legs when I'm not looking, alright? I'm trusting you on this.

Laura's Diary
Tuesday, September 28th

Dear Mum,

Atchoo!

I have a cold.

A nasty, stinking early Autumn cold.

I caught it at the book conference we've just been at for the past three days. I can even hazard a guess as to who gave it to me. It was the bloke on the tube first thing Saturday morning, as we were making our way to Danesborough Halls, where the three day event took place.

The bugger sneezed on my cheek.

I'm sure he didn't mean to, but it was one of those explosive sneezes that erupt from your face without warning when you are stricken with a cold.

'I'm so dreadfully sorry!' he stammers, as I wipe away his nasal excretions with the collar of my jacket.

I should scream and shout at the poor man for not having better manners, but it's 8am, and I haven't even had a decent cup of tea yet, so can't manage more ire in my response than a slight growl. 'Don't worry. Perhaps you should buy yourself a handkerchief?' I say to him.

His face blanches. He would probably keep apologising, were it not for the fact that the tube train has started to slow, indicating that it's coming into the next station. 'This is my stop,' the red nosed man tells me.

'Oh good. At least I won't have to worry about you peppering me with any more sputum,' I reply in a haughty tone I don't really like the sound of.

As the tube doors open, he gives me one last look of embarrassed regret, before piling out of the train with the rest of the exodus.

'I hope that doesn't set the tone for the day,' Jamie says, from where he is stood with Poppy to one side of me.

'I've got a tissue in my pocket,' Dad says, rummaging around in his coat for a moment, before producing a small packet of Kleenex and handing it to me.

'Thanks,' I reply, taking one of the tissues and wiping my neck with it.

Now, don't be mad, Mum. I know you might not like the idea of Dad coming along on a family trip like this, but we've been getting on very well in the past few months, and I felt it was about time to start including him more in Newman family activities.

This trip to London has been in the calendar for months now.

Jamie and I are speaking in two sessions at the Contemporary Writers Conference - one this morning, and the other on Monday. Coincidentally, Poppy's school has an inset day on Monday as well, and we took this as a sign to turn the whole thing into a proper weekend away. The conference organisers are footing our expenses, so it seemed like a no-brainer.

Dad coming along was a spur of the moment thing last week, after he came around for a coffee. It was while he was playing on the floor with Poppy and Winky that the idea occurred to me.

'You should come with us this weekend, Dad,' I suggest.

'What?' Jamie splutters from around his coffee cup.

Dad grins. 'That would be lovely, Laura.' His eyes dart to Jamie. 'But are you sure?'

'Yes. Definitely.' I can feel Jamie's eyes trying their best to burn a hole through the side of my skull. I turn to look at him. 'Dad could probably look after Poppy for us one night, Jamie. What do you think of that?'

Jamie's expression instantly softens as he realises the import of this statement. If Dad babysits Pops, we can have an evening alone together, with all the fun and games that might entail. 'Oh. Er. Yeah.' He looks at Dad. 'Would you mind having Pops for the night, Terry?' He pauses for a second. 'Maybe two?'

Dad might be an aging hippy, but he's not an idiot. 'That would be fine, Jamie,' he replies with a smile, before looking at Poppy, who is busily poking a finger into Winklehoven's ear. 'Would you like that, Poppy? Would you like to spend the evening with Grandad?'

Poppy's eyes widen. 'Can we watch Frozen again?' she says.

Dad's eyes twitch momentarily. 'Of course we can sweetheart.'

Jamie picks up his mobile. 'I'll call the Premier Inn and ask them for another room,' he says, finding the number in the phone's memory as he does so.

You'll note that we're staying in a Premier Inn, rather than The Dorchester this time. The Contemporary Writer's Conference may be one of the largest events in the publishing industry calendar, but that doesn't mean it isn't tighter than a gnat's naughty parts when it comes to how much it pays in expenses.

Poppy gasps. 'But what about Winky?' she says, with a healthy dollop of melodramatic distress.

'Oh lovely, that's just excellent,' Jamie says as he looks up from the ringing phone, a smile of such malevolence crossing his face that I start sketching the sign of the cross. 'Mum and Dad. Mum and Dad can have Winklehoven for the weekend. I'm sure they wouldn't mind.'

I'm not sure whether it's his parents or the dog that my husband is aiming his malevolence at.

To be frank, I'm not just using Dad as a babysitting service, I also want him to come along and see what it is that Jamie and I actually do for a living. I'm very proud of what we've managed to accomplish, and I see nothing wrong with wanting to flaunt that success to a father who absented himself from my life at such an early age. He had nothing to do with making me the woman I am today, and I want him to know that I didn't need him to become the person I am. We may have mended some bridges, but they're still under construction, and I'm not entirely comfortable with the old man *just* yet. It'll do me the world of good to show off to him a bit, I think.

It'll also give Dad an insight into the writing world - something he's never had any part of before. I must get my writing ability from your side of the family Mum, because my father has no tendencies towards it at all. It transpires that the longest thing he's ever written is a shopping list. Sometimes I do wonder how I'm his child, given how different we are as people. When talking to him, I am left in no doubt that I am my mother's daughter. I just don't see much of myself in him at all. Your genes must have been the stronger of the two, Mum!

Having said that, he is prone to moments of kindness that have surprised me greatly. Jamie might hate Winklehoven, and even I sometimes feel a little overwhelmed by the tiny dog, but Poppy adores the Chihuahua with a love so unconditional that it brings tears to my eyes. If I am ever in a low mood, all I have to do is watch her cuddling Winky, and it makes me feel so much better.

And so, it felt right to ask Dad along this weekend. If nothing else he can sit in the audience with Poppy to stop her squirming all over the shop when she gets bored.

The tube train arrives at our station, and I'm very grateful to get off it before somebody else evacuates a bodily fluid over my person. I won't realise I've caught a cold for a while yet, so I put the sneezing episode behind me, and stride purposefully towards Danesborough Halls - and whatever fun and games will greet us there.

Today, Jamie and I are taking part in a discussion panel with another two authors about the way the publishing industry is changing for writers in the 21st Century. This will largely consist of a lot of people in the audience trying to pretend that Amazon isn't as powerful as it is - and that it *was* the right decision to sign that contract with a small traditional publisher for a £200 advance and 12% of the ebook royalties.

On the panel with us are two writers who couldn't be more different from Jamie and I if you bussed them in from a parallel universe. One is Joy Mannings, a middle aged author of cosy mysteries, usually involving a four legged animal of some kind. If this woman doesn't have The Littlest Hobo on blu-ray box set at home somewhere, I'd be amazed. Still, her dog related mystery stories sell by the truckload, so there must be someone reading them. I could never suspend disbelief enough to accept that a kangaroo, horse, dolphin or dog could provide assistance during a missing persons investigation, so the whole thing is rather lost on me.

The other writer is Jack Hannigan, a tall, strapping American man in his mid sixties, who writes robust and exciting military action fare. Again, not a genre I'm familiar with, but I know it has many followers. Most of them sporting a small penis and an inferiority complex possibly, but you can never underestimate a man's desire to read all about the defusing of nuclear bombs with just one second left on the countdown timer.

Before we get to the panel though, we have to sign in.

'Laura Newman, with her husband Jamie, daughter Poppy, and father Terry,' I tell the harassed and bespectacled woman sat behind the reception desk in the large, echoing foyer of Danesborough Halls.

'Are you the comedy people?' she asks us, in a manner as brisk as you'd expect from a grey haired woman in slightly too much tweed. I assume she's referring to the books we write, and is not passing comment on our dress sense, or general demeanour.

'Yes, that's us,' I tell her.

'Ah, well then. Here are your I.D cards.' She gives me a stern look as she hands them over. 'Do not lose them!' she orders, as if we were taking possession of expertly forged passports for transport through the Iron Curtain, and not bits of paper stuffed into rather flimsy lanyards.

'Thanks,' I reply, and hand the lanyards out.

'There is a green room available to our speakers,' she tells us. 'Go left down those stairs and follow the signs.'

I try to thank her for her help, but she's already turned to the next person in the long queue snaking across the foyer. 'Well, let's go get a cup of coffee then,' I say to the others, and make my way towards the stairs as instructed.

The green room is not green of course, it's more of a dull beige. A few tables and chairs have been haphazardly strewn across the small room, and a table has been erected at the far end, on which sits a coffee machine and some bite sized snacks, sweating under the warm strip lighting above. Luxurious, it is not. Still, it's somewhere to sit and have a rest until we're due on stage in half an hour.

Our two fellow speakers join us in the next ten minutes. First Joy Mannings makes her appearance - with a small shitzu in tow. The dog looks about four hundred years old and moves like it just wants to lie down and die. A few minutes later, silver haired Jack Hannigan walks in, and gives us all a broad American smile, before making his way to the coffee machine, where he looks quite distressed at the prospect of having to drink more British coffee.

We pass the intervening few minutes in idle writer's conversation with them both. Jamie always enjoys the chance to swap stories with those in the same line as us, so he's quite animated in the discussion, Poppy sat on his lap and busily munching a flapjack. Dad seems less enthused. All this authorial talk goes over his head a bit, and I also think the natural hippy in him baulks at Jack Hannigan and his military bearing. You couldn't get two men more different.

Eventually it's time for us to go do our thing, so Dad takes Poppy to sit in the audience, and the four of us make our way to the back stage area.

'There's a lot of people out there,' Joy Mannings says with some surprise.

'Smashing!' Jamie responds, ever the show off.

'Hmmm,' I mutter.

Jack Hannigan gives me a smile. 'I know what you mean,' he says, picking up on my reticence. 'It doesn't matter how many of these things I do, I still get nervous every time.'

Well, if a big, strapping man like that can be nervous, then there's no shame in skinny, ex-chocolateer Laura Newman feeling the same way.

We're introduced on stage, and all four of us walk out to some rather half hearted applause. Those gathered are other writers, after all, not fans of our work. They're here to get tips and advice, not bask in the reflected glory of their favourite authors.

The most disconcerting thing about the set-up for this talk is that there is a man with a camcorder directly in front of us, getting close ups of our faces as we speak that are beamed onto a large screen behind our heads. This is to give those at the back a better view I'm sure, but I really could do without my head being projected twenty feet high every time I open my mouth. I'm just thankful the screen is right behind us so I can safely ignore it as much as possible. It can't be all that beneficial to the crowd anyway, because there appears to be a delay between what's being filmed, and what's shown on the screen. If I move my head quick enough I can see my own face briefly, before my twenty foot high head turns to look up. It's a very odd experience.

The next forty five minutes are actually quite pleasant. We all take turns answering a variety of questions from the audience.

Jamie naturally does most of the talking for us, but I am able to make what I think is a rather good comment about how self publishing has democratised the publishing industry, and made it easier than ever for someone to have their work published, no matter how niche or strange it may be.

I would probably have said more, but about half way through the panel, I am aware of a tickle in my nose, and a soreness in my throat that forces me to drink a lot of the sparkling water on the table in front of me.

I put it down to having to speak in public and try to ignore it, thinking it'll go away once we're done.

Completely wrong, of course, but I've never had a cold take hold this fast before, so I think I can be forgiven for my error.

By late afternoon that day, I am feeling decidedly rough. My head is swimming and I've developed a throbbing headache. My face feels like a radiator, but my fingers are frozen. My throat is now a scratchy mess and I'm starting to sound hoarse.

'Are you okay baby?' Jamie asks me as we ride the tube back from the centre of the city, towards our Premier Inn on the outskirts.

'Oh yes, I'm fine,' I say, not really believing a word of it. As human beings, we do tend to enter into a stage of denial when we're coming down with an illness. 'Probably just tired.'

Jamie looks at me uncertainly, but doesn't press the issue.

There's a five star rated Chinese restaurant just down the road from the hotel, so we elect to go there for our evening meal. By the time the main course comes out, I'm starting to feel properly rough, and only manage to eat about a third of my chicken in black bean sauce, before putting the knife and fork down.

I am grateful when Dad takes Poppy off to watch Frozen in their room, but not for the reasons I originally thought. It's less about wanting some space for sex, and more about just wanting to lie down somewhere quiet.

I still give it a go though - the sex, I mean. As has been stated many times, we don't get much Poppy free time for these kinds of shenanigans. Pounding headache or not, an orgasm sounds like a mighty fine way to end what has been a very tiring day.

Unfortunately, the cold virus is not one for allowing such things, especially when in its early stages.

'Baby, you're not really enjoying this are you?' Jamie says to me, looking down at my pale face and bloodshot eyes.

'Yes I am!' I try to reassure him, knowing the frailties of the male ego.

He sees right through this. 'Sweetheart, we've been married for years, I'm not going to collapse into a heap of neuroses if you want to stop.'

I take a deep breath. 'Oh, thank God for that, I feel terrible,' I say, letting out the breath explosively.

Jamie winces and leans back. 'Well, don't give it to me woman.'

'I'm not sick,' I insist. 'Just a little tired.'

'Yes, I always look like the ghost of Christmas Past when I'm feeling a bit tired too,' he says in a derisory voice. 'You've never let being tired put you off sex, Laura. You're sick. Now get into bed while I run down to the Tesco Express to pick you up some Lemsip.'

He does have his moments, my husband. He really does.

The cold takes proper hold overnight, and by morning I am a walking mucus factory. If you think back many years to my one and only experience in a microlight aircraft, you will recall that I am an absolute horror when my nasal secretions go into overdrive. As Jamie lets Dad and Poppy into our room, I am sat at the table by the window, trying my level best not to cover everything in sight with a thin, shiny film of mucus.

'Mum,' Poppy says hesitantly, seeing the state I'm in. 'I don't think I'm going to give you a morning kiss today.' I would feel hurt about this, but I'm fairly sure that licking a slug would be preferable to planting a smacker on my face right now, so can understand her feelings on the matter.

Dad does give me a kiss on the forehead, which is nice. 'I think you'd better stay in bed today,' he says to me.

'Your Dad's right,' Jamie agrees. This is officially the first time Jamie has agreed with him - or referred to him as my Dad, for that matter. We'll call that progress.

'But we were going to take Poppy to the zoo today,' I whine, before a fit of sneezing hits me, forcing all three of them to stand back.

'We can still take her,' Jamie says.

I want to argue, I truly do. I want to fight my way through this thing and enjoy my day, but I am a woman self aware enough to know that I will actually do nothing of the sort. I picture myself soaking the chimpanzees in phlegm before keeling over in a dead feint, and mentally decide to take my husband's counsel on this matter.

'Alright, I'll stay here in bed. Hopefully the rest will do me good.'

'I'm sure it will,' Dad says with a reassuring smile.

Normally, Poppy would kick up a stink at this point. She likes it when Jamie and I are together when we go out on a day trip, but I think her desire to spend the day with both parents is superseded by her desire not to spend that day covered in one parent's germs.

All three of them troop out of the hotel room an hour after breakfast, leaving me bundled up and full of hot lemon flavoured drink. I do feel quite, quite awful, but the duvet is warm, the pillow is soft, and there is peace and quiet in my world. I drift off to sleep, hoping that by the time they get back, I'll be feeling more myself again.

The low fever I've had from the cold breaks mid-afternoon, leaving me feeling more human. I have a rather delicious shower, followed by a bagel with cream cheese from room service. I'm still sneezing every thirty seconds or so, and I'm bunged up to the nines, but I do have a bit more energy, and am pleased that I apparently just have a rather nasty cold, rather than a full blown case of the flu, which would have been disastrous. With a cold I can attend tomorrow's conference panel, even if I will do so carrying a packet of tissues. The flu would have laid me up completely for a good couple of weeks, and I just can't afford to take that much time out.

'Well, you do look better,' Jamie says with a smile when he sees me sat up at the table, playing around with my iPad.

'Yep. I think id's only a cold,' I tell him through the snot. 'I feel a lod better than I did dis mornind.'

Jamie takes a few moments to process this, and mentally change all those d's for the correct syllable. 'Good stuff. Take it nice and easy this evening then, and we'll see how you are tomorrow.'

'How wad the zoo, Pops?' I ask my daughter.

Poppy's mouth bows downwards. 'A bit disappointing. All the animals were hiding,' she says.

That's the problem with zoos. The inhabitants never do what you want them to. Having said that, there's every chance my seven-year-old is actually disappointed because she didn't get to poke anything.

We all end up eating in the Premier Inn restaurant downstairs that evening. I manage to finish all of my chicken and chips, signifying that I am starting to get over this virus. By 9pm though, I'm knackered again and in need of sleep. Dad and Jamie keep Poppy down in the bar with them as I make my way back to the room, and fall more or less instantly into a gratifying deep sleep.

The next morning I am rested enough to tackle the second of our two speaking engagements at the CWC. This one is the main event for us. Entitled 'Writing As A Couple', it involves Jamie and I, along with another pairing of similar age to us, who write erotic fiction. Their writing names are Marie and Pierre Rougemont, but I'm led to believe their real names are Mary and Peter Redhill. I've never heard of their books, but Jamie professes to having scanned through an ebook version of 'Whipped Into A Frenzy', the couple's first bestseller.

'It was a bit weird,' he tells me as we're getting dressed. 'I'm not a prude or anything, but even I draw the line when large rubber implements start getting inserted into every orifice. Their characters act like they're sexually aroused every second of the day. It all sounds exhausting.'

'Well, don't say thad to dem,' I warn. 'Dey might think our books aren't fuddy.'

'Fuddy?'

'Yes, *fuddy*. You know... *ha ha ha*?'

Jamie looks thoughtful. 'Maybe I should do most of the talking today, eh?'

I roll my eyes. 'You dormally do anyway, Misder. Why would dis be ady dibberent?'

My husband does make a point though. I sound barely intelligible at the moment.

A quick detour to Boots on the way to the tube station solves this issue - at least to a certain extent. I find the strongest nasal decongestant I can, and shove it up my nose as we board the train.

'Thas better!' I say, as I feel the chemicals start to cut through the thick lining of mucus. 'I can talk again!'

'Eww Mum! You're snotting!' Poppy points out. She's right. The problem with decongestants is that they really do decongest. Right onto your top lip, if you're not careful. Still, I'll take a bit of drippage over sounding like I have a ball of cotton wool stuffed in my nose any day of the week.

We arrive back at Danesborough Halls a good half an hour early again, so have another chance to sample the delightful machine coffee and stale flapjacks on offer. We also get the chance to say hello to Marie and Pierre Rougemont's alter-egos, who have arrived before us.

'Morning,' Jamie says cheerfully to the couple, as we enter the beige green room. I am somewhat surprised to see that neither one of them is dressed head to toe in black rubber, and am slightly disappointed by the fact.

Mary is resplendent in the same blue M&S ladies suit I rejected a few months ago because the skirt was too short to hide my atrocious knees, and Peter looks equally as smart in what I can only assume is the male equivalent.

I suddenly feel completely under-dressed, togged out as I am in Jane Norman jeans, Fat Face long sleeved top, and Asda George bodywarmer. Jamie looks even more scruffy. I really should have dissuaded him from wearing that Batman hoodie, but the cold has knocked me off my game a bit.

'Good morning,' Peter and Mary echo in formal voices. For a couple that writes erotic fiction, they come across as people you'd think would be more at home filling in tax returns or insurance claims.

About ten minutes later though, I get a good idea of what's going on under all that pressed polyester, when I go into the ladies toilet to get some more tissue, and see Mary Redhill coming out of the cubicle, holding her jacket. The shirt she has on underneath is short sleeved, and poking from out of both arms I can see tattoos that run almost to her wrists. The shirt itself is very tight, showing off a sleek, toned figure and perfect breasts that must take a huge amount of work (and probably money) to maintain. Mary notices my wide-eyed expression and smiles a rather wicked smile. 'The suits are all part of the act,' she says in a smoky voice, answering my unspoken question. 'After all, it's only sexy if it's not on show all the time, isn't it?' One of her eyebrows arches suggestively. 'The tease is what pulls them in.'

There's a blatant sexuality to this woman I couldn't hope to replicate with several shots of vodka and a very long run up. I have to take a couple of deep breaths after she's left the toilet.

When it comes time for us to sit down in front of the large crowd gathered in the hall, I make a point of placing myself between Jamie and Mary. I don't want to have to do all the talking today, and if Mary takes that jacket off again while she's sat next to him, Jamie's brain will no doubt freeze up, and I'll be a one woman show.

The bloody cameraman is back of course, zooming in on us individually every time we answer a question. If I was disconcerted by its presence on Saturday, you can imagine my delight at having it here now I'm thick with cold. But there's nothing I can do about it, so I have to soldier on.

The first few questions from the crowd are fairly easy. *What's it like to write half a book each? How do you cope with being in each other's pockets all day? Do you edit each other's writing?* The usual kind of stuff that we've answered many times before.

The one thing I do take note of is that Mary and Peter are far better speakers than my husband and I. They are smooth, witty, and both speak in a clear, confident tone that the audience laps up with every question answered. I guess being a sadomasochist must make you a good public speaker. If you don't get embarrassed when someone's slapping your boobs with a wooden paddle, I wouldn't imagine talking about your day to day life with a couple of hundred strangers is any problem at all.

I inevitably start to feel envious. The two eroticists are making Jamie and I look bad.

I can tell Jamie feels the same way, as he keeps giving me a pained look every time Mary or Peter say something cool and eminently quotable to the rapt audience.

Right, the next question that gets asked, I'm going to wow the crowd with my answer, I think to myself, with badly misplaced determination. I can't really hope to compete with tattooed Mary and her bold sexuality (especially carrying a bad head cold) but my ego has woken up, and needs feeding.

I get the chance to make a fool of myself when a question comes from the audience that seems perfect.

'Do you argue much over what goes into the book?' a pleasant faced young girl asks from the front row. I can see Mary leaning in to speak into her microphone, so I lunge forward to get there before she does.

'Somedimes!' I spit down my mic. I can see Mary is a bit non-plussed by my eagerness, but she does sit back to let me continue. 'We udually made sure we're bode habby wid whad de odder perdon had wridden,' I tell the girl, sounding like I'm a half South African, half Caribbean, virus carrying lunatic.

When Mary answers a question the audience laughs and nods appreciatively. When I do it, they look confused and a little bit revolted.

Time for drastic action. 'Excude me, I hab a cold,' I say, and reach for the decongestant. I take a massive snort away from the microphone, put the bottle back in my pocket and lean in again. 'As I was saying,' I continue, this time with recognisable pronunciation, 'Jamie and I usually make sure we're both happy with what the other person has written. There are enough reasons to argue in a marriage, we don't need to add any others!' This time, my answer is greeted with laughter and a few appreciative nods. I smile indulgently. I am winning the crowd back.

'Who gets the last word on the final draft?' the girl asks me. I am delighted to note that her attention is entirely on me now. She isn't looking at Mary or Peter at all. I flick a quick glance at Jamie, who looks as pleased as I am. Time to really turn on the charm.

'What's your name?' I ask the girl.

'Angela,' she replies.

'Well Angela, let's just say that my husband has a way with words, but I have a way of making those words even better,' I tell her in a tone so smooth, it's a wonder I don't slide right off my chair and under the table. Jamie chuckles ruefully, and even Mary and Peter are forced to raise a smile. 'And let me just add,' I carry on, 'that writing together really is all about co-operation. You have to - '

ATCHOO!

The sneeze comes from nowhere, much like The Big Bang. And, just like The Big Bang, it is enormously explosive and travels at the speed of light.

Mucus splatters the table in front of me. The microphone is instantly covered in phlegm.

I look up at the crowd in horror, but only for a moment, because another gigantic sneeze is forcing its way out of my nose. This one is so apocalyptic that my head jerks forward and I head butt the microphone, sending a loud report echoing around the conference hall.

That isn't the end of it though. Another three sneezes blast out in quick succession, and by the time the third one has left my nose, my hand is covered in nasal slime.

The crowd looks horrified. And who can blame them? There's every chance they are trapped in a room with someone carrying the kind of disease they talk about in the news headlines. I may know I've only got a cold, but as far as they're concerned, any disease that can make your face explode the way mine just has, must be fatal.

All the sneezing has made me feel quite light headed, so I slump back in my chair and go delving in my pocket for more tissue, an apology forming on my lips to everyone gathered.

Now, as you know, the Law of Sod exists to haunt us at our every move. Well it haunts me, anyway. And what more perfect way can there be for the Law to raise its ugly head than right now, when I am in most need of something to wipe my nose with?

I am out of tissues.

I look at Jamie in pleading misery. He looks back at me with husbandly revulsion. 'What's der madder?' I say to him, my nasal walls inexplicably blocked again already.

Jamie points at his top lip. 'You, er, you have a little something here,' he says. His eyes then flick up to the screen behind us and his face goes white. 'You, um, might want to take care of it?' His voice is thin and reedy.

I quickly turn my head to look up at the screen, and thanks to the delay between camera and display, I get a brief, but oh so terrible, look at my face. There is a long gob of green mucus hanging from my nose like a fucking punch bag. As I whip my head back towards the crowd again, I feel it slap against my top lip. Of course, this brings my face back round so the camera - and by extension the crowd - can see my thick new nasal friend in all its shiny green glory.

I swiftly turn my head again to look back at the screen and stop everyone from having to gaze at my revolting excretion. This allows me yet another brief view of it myself. All the head turning has lengthened my nose baby to the point that it might well drop off any second, but I have no tissue to catch it with, so I can't let that happen.

There's only one thing I can do.

Have you already guessed what it is?

Are your toes curling as you imagine what I'm about to do?

I squeeze my eyes closed, take a deep breath, and inhale as hard as I can.

Oh, for the love of all things holy and right in the world, what have I become?

The mucus shoots back up into my head like a wet, slimy missile. Unfortunately I've sniffed a little too hard, and the bogie continues up through my nasal canal and back down the other side into my mouth.

I feel the clammy, sticky mass hit the back of my throat and unbridled disgust overwhelms me. As does the immediate coughing fit that directly follows.

'Laura? Are you okay?' Jamie asks, patting me on the back.

Nothing that a little light suicide won't cure, husband of mine.

There's nothing for it, I'm going to have to leave the stage as fast as my knobbly knees will carry me. For the last time I turn back to the crowd to try and issue that apology that still hasn't made its way out of my mouth, but as I'm choking on my own phlegm, it's not going to happen.

Giving the whole thing up as a bad deal, I get up from the table and scuttle off to one side to get out of the public glare. The cameraman, knowing full well that this will be the best thing he films today, pans to follow me off the stage, before panning back to show Jamie, Mary and Peter all looking off stage in stunned silence.

'Um, excuse me?' Angela asks the three of them. They all turn back. 'So, who does get the last word on the final draft then?' she asks, proving that writers are tremendously single-minded when they want to be.

Jamie points one finger in the direction I went off in. 'Er, she does?' he answers. I'm quite sure that neither Angela, nor the rest of the audience actually believe a word of this. I am quite clearly a woman with no control over her own bodily functions, so how the hell am I supposed to have the final say on what goes into a book? About the greatest contribution to the finished article I can provide must be an enormous gob of phlegm that I deposit between pages 93 and 94 before it goes off to the printers.

Of course I'm not privy to any of this - Jamie has to fill me in later. While he and Mr and Mrs Erotica are attempting to carry on with the show, I am back stage, coughing up my lungs.

By the time they wind the talk down ten minutes later, I have myself under control and wiped down. My face is flaming red though, partly because of the cold, and partly due to embarrassment.

'I wand do leave, and I wand do leave *right now,*' I tell my family as they join me back in the green room downstairs.

'That's a nasty cold you've got there,' Mary says to me in a sympathetic voice, coming over and laying one arm over my shoulders. 'I always have a cup of hot water with cinnamon and cayenne pepper in it. Works wonders.'

I refrain from asking whether she means I should drink it, or rub it over my genitals. It could be either. 'Thank you Mary. It wad nide to meet you and Peter.'

'Likewise,' she replies with an amused expression. 'I like to think we make the best impression at these talks when we do them, but I don't think anyone's going to be talking about us tonight.'

Oh do fuck off, you smutty bitch.

'No, probably nod,' I reply, offering her a weak smile.

'Time to go, I think,' Jamie says, replacing Mary's arm with his own. This feels much better.

He escorts me from the green room and up into the crowded foyer above. As we make our way to the exit, I can see people doing one of two things. They are either taking a step back with their hands in front of their faces, or taking a step forward holding out a handkerchief. So, now I have a new resolution, Mum. At the slightest hint of a tickle in my nose, I will confine myself to the house until I am one thousand percent sure I am well again. That way I will be spared any more humiliation, and the world will be spared a light covering of my mucus.

Lub you and mid you, your bunged up daughter, Laura.

XX

Jamie's Blog
Sunday 10 October

Six days ago I get a phone call. A very excited phone call.

'Jamie!' Craig bellows down the phone. 'I've got some great news!'

'Are you having your vocal chords removed?' I reply, holding the phone away from my head.

'What? No! What are you talking about?'

'Never mind, what great news have you got Craig?'

'I've got you invites to the premiere of Lost Lives And Broken Hearts!'

This means nothing to me. 'Is that a movie?'

'Well of course it's a movie! A big one too. They say it could go all the way to the Oscars! There will be loads of celebrities there. You'll love it.'

'And you've got us tickets to the premiere?'

'Yeah!'

'Why?'

'What the hell do you mean, *why*?'

'Well, precisely that Craig. Why?'

'Because it'll be great for your public profile!'

'I'm quite happy with my public profile thanks. It's nice and low.'

'Oh, come on Jamie. This is the kind of thing that can really help your career. It'll be a great night out as well.'

My idea of a great night out and Craig's are obviously vastly different. For me, I like nothing better than a meal in a nice restaurant with Laura, followed by some sex. I am a man of simple pleasures. Attending a film premiere with a bunch of famous types for me to feel awkward around sounds awful.

'Is that Craig?' Laura says, coming into the front room.

'Yep.'

'What's he want?'

'He says he's got us tickets to the premiere of some movie called Lost Lives And Broken Hearts.'

Laura becomes ninety percent eyeballs. 'What?!'

'You've heard of it?'

'Heard of it!? Jamie, they're saying it's the next English Patient! Or the next King's Speech!'

'Really? Can it be the next Bourne Identity instead?'

She rolls her eyes. 'Oh Jamie, you're such a philistine. Give me the phone.' It gets snatched out of my hand. 'Craig? It's Laura. Are you serious about this?'

Craig is *indeed* serious about this. He scored a load of tickets to the premiere from the agent down the corridor who represents the author of the book the movie is based on. I guess I should feel honoured that Craig wants to bring us along, but then I remember we're his best selling clients at the moment, so I guess it makes sense for him to keep us sweet.

Frankly, he could have kept me sweet by buying me a new game for the PS4 and letting me stay at home to play it, but that isn't the way things work in the glamorous world of show business. It's a little hard to schmooze someone when they're sat in lounge pants, playing Call Of Duty.

Laura continues talking to Craig in a highly animated fashion while I pick up the iPad and do a little Googling.

Okay, so the cast of this flick looks quite impressive. Ralph Fiennes is in it, of course. You can't have a potential Oscar winning film made in the UK without Ralph Fiennes in it. I think if they ever make a movie version of Love From Both Sides I'll kidnap him, concuss him with a dildo truncheon, and stick him in the back of every shot.

Oh look, Keira Knightley's in the movie as well. What a *huge* surprise. I wonder if she's playing an English rose, who learns a valuable lesson about love while in the aftermath of personal tragedy?

Those are the two main stars, but any British Oscar contender worth its salt must feature a couple of people who have been given a title by the Queen. And indeed, Dame Maggie Smith and Sir Ian McKellan are playing Keira's grandparents. There's nary a mention of Keira's mother and father in the IMDB credits list though, so I think we can safely assume that this is the personal tragedy I was referring to earlier.

The rest of the cast is the usual collection of British thespians. You always recognise a few from the TV shows they're more famous for being in, and there's always one cast member who you thought was dead, but inexplicably isn't. In Lost Lives And Broken Hearts, it's Ian Lavender from Dad's Army. I was convinced Private Pike had popped his clogs, but I think that's just because every other member of the cast has gone to meet their maker, and I was killing him off by association.

The plot of the movie sounds dreadful.

Not in a badly written way, just in a 'this is pretentious rubbish and I'd rather be watching something with Bruce Willis in it' kind of way. It's set in the sixties, a time period that popular culture still has a strange fascination with. Keira plays a sexually repressed young woman, who finds love with travelling musician Ralph Fiennes. She then discovers Ralphy boy is not everything he's cracked up to be, what with his burgeoning drug habit and casual approach to female equality. What follows is a domestic drama of such po-faced sincerity it's enough to make you chew your own foot off. According to IMDB, Lost Lives & Broken Hearts is based on the book of the same name by a rather odd looking small man of Sri Lankan descent called Sanjapat Hathiristipan - or 'Sanja' to his mates.

Sanja is seventy years old, and a product of the upper class boarding school system, thanks to how fabulously wealthy his parents were when they emigrated to the UK in the fifties. The old boy has written two books - this one, and a non-fiction piece about the Sri Lankan civil war. He must have been delighted when Warner Bros picked his drama to be their Oscar contender for the year. I know I would have been.

I wouldn't usually be caught within a hundred miles of this kind of film, but judging from the excitement in Laura's voice as she speaks to Craig, that perfectly reasonable stance is about to change.

'Okay Craig! We'll see you on Thursday!' Laura ends the call with our agent and gives me an animated grin. 'Isn't that great Jamie? I might get to meet Ralph Fiennes!'

'Yes.'

'And Keira Knightley!'

'Yes.

'And the one who's not dead from Dad's Army!'

'Yes.'

She folds her arms. 'You seem less than enthused.'

'Yes.'

'Oh, what's your problem? Not many people get to go to these things, you should be pleased.'

I too fold my arms, so we're both taking up defensive positions. 'Right Laura, let's just analyse this for a moment, shall we?'

She sits down in the armchair and regards me carefully. 'Okay.'

'This is going to be a star studded event, no doubt followed by the national media, correct?'

'Yes, I suppose so.'

'And we are the Newmans.'

'What do you mean by that?'

I hold one hand open and start ticking things off on my fingers. 'Vomiting at a job interview, ordering nasal discharge in a coffee shop, stealing a Chinese baby, the beach whore swimsuit, the breakdown at work - '

Laura holds up her hand. 'Whoa, boy. What's the point in all this?'

I grimace. 'We are *awful* in public, Laura. If there's an opportunity for one or both of us to make fucking idiots of ourselves in front of complete strangers, then we'll grasp it with both hands and damn the consequences. We are the 21st century equivalent of Laurel and Hardy. I've lost count of the amount of times I've had to apologise to someone I've never met before.' I look at the ceiling. 'It's like we're cursed. Someone up there really hates us, and likes to make us suffer as much as possible for their own sick entertainment.'

'You're being melodramatic.'

I start counting off on my fingers again. 'Covering a woman in dog piss, death by pedalo, mucus explosion during a speech - '

'Yes yes yes! Alright, you've made your point.'

'Can you imagine what minor hell awaits us if we go to this premiere? What ample opportunities exist for us to look like utter bell ends? Not just in front of complete strangers this time, but celebrities and the bloody paparazzi?'

'No-one's going to be paying you and me any attention,' Laura counters. 'We're nobodies.'

I lean forward. 'Well, we won't be nobodies when I sexually assault Keira Knightley by accident, or you end up elbowing Sir Ian McKellan in the face, will we?'

Laura opens her mouth to argue, but I can see the cogs whirring in her head as she comes to the sad but inevitable conclusion that we are a couple of prat-falling lunatics once we step out of the front door, and that attending this event may end in disgrace, injury, and possible criminal charges.

'See what I mean?' I tell her. 'It's far better that we just decline the offer and watch the bloody thing on Sky News.'

The edges of Laura's mouth sag. Then they go straight again as determination replaces disappointment. 'I want to go anyway,' she says.

'What?'

'I want to go anyway, Jamie. We *can* act like normal human beings. We don't have to end up with egg on our faces wherever we go.'

'Yes we do. It's our thing.'

'No!' She stamps her foot. 'I want to go! I want to meet Ralph Fiennes in a brand new evening gown!'

'Why would he be wearing an evening gown? He's not Eddie Izzard.'

'Me, you idiot! I'm wearing the evening gown!'

'Oh, I see.'

The look of determined resolve hardens. 'We're going, Jamie. We're going, and we're going to have a lovely time, with no problems, issues or cock-ups.'

I let out a loud bray of cynical laughter. My wife has taken leave of her senses.

However, she also has a look on her face that tells me that if I don't go along with her on this one, I will not be receiving any blow jobs for the foreseeable future. I will also never hear my one word birthday present again. I do hate being such a two dimensional man, but I sadly have no choice in the matter. Even at the risk of making a fool of myself on the national news, I will do anything if it means I can still have a pair of woman's lips wrapped around my penis at some time in the near future.

Laura smiles. She knows exactly what I'm thinking. Damn her for knowing me so well - and for looking so fantastic in black lingerie.

I suck air in through my teeth. 'I'll have to get a bloody tuxedo,' I say unhappily.

Laura comes over and puts a hand on my thigh. 'And you'll look *very* sexy in it, baby.' The voice is husky. I feel as if I'm a dog that's about to get a treat for being a good boy.

I'm not complaining.

In the end, I rent a tuxedo from a local place in town. There are only ever going to be a few occasions in life when I'm called upon to wear such a silly outfit, so I really don't see the point in buying one.

Having said that, they do make you look good. Even I had to admire the dashing image I cut, standing in front of the rental shop's mirror, looking like a low rent James Bond.

Of course, there's no renting going on when it comes to Laura's dress. That just wouldn't do at all. If a woman is called upon to attend a swanky event, she *must* wear a brand new outfit that has never seen the light of day. One costing a truckload of cash. This is just one of those universal truisms, so it's best we don't dwell on it too much and get on with our lives.

Given that there are only two days between invite and premiere, Laura has to make her mind up about which dress she wants far quicker than she would have liked. I'm not going to go into details about the hunt for the dress right now. Suffice to say that I've seen the inside of one too many designer clothes shops over the past forty eight hours.

Laura eventually settles on a flowing grey number, replete with a splash of sequins. This was after rejecting a smart black off the shoulder job that was too tight around the boobs, and a long, silky, white strappy dress that she thought made her calves look fat. The grey dress suits her figure down to the ground - and now I'm going to stop talking about ladies dresses before you mistake me for Gok Wan.

There was a brief shining moment I thought we might get out of our public appearance, when we struggled to get a babysitter for Poppy. We usually rely on a sweet, good natured girl called Amber who lives down the road from us, but she was busy the night of the premiere. Luckily - for Laura, not me - Terry steps up to the plate once again, and agrees to take our daughter for the night.

I am rather worried that Terry is becoming very useful - and indeed, indispensable. I'm still waiting for him to do something hideously wrong, but as yet, he's been everything he said he would be upon his return. This obviously pleases Laura no end, but she isn't blessed with my rampant cynicism, so I am still concerned that a moment will come when the house of cards will fall down, and the man that buggered off and left his child in the formative years of her life will return with a vengeance. For now though, I have to grudgingly accept that Terry is being every inch the apologetic father, and doting grandfather. Even if he did introduce Winklebastard into my life, *and* prevent me having a decent excuse not to trudge down a red carpet in a rented tuxedo, I have to give him some credit, don't I?

The gala premiere for Lost Lives And Broken Hearts is at the Odeon in Leicester Square - the site of many a movie's opening night over the years. Given the fact that we're in for an evening out in London, Laura and I have to spend yet *another* night this year at a hotel in the city. I'm starting to understand why the rich buy a second flat here. I know I would if I could, just to know for certain what kind of bed I'd be sleeping in.

This time around, we spring for a night in a decent boutique hotel in Kensington called The Radley Suites. This lies somewhere between the opulence of The Dorchester, and the down to Earth austerity of the Premier Inn. We don't feel completely out of our depth, but we also don't feel like we're slumming it.

I say 'don't feel like *we're* slumming it', but you probably know me well enough by now to know that I would have been quite happy with the cheapest option. My wife on the other hand, has different ideas. 'I'm not attending a star studded film event, and coming back to a ruddy Premier Inn, Jamie,' she told me. 'Book us somewhere a bit nicer, and a bit more appropriate.'

I think £59 for a night in London is *perfectly* appropriate, but then I have absolutely no taste, given that I am a man, and am therefore an idiot.

At least Craig and his agent friend have arranged the transport for the evening. A chauffeur driven limousine, no less.

It'll have to be a large one, as Craig has informed us that we will be travelling to the premiere with him and his girlfriend Maxine, Sanjapat Hathiristipan and his wife, and the old man's agent Caroline Denham, with her partner Alberto. Four couples in total - only two of which have any real business being at the event.

If there were a time to take on the legendary role of spare prick at a wedding, then this is truly it.

'We'll be fine, Jamie,' Laura again has to reassure me as we stand in the foyer of The Radley Suites, waiting for Craig and his entourage to arrive.

'How much do you want to bet me?'

Laura thinks about this for a moment. 'A month's loading the dishwasher?'

'You're on.' We shake hands, and I start to feel a bit better. I may be about to accidentally touch one of Keira Knightley's boobs while Sky News films it, but at least I won't have to scrape food into the bin and try to neatly stack plates in a dishwasher for the next few weeks.

The limousine arrives and Laura and I get in. The interior is just what you'd expect. Black leather seats, dark blue carpet, tinted windows. You know, the type of thing that twats like to ride around in.

'Evening Jamie and Laura!' Craig barks, holding out two champagne glasses. 'Have a drink!'

Oh fabulous, I'm going to be hammered by the time we hit the red carpet. Craig will have shoved half a bottle of fizzy plonk down my throat before we hit the congestion charge zone. But then I remember that Laura is here, and that her control over me is even greater than Craig's. She won't let me get drunk. We're on our best behaviour tonight, after all. I therefore take the champagne in the secure knowledge that it will be the only alcohol I have access to this evening.

Laura and I sit down in two of the plush seats that ring the limo's interior while Craig does the introductions. Caroline Denham is a tall, thin-lipped woman of indeterminate age. She might be thirty or fifty under all that make-up, I have no way of knowing. Alberto is a trophy husband of the highest order. He's Italian. He must be. He has thick, black, swept back hair and is wearing a lime green suit that he actually manages to *pull off*. Italians are the only people in the world who can get away with clothing of such a hideous colour. It's genetic.

Sanja is a small, prune like individual, with dark brown wrinkled skin and bright, searching eyes. He is dressed in a sombre grey suit that is a little too large for him, and looks quite, quite furious about something. He's trying to hide his anger, but you can see it trying to bubble to the surface when he speaks. He's all eye twitching and lip curling. As someone who knows what it's like to suppress your frustration at the world on a horrifyingly regular basis, I know the signs of someone forming an ulcer in their stomach from a mile away.

'Good evening,' he says to us, his accent perfectly English, other than a hint of exotic Far Eastern spice attached at the ends. 'This is my wife, Sunil.' He indicates a rather worried looking Asian woman sat next to him in a sari. She knows her husband is mad about something, that's for sure.

'Hello to you both,' she says.

Last, Craig introduces Maxine, who I'm fairly sure is an escort girl. I don't mean that Craig has paid for an escort girl for the evening, I just mean that Craig likes to *date* escort girls. This is supreme evidence of Craig's enormous self confidence, and should be applauded by every straight man in England. Maxine looks like a walking blowjob in Manolo Blahniks. I make a point not to look directly at her. I know which side my bread is buttered, and Laura is holding the knife.

'Are you excited, Laura?' Craig asks, knowing full well that my wife is beside herself, and probably wearing one of the other dresses she rejected yesterday.

'Yes! I'm hoping to speak to Maggie Smith. I love her!' I have to grin at Laura's open fan girl enthusiasm. Even if I'm looking forward to this about as much as root canal surgery, she's excited enough for the both of us. She turns to Sanja. 'And it's an honour to meet you Mr Hathiristipan.' How the *fuck* did she manage that? 'I thought your book was just wonderful.'

This gets a warm smile from Sanja, which temporarily breaks through all of that suppressed anger. 'Thank you, my dear. I'm so glad you liked it.'

'I did! I'm hoping the film does it justice.'

Sanja's face darkens immediately.

Aha!

I think we've come to the root of the matter. Sanja isn't happy with the movie for some reason. It's written all over his face.

'We shall see,' he answers noncommittally.

'It'll be *wonderful,*' Caroline Denham assures him, patting one of his wrinkled little hands. Sanja's having none of it, and regards her with cynicism.

I'm really starting to like this little fella, for some reason.

The rest of the limo journey passes in idle chit chat. Alberto and Maxine don't say much, but they're essentially ambulatory fashion accessories anyway, so that doesn't come as much of a surprise. Amazingly, Sunil has read Love From Both Sides. I don't know whether to be pleased or worried, given how much of an insight it is into what pillocks Laura and I are.

Luckily, before Sunil has chance to ask us about how true the fajita incident is, we turn into Leicester Square, and a rather large crowd of people.

It's rather large, as opposed to *enormous*, because this is a period drama, rather than the latest Marvel blockbuster. If Keira and Ralph wore capes and fought Sir Ian McKellan in a helmet, the crowd would be three times the size, I have no doubt. The media are still out in force though. Nobody likes a good film premiere more than the 24 hour news cycle.

As the limo approaches the cinema entrance and the legendary red carpet, I start whispering a mantra under my breath. "Don't do anything stupid, don't do anything stupid, don't do anything stupid." I will approach this event as one might approach a pit of exploding scorpions. *Very carefully*. If Laura and I can just negotiate our way through the public aspect of this premiere and get into our seats, things might not go too badly for us.

Stop making that face. *Stop it!*

The limo parks up directly in front of the cinema. 'After you Sanja,' Caroline Denham says, waving a hand in the direction of the door. Sanja is up out of his seat like a man who just wants to get this shit over and done with. The door is opened by the chauffeur, and the little man steps out onto the carpet with a decidedly unimpressed look on his face.

No-one in the crowd pays him the slightest bit of attention. This is to be expected, of course. We don't get into the writing game for the public fame and adulation, after all. That's the job of the actors who have already arrived at the premiere, and are being papped to within an inch of their lives.

The rest of us bundle out of the limo and find ourselves at the back of a queue. The queue is being held up by Ralph and Keira, who are taking part in interviews for Sky and the BBC respectively. Miss Knightley looks as glamorous as you'd imagine. The girl needs to eat a bloody pie though. There's nothing of her in that grey, sequined dress she's wearing.

Oh shit.

Her dress looks like Laura's. *Exactly* like Laura's.

Now, do I turn to look at my wife's expression? Or should I just pretend she doesn't exist for the next few hours?

I take a chance. 'Don't worry sweetheart, I think you look much better in yours,' I say, as I see the thunderstorm brewing.

'Don't be such a fucking idiot, Jamie,' she replies. 'That's Keira Knightley. She'd look beautiful in Poppy's chicken costume.'

I take her hand. 'Okay, but please just try to relax. We're not here to cause a scene, are we?'

Laura manages to successfully wrestle her emotions under control. She's as determined as I am that we don't make fools of ourselves tonight. That starts with not flying off the handle because one of the biggest movie stars in the world is wearing a more expensive version of the same dress. Laura counts to ten under her breath... and we're back in the game.

Caroline grabs Sanja and Sunil, and leads them off in the direction of the Sky News camera, lining up behind Keira for a chat with Kay Burley.

'Come on, let's get inside,' Craig says. 'I believe there's a free bar here tonight.'

He takes Maxine by the arm and stamps off up the red carpet, pushing past poor old Ralphy boy as he does so.

Laura gasps. 'There's Maggie Smith!' she says, looking just past Fiennes, to where the Dame is standing close to the cinema's entrance.

'Do you want to meet her?' I ask.

Laura suddenly looks very nervous. 'I'm not sure.'

'Yeah, come on! You'll never get the chance again!'

Laura doesn't move. 'But we might be *morons*, Jamie. In front of Maggie Smith!'

'She's been in the movie industry for decades, baby. I'm sure she's met countless morons before.' I move in the Dame's direction, dragging Laura with me.

We have to wait a few moments for her to finish her interview with ITV, but that's fine, as it gives Laura a chance to calm down a bit. As the actress moves towards the entrance, I intercept her with a friendly wave. 'Excuse me, Dame Maggie?'

'Hello young man,' she replies with a smile.

'Sorry to interrupt, but my wife is a big fan. Can she say hello?'

'I can speak for myself, Jamie,' Laura snaps, and steps in front of me. Dame Maggie Smith rolls her eyes in a show of female solidarity at my blatant chauvinism.

'I'm so pleased to meet you, Dame Maggie,' Laura continues. 'Downton Abbey is my favourite show.'

This is utter shit.

Laura's favourite TV show is Location, Location, Location. However, there's no sign of Phil and Kirsty, so we'll let her get away with this white lie for the sake of a peaceful evening.

My wife engages the enigmatic actress in a conversation for a few minutes as we all walk into the cinema, leaving the crowd of on-lookers and media representatives behind.

Inside, it's even more crowded in the enormous foyer. Hundreds of well dressed and well heeled people stand gathered, holding free drinks and talking amongst themselves. If I breathe in deeply enough, I can smell the pretentiousness emanating from every pore.

Still, we're a good ten minutes into this charade and neither Newman has done anything to embarrass themselves yet, so it's so far, so good. We're well past the cameras now as well, which is a bonus. Laura even manages to finish her brief chat with Dame Maggie without coming across as a moron.

'I did it!' she says with triumph as she rejoins me. 'I was smooth. I was charming. I didn't talk bollocks.'

'Well done baby!' I tell her, and give her a celebratory kiss. 'Let's get a drink.' Laura gives me a look. 'A *soft* drink, I mean.'

We go to find Craig at the bar, who has been joined by Caroline, Sanja and their respective partners.

'All going well then?' he asks us all.

'I met Dame Maggie Smith!' Laura says happily.

'Well done you!' Craig replies, trying to sound as non-patronising as he can, but failing miserably. 'How was Sanja's interview, Caroline?'

The agent goes even more thin lipped than usual. 'It was okay. Sanja was a bit nervous.'

The little man gives her a look of contempt. 'I was not nervous! I was merely pointing out to the lovely ginger lady that I'm not happy with some of the changes that that smarmy fool has made to my book!'

I give Craig a confused look. He mouths the words 'I'll tell you later'.

I lean forward on the bar and order Laura and I a Diet Coke. As this is a bar for celebrity show business types, I don't have to wait too long. I hand Laura her drink, take a sip of mine, and let out a deep breath.

'You okay?' Laura asks.

'Oh yes, I'm fine. Just happy we've made it this far without any probl - '

My arm is jostled, spilling my drink. I turn quickly to see who has bumped into me.

'Oh, I am so sorry, I didn't see you th - '

The man's apology dies on his lips as he realises who I am.

It's Sylvester bloody McCoy. My pedalo nemesis.

'You!' we both say at exactly the same time.

'What are *you* doing here?' McCoy asks in disgust.

'I might ask you the same thing, Doctor!' I spit.

Laura, seeing that this could end in disaster - despite there being no fibre glass boat for a hundred miles around us - steps between the old man and I. 'Now stop it, the pair of you!' she commands. 'This is a lovely evening out, and we're not going to spoil it with an argument... *are we, Jamie?*'

I open my mouth to protest that this isn't my fault. But then I remember that of course it *is* my fault, so I close it again.

'You look lovely Laura,' Sylvester says. 'How is Poppy?'

Blimey, he remembered both their names.

'She's very well Sylvester, thank you.' Her head whips back to me. 'You remember how I told you how helpful and caring

191

Sylvester was to our traumatised daughter when you went gallivanting off in that bloody pedalo, *don't you Jamie?'*

If I didn't, I certainly do now.

I heave a reluctant sigh. 'Thank you for taking care of Poppy, Mr McCoy,' I tell him, in the tone of one who knows when he's been chastised.

The seventh Doctor's face softens. 'A pleasure. And I assume you recovered from your sun stroke, young man?'

'I did, thank you.' My face creases. 'Why *are* you here, by the way?'

McCoy points over to where Sir Ian McKellan is standing. 'Ian invited me along.'

I make the connection. 'Ah! Of course. You were in The Hobbit together.'

'Oh my God, you were in The Hobbit!' Laura exclaims loudly.

I give her a withering look. 'Yes dear. And he was Doctor Who? Remember me telling you?' I shake my head. 'You really need to pay more attention to movies and TV you know, sweetheart. I keep telling you that.' I give McCoy a 'you just can't get the staff these days' look that makes him smile. I take another sip of Coke and reach a decision. 'I am so sorry about my behaviour on that island, Mr McCoy. I don't think you were worse than Colin Baker at all. In fact, The Curse Of Fenric is one of my favourite Who stories.'

'Well, thank you very much, Mr Newman!'

'Call me Jamie.'

'I shall. And do call me Sylvester.'

'What the hell's a Fenric?' Laura asks us both.

Sylvester and I both chuckle indulgently at Laura's evident confusion.

The seventh Doctor and I have managed to successfully bond over my wife's lack of geek credentials. It means that Laura will be mad at me for the rest of her natural lifespan for using her as a tool to break the ice, but at least I am no longer at loggerheads with Doctor Who.

I'm about to ask Sylvester what he thinks of Peter Capaldi's interpretation of the character when a roar of anger interrupts me from behind.

'You have done what?!' Sanjapat Hathiristipan bellows. Bellowing isn't something that comes easy to a man who can't be much over five foot two and eight stone, but he achieves it magnificently.

I turn round to see Sanja standing opposite a man who's wardrobe marks him out to be a wanker of the highest order. We're talking tenth level pretentiousness here, folks. For starters, that is *indeed* a dark blue beret parked on his pointy head. The glasses perched on his nose are small, round and ever so thin. The beard is as pointy as his head. The shirt is black with small white polka dots, and the cravat is the same shade of deep blue as the beret. The velvet smoking jacket is urbane, and the black spats on his feet are highly polished. I want to punch this man repeatedly until the beret turns red.

It seems Sanja feels much the same way. 'You said the ending would not change!' he storms, squaring all of those five feet two inches up to the much taller man. 'You said Verity would still die at the end!'

Oh thanks Sanja. Now you've ruined the ending of a book I was never actually intending to read. How could you?

'But Sanja, my friend,' the beret wearing codpiece replies, 'the test screenings weren't positive. We simply had to reshoot the ending to something more palatable to an audience!'

'With Verity living, marrying David, and buying a cottage in the bloody Cotswolds?!' the old man screams.

Oh thanks Sanja. Now you've ruined the ending of a movie I was going to pay absolutely no attention to. How could you?

'Yes! The second test audience loved it!' the twat in the cravat simpers.

'It ruins the story! Destroys its meaning! You've turned my diatribe on loss and emotional detachment into an episode of Escape To The fucking Country!'

I don't know what I'm more surprised at, Sanja's use of the F word, or that he knows what Escape To The Country is. He looks far too upper class for a bit of Jules Hudson of an afternoon.

'Oh dear,' Sylvester says under his breath from my side. 'This could get nasty.'

'What's going on?' I ask out of the side of my mouth.

'That is Lionel Moncrieff, the film's director. I knew him back when he was just Lionel Sidlington. A tiresome man, I found.'

Sylvester doesn't have to say any more. The cravat and the name change are all I need. 'I gather poor old Sanja doesn't like some of the revisions to his book.'

'Doesn't look that way, does it?' Sylvester turns to leave. 'I think I'll just go and talk to Ian for a while.' And with that he disappears like his Tardis, only with slightly less wheezing. I can't say I blame him. I wish I knew someone rich and famous who I could go and have a chat with right about now. Sadly, everyone I know is standing in a semi-circle watching the argument unfold.

Moncrieff is still simpering. 'But that's what the audience wants, Sanja! We have crafted a fantastic story, and I'm sure it will go down an absolute storm.'

'*We*? We have crafted?! All I see is that you've taken *my* story and bent it out of shape to suit your money men!'

'Nothing could be further from the truth!'

'Lies! All lies! You people are all the same. Taking an author's work and ruining it for the sake of the almighty dollar! Isn't that right Jamie and Laura?'

What?

'What?' I exclaim in shock. Why the hell is he dragging us into this? We're just along for the ride tonight. We're background artists, not main characters!

'You're writers,' the little man continues, 'help me explain to this idiot what it feels like to have your book so badly mistreated!'

I go a bit pale and look at Craig, who is shaking his head quickly back and forth and giving me the bulgy eyes. No help there, then. I turn and stare at Laura, whose letterbox shaped mouth is no help either.

I then look at Lionel Moncrieff, who now has the bearing of a man studying a small lemming like creature as he regards me, awaiting my opinion.

I'll have to say something, won't I? I can't just stand here in front of all these toffs with my gob hanging open.

And the evening was going so well, wasn't it?

We'd done so well to avoid any problems, hadn't we? There were no mistakes on the red carpet. I didn't trip up. Laura didn't vomit on anyone. Neither of us said anything rude or embarrassing to a celebrity. We made it into the cinema fine. I even made friends with Sylvester McCoy, and you'd have thought *that* would have been the perfect opportunity to make a fucking idiot of myself again. But no! It all went swimmingly.

We'd got to the point where all we had to do was stand around holding a drink for a few minutes, before going to watch a movie. That was it. That was all.

It would have been *fine*.

But then Sanjapat Hathiristipan happened.

Please remember that.

It wasn't *my fault this time.*

'Er, as a writer, you do get attached to your work,' I offer, keep things nice and diplomatic. I look at Laura again, hoping she's going to back me up, but she just nods her head and takes a sip of Coke, before looking off in another direction.

'Who are you?' Moncrieff asks, looking down his nose at me.

'Um. Jamie Newman?' I reply, sounding somewhat unsure of myself. 'I write comedy books?' From his expression, I might as well have said I was the guy who filled up the popcorn machine.

'Well, I'm not sure you're qualified to have an opinion on this discussion,' Moncrieff tells me, lighting the blue touch paper.

I instantly change from awkward to furious. I may just be a hanger-on here tonight, and I may write the kind of books that this ludicrous human being wouldn't go within twenty feet of, but I will not stand here and be talked down to in public. That only happens back at home.

'Really? That's what you think, is it?' I say to Moncrieff, the venom in my voice plain to hear. I look at Sanja, who's flat, irate expression matches mine. 'Well, I think that anyone who changes a writer's work just to turn a fast buck should be struck off the creative register.'

That should do it. Moncrieff is definitely one of those beret wearing morons who believes that they are permanently creating great art, even when they're taking a crap. To have his creative credentials questioned is the worst insult I could throw at him.

Craig knows this too and is slowly trying to put himself between me and the director. I can hear a high pitched keening noise coming from the back of his throat as he mentally works out how much money I'm potentially losing us all right now. Show business is a small world, after all. This will get around in no time.

'I'm sure Jamie doesn't mean you, Mr Moncrieff. We all know how fantastic your reputation in the industry is. You've made some wonderful movies.'

Is it? Has he?

I've never heard of this bloke. But then I like movies that feature explosions and boobs, so what the hell do I know?

One thing I do know for sure, is that Sanja thinks he now has an ally in this argument, and is made all the bolder because of it. 'Jamie is right!' He points a stiff finger at Moncrieff. 'This charlatan has no creative merit! He is a puppet of studio executives!' The finger then gets pointed at Caroline Denham. 'I *knew* I should never have let you talk me into accepting the deal!'

'But Sanja, it was a great contract! The film will be marvellous!' Caroline objects, fear etched onto her face. She knows this is going south fast - and with it her next pay check.

'No it won't!' Sanja argues.

Moncrieff steps forward. A definite change has come over him. The faked concern for Sanja's wellbeing has gone. In its place is something far more honest, I'm sure. 'Look, just be happy the film got made,' he snaps. 'You've been paid a lot of money for me to make your story into something an audience will want to see. You should be grateful.'

There is an audible intake of breath from everyone in the crowd. When Lionel Moncrieff shows his true colours, he doesn't muck about.

There are several ways Sanja could have handled this. He could have continued to argue with the beret wearing git. He could have stormed away from the conversation with his wife in tow. He could have broken down in tears and apologised to Moncrieff for daring to question his artistic integrity.

He does none of those things however. He just slaps Lionel Moncrieff across the chops.

The blow is smartly delivered. There's not a huge amount of power behind it - this is an elderly gentleman after all - but it's enough to leave a red mark on Moncrieff's cheek. The director lets out a squeak of shock and his hand flies to his face.

'You hit me!' he exclaims in profound disbelief. 'You actually hit me!'

Sanja doesn't reply, he just kicks Moncrieff on the shin. Again, no real damage is done, but you can tell the blow smarts as Moncrieff squeaks even louder and starts to back away, limping slightly.

'Keep away from me!' he cries, but Sanja is having none of it. Leaving the rest of us standing dumbfounded, the little man stalks towards Moncrieff, rage still burning in his eyes. He looks like The Terminator after three hours on a hot wash.

The surrounding crowd of smartly dressed show business types start to notice what's going on. It's a little hard to miss the shrieking director of the film you're about to watch being pursued across the foyer by an enraged Sri Lankan man in a grey suit.

I take off after them both in hot pursuit.

I can't help thinking that my remarks to Moncrieff *may* have exacerbated the situation just a tad. The fool made me angry though.

If I can catch up to Sanja and calm him down a bit, maybe complete disaster can be averted.

'Jamie! What are you doing?' Laura calls after me, but I don't respond, as every moment here is vital.

By the time I do reach Sanja, Moncrieff is out through the large glass double doors again and back onto the red carpet. This comes as a complete surprise to the crowd outside, who were all starting to shuffle off, thinking that they'd had their evening's entertainment. The TV crews that are packing up look a bit startled, as Lionel Moncrieff, director of high brow cinema, comes stumbling towards them, warding off Sanjapat Hathiristipan, writer of high brow literature.

'Sanja, stop!' I exclaim right behind them. 'Just leave him alone. It's not worth it!' I now sound like a drunk working class girl trying to stop her tattooed boyfriend from beating up the bloke who spilled his eighth pint.

Sanja's having none of it though and reaches Moncrieff without breaking his stride. This time he pokes the director in the stomach, which makes the man wail in pained surprise and instantly bend double. The beret comes flying off to reveal a gloriously bald pate.

Which Sanja slaps.

Hard.

Sky News can't get their camera rolling fast enough. Kay Burley has a combined look of shock and triumph writ large across her face. It's been a slow news day thus far, but this will liven things up a treat.

I have to get in the middle of this fight and break it up before any more damage can be done. It has to be me, as no-one else is taking any steps to stop it. I can only put this down to the fact that none of them have ever had to deal with a situation this ridiculous before, and it has rooted them all to the spot. On the other hand, I deal with this kind of shit on a seemingly daily basis, so I have no such issues.

Maybe I should join the police when I'm done here. I'd look quite fetching in a stab vest.

Channeling all the episodes of Cops I've seen over the years, I step between Sanja and Moncrieff. 'Now stop it!' I command. 'This is a film premiere, not an underground fight club!'

This just earns me a look of distain from Sanja, and a kick on the shin for my troubles.

'Ow!' I shout, clutching my leg. 'Why did you do that?'

'I thought you were on my side!' Sanja snaps in a betrayed voice.

'I'm not on anyone's side!' I argue.

'Then why did you support me against this buffoon?!'

'I don't know! You dragged me into it! I just wanted a quiet bloody evening where I didn't sexually molest Keira Knightley!'

Both Sanja and Moncrieff regard me with horror. I must remember not to speak out of context. It does me absolutely no favours.

'What's going on, Mr Moncrieff?' Kay Burley shouts, holding a microphone out to the harassed director. 'Why are you and the writer fighting? Who's the other man in the bad tuxedo?'

'Oi! Fuck off!' I object, forgetting where I am for the moment. 'This thing is costing me a fortune for the night!'

Moncrieff waves a shaking finger at Sanja. 'This maniac attacked me Kay! He assaulted me!'

I wave my hand. 'Oh, he did nothing of the sort. Look at him. He's way too tiny to do you any damage.'

'You ruined my story!' Sanja barks at the bald man, ignoring the back handed insult I've just thrown his way.

'You should be grateful I agreed to make the bloody thing into a decent movie!' Moncrieff counters.

Kay is loving this. She turned up expecting just to get a dull interview with Ralph Fiennes, but now she's getting a full blown domestic right on the red carpet.

Behind me I see Laura, Craig, Caroline Denham and a score of other people emerge back out into the open air. Much to the delight of the crowd, Keira and Ralph have reappeared as well. It looks like even the stars of the show know when they're being eclipsed, and want to see what the hell is going on.

And *still* nobody is stepping forward to calm the situation.

This leaves Jamie Newman as the only person here present with enough gumption to take a degree of control. Do you have any idea how *dire* a scenario has to be for that to happen?

My arms go out sideways and I step back between the warring enemies. 'Now, come on you two. Let's just calm down a bit and take a few deep breaths. We are on TV, after all.' I give Kay a smile.

'Who are you exactly?' she asks, microphone now pointing in my direction.

'My name is Jamie Newman,' I tell her. The blank expression I get in return proves that Kay Burley doesn't read romantic comedies. 'I'm a writer and a friend of Sanja's,' I add.

'And why are Mr Moncrieff and the author of the book fighting?' she demands in that strident way reporters use when they know they're on to a good thing. You'll note that Kay doesn't try to pronounce Sanja's name. This is probably wise on her part.

'Oh, it's nothing to worry about. Just a few nerves before the big show. You know how us show business types can be, eh Kay?' Hark at me, referring to myself as a show business type. I will be committing suicide the second I get home.

Kay Burley actually laughs. 'You seem like a funny fellow,' she tells me.

'You should read my books!' I look directly down the camera. 'Love From Both Sides, available in ebook and paperback from all good stores,' I tell the viewing audience.

From the crowd I hear Craig shout 'Yes!' triumphantly.

'Anyway,' I continue, returning my attention to the matter at hand. 'I think we should all go back inside now. I'm sure Sanja and

Lionel would like to have a chat and make up. *Wouldn't you gentlemen?'*

Both of them have the good decency to look sheepish. 'Yes,' they both reply.

'Good!' I turn my head. 'And perhaps, from the crowd of bloody statues behind me, someone with a little more authority to deal with this kind of thing could *step forward and take over?'* I give the crowd an evil look until several people break their stunned vigil and move towards where I'm still standing with my hands held out. One of them is Caroline Denham, who has no doubt kicked into career preservation mode.

She gives Kay Burley the widest berth possible, puts an arm around Sanja, and escorts the little man back inside. The only people who come rushing to Moncrieff's aid are a couple of the cinema's smartly presented staff, which should give you an idea of how popular the man actually is with his colleagues.

I have to admit that at this point I'm basking in my own glory a little bit. Not only have I been an effective peacemaker in an argument between two emotionally charged men, I have done it in front of a large crowd.

I think you'll find that doing *anything* successfully in front of a large crowd is a great ego boost.

Yes. Including that.

'Well done, husband,' Laura comments as she joins me.

I give her a look. 'And where were you when all this was going on, woman?'

Laura takes a deep breath. 'I thought I'd leave you to it. You look like you had the situation handled.'

I put one hand up to her forehead. 'Are you sick again?'

Laura bats it away. 'I'm fine. I do trust you to do the right thing, you know.'

'Do you?'

'Yes. Provided there isn't a pedalo or Chihuahua in sight.'

'Excuse me?' Kay Burley says from where she is still standing behind the barrier. The camera is now fixed squarely on Laura and I.

'Oh Christ,' Laura moans, and sticks her head behind my shoulder.

'What's up Kay?' I ask the ginger newshound.

'Would you do an on-air interview with me in a moment? About everything that just happened?'

Laura moans again. I rub my chin. 'Well, I'm not sure that'd be a goo - '

'Of course they'll do an interview!' Craig roars, coming between us, and propelling us inexorably at the Sky News camera with his arms around our shoulders.

'Oh, I don't think we should!' Laura protests.

'Sky News is watched by millions of people,' Craig stage whispers out of one side of his mouth. 'This interview could sell you a hundred thousand books.'

A brief war goes on behind Laura's eyes, between her inherent reluctance to appear on national TV, and pure unadulterated greed. I'm proud to say that the greed wins out. She plasters on a dazzling smile and looks at Kay Burley. 'Pleased to meet you, Kay. I'm Laura Newman. The brains behind the operation. Can I just say how lovely your hair looks this evening?'

The interview goes well. Kay asks us lots of searching questions about why Sanja and Moncrieff were arguing, which we ignore like crazy in favour of talking about our books. After five minutes, she wraps things up with a wry smile on her face, knowing full well that we've just turned her interview into one long book advertisement. Still, we were both as charming and as witty as it's possible to be when there's a camera shoved in your face, so hopefully the folks at home liked us... and will therefore buy our entire back catalogue.

In the end, neither of us get to see the movie. By the time we're done with Kay, everyone else has trooped in already and sat down. It's either go in late and have to climb over people, or stay out here at the bar with Craig for a while, before sloping off home. The bar seems the obvious choice, given that if I had to climb over anyone, it would no doubt be Keira Knightley, and there would therefore be a sexual assault charge coming my way in no time at all.

Our cue to leave occurs when Sanjapat Hathiristipan comes storming back through the foyer about an hour and half later, screaming obscenities at the top of his voice.

Craig pulls out his mobile phone. 'I'll get the car to come round,' he says in a resigned voice, draining the last of his scotch.

As we amble our way back to the limo, I make a firm decision. 'Craig?'

'Yep?'

'If anyone wants to make a movie out of Love From Both Sides, they are more than welcome to. On one condition.'

'What's that?'

'I get to vet the director beforehand to see whether I can have him in a fight or not.'

Our interview is repeated on Sky News later that evening, so Laura and I get to watch it when we get back to the hotel room.

We then have epic sex... because you would, wouldn't you?

For once, just for once, we're going to put this one in the win column.

Don't worry, I'm sure normal service will be resumed shortly.

Laura's Diary
Tuesday, November 2nd

Dear Mum,

A funny thing happens when you appear on TV, and have a YouTube video go viral. You suddenly become popular with people who haven't paid you the *slightest* bit of attention previously.

Jamie and I have written three books so far, but haven't had much interest from the major media outlets. But you break up one fight at a film premiere, and get one dildo waved at you by a man in a Sherlock Holmes costume, and suddenly all sorts of people start popping out of the woodwork.

Today, we are being interviewed by the BBC!

An email arrived last week asking us if we'd be interested in appearing in a new documentary about comedy writers, commissioned by the BBC for broadcast in the spring. They needed someone to talk about writing humorous novels, and apparently neither Terry Pratchett nor Helen Fielding were free, so they settled on two idiots with no media training instead.

While I was less than initially willing to be interviewed live on Sky News by Kay Burley, I am much happier to let the BBC into my house, given that I have ample time to prepare my hair and make-up. They are due to arrive at 9am, so I'm up at 7 to give it a good hour to make myself look beautiful. First I safely lock all of the self tanning cream away in the cupboard. I'm not falling for that one again.

It promises to be a long day. According to Jonathan Lightfoot, the documentary's producer, the shoot could go on for several hours, depending on what footage they want to film when they get here. Mostly it'll just be a talking heads interview with me and Jamie sat at our dining table, but Lightfoot also wants lots of flavour to add to the segment, so there will be additional footage shot of us doing all those things that the public expect authors like us to do on a day to day basis. There will be shots of Jamie and I sat writing,

Jamie and I sat reading, Jamie and I taking a brisk walk to cure writer's block, Jamie and I playing with Poppy and Winklehoven, Jamie and I having a massive argument over who should have turned the dishwasher on last night, because now the thing stinks of curry.

Actually, not that last one. That may be exactly the kind of thing that happens on a day to day basis for the Newmans, but it's hardly the kind of thing that's suitable for a well intentioned documentary on humour. Things will be kept light and fluffy, in no uncertain terms.

Given the length of the shoot, I've asked Dad to come by and help look after Poppy. Once the excitement of seeing all the cameras and lighting equipment has passed, my daughter will become instantly bored. We'll need someone there to occupy her while we film the stuff without her, and Dad is perfect for that. We've also shut poor old Winklehoven in the utility room for the duration. The interview will not go well if Jamie's toes get bitten off half way through it.

By 8.50am I am just about done with my preparations. The make-up is thick, the hair is sprayed, the knees are covered. I've elected to go with a daytime chic look, comprising of a smart but cute white shirt, and a pair of dark blue power trousers that I haven't worn since I ran the chocolate shop and had to go to meetings with suppliers. I am delighted I still fit into them.

'Going to a job interview, are we?' Jamie remarks when he sees me coming down the stairs.

'Quiet you. This is the BBC. I want to make a good impression.' I squint at him. 'And so do you. Take off that bloody hoodie and go put on a shirt.'

Jamie grumbles his way past me and I venture into the living room, where Dad is already holding a giggling Poppy up by her ankles.

'Please don't make her sick, Dad,' I admonish, and go to the dining room mirror to check my eye-liner for the tenth time in as many minutes.

At 9.30, the doorbell rings.

'Good morning Mrs Newman,' Jonathan Lightfoot says as I open the door to him. 'Sorry we're a bit late. Pete's Tom Tom took us the wrong way down the motorway for ten miles.'

Lightfoot is a man of about fifty, wearing a rather crumpled blue suit with no tie. Pete is short, chubby and balding, wearing jeans, a black waistcoat and a BBC production crew t-shirt. He's obviously the cameraman, given the three large bags he's carrying awkwardly over both shoulders.

'No problem.' I reply. Best to keep these two on-side. I want them to film me in the best light possible, after all. 'Do come in. Would you both like a cup of tea?'

'Oh, just water for me,' Lightfoot replies.

'Yes please love,' Pete says with a grin. 'White, two sugars, thanks.'

I leave them both with Jamie, who has managed to squeeze himself into a half decent blue shirt, and go to make Pete his cuppa.

By the time I hand it over to him, both men have been introduced to Poppy and Dad.

'I wasn't aware your father was going to be here,' Lightfoot says as he sips his water, 'maybe he could be included in the interview as well?'

Dad beams. 'Really?'

'Yes, why not. The proud father commenting on his daughter's success. It'll add a lovely bit of colour.'

Dad gives me an expectant look.

This is it then.

This is the moment when I either accept Dad into my life again 100%, or I don't. Once I acknowledge his relationship with me on live television there's no going back.

I hope you don't mind Mum, when I say that the decision is not all that hard for me to reach. Over the last eight months, Dad has done just about everything right. It's time to let the barriers down completely.

'Yeah, sure. It'll be nice to have him in it with us,' I tell Lightfoot, and give Dad a warm smile. Even Jamie doesn't seem bothered by the idea. We must be making progress.

Lightfoot looks at Jamie. 'Seems a bit unfair to just have Laura's parent included though. Would you like yours to be part of it too Jamie?'

My husband's face goes instantly white and he lets out a strained laugh. 'Um... no. No, that's fine Jonathan. We'll just have Terry in it. That's more than enough.'

I can't say I blame his reaction. If Jane Newman gets on camera and starts talking about her son and daughter in law, there's no telling where it might end up. In court, possibly. Or hospital. The psychiatric kind.

'Fair enough!' Lightfoot says, and bends down to address Poppy. 'And no forgetting about this little monkey, eh? She's the real star of the show.'

This is the best thing anyone has ever said to our daughter. She couldn't love Jonathan Lightfoot more now if he produced a life-sized animatronic Simba from his back pocket and started singing Hakuna Matata.

The BBC producer tells us he'd like to start with filming all the extra material first and the interview second, so we obligingly wait for half an hour while he and Pete bash out what they want to film.

For the next three hours Jamie and I get a flavour of what it feels like to be a professional actor - and it's one career that I wouldn't want for all the tea in China. By the time lunchtime rolls around I'm exhausted. We've had to repeatedly drive up to our house and walk in through the front door 'to establish geography', as Pete puts it. We've had to sit at our computer and write nonsense over and over again so they can get some good shots of us working. Jamie and I are never in the room at the same time when we're actually writing, but Lightfoot has my husband stand over me with a studious look on his face as I type whatever gibberish comes into my head. It's a load of old bollocks, but Lightfoot assures us it'll look good.

Never, ever believe what you see on the TV. That's one lesson I'm learning here today.

If that felt fake, then walking along the street with shit-eating grins on our faces, while we merrily swing Poppy between us is a thousand times worse. I have to cringe every time a car goes past. It wouldn't be so bad if we only had to do it once, but the two BBC men have us walk down the same bit of pavement at least twenty times, just to get the shot absolutely right. By the time we're done, my arm feels like it's going to come out of its socket, and Poppy has gone a bit green from being swung around so much.

'My jaw hurts from all the smiling,' Jamie says as we go back into the house.

'I know what you mean,' I reply. 'I've never felt so miserable having to look so happy.'

'Let's not become movie stars any time in the near future, eh?'

'Pfft. Some chance of that happening. Lionel Moncrieff has probably told every director in the world not to come within a mile of us.'

'Thank heavens for that.'

Dad pops up to Asda to buy us all sandwiches for lunch. This I am very grateful for, as if I try to butter any bread right now, my arm will fall off. Lightfoot pays for them, which is a bonus. Even he can see how tired we're getting from all the happy walking to and fro, and probably buys lunch as some kind of peace offering.

At least the rest of the filming will just be the interview. All the extraneous stuff has been done. We can sit with a nice cup of tea and talk bollocks for a couple of hours.

Pete sets up the camera so the garden can be seen through the patio doors. Given that it's a crisp autumn day, and the fact that Jamie spent most of yesterday picking up fallen leaves, it's a very pleasant backdrop to have behind your head as someone grills you about how hard it is to write comedy.

Lightfoot sits Jamie and I behind the dining table, and tells us to look casual. This is not easy when someone is pointing a camera lens directly at your face. It's not quite as bad as a gun, but it's not far off. I am suddenly aware of all the pits and cracks in my face. The cavernous crow's feet extending from my eyes will look terrific in glorious HD, I'm sure.

'Er, can I just pop to the loo?' I ask the BBC men.

'Didn't you just go?' Jamie says, earning himself a dig in the ribs.

'Of course, we're still checking light levels, so please do,' Lightfoot replies.

I get up and make my way upstairs to the bathroom, where I spend the next ten minutes applying a month's worth of foundation and a year's worth of eye liner. This means that in my BBC debut I will look like a whore. But I will be a whore that isn't covered in wrinkles, so I have no problem with it whatsoever.

A horrid thought then springs into my head. I have now been up here quite a while. Everyone downstairs will naturally assume that I am having a poo. It's a testament to my desire not to look old and haggard that I find I really don't care that much. I will just be a whore with irritable bowel syndrome.

By the time I get back to the dining room Pete has set up a couple of small lights that brighten the room like it's a summer's day outside. I consider turning on my heels to go back and apply even more foundation, but common sense gets the better of me. Looking like a whore is one thing, looking like Barbara Cartland is entirely another.

Lightfoot sits himself down opposite us, to one side of the camera. 'Now then, folks. This should be quite easy. All I want to do is interview the two of you on your own for a while, and then we can do a bit with Poppy and Terry together as well at the end.'

I look round to see Poppy pouting from the kitchen doorway. She obviously thought she was going to get in on her mother and father's interview, and is not happy about being relegated to 'a bit at the end'. Jonathan Lightfoot had assured her that she was the star of the show, but this is not proving to be the case. My daughter is learning a valuable lesson about show business here: people will lie to your face just to shut you up. It will hold her in very good stead, I'm sure.

I regard her thunderous expression for a moment. 'Poppy? Do you promise to be quiet while we do the interview, or should Grandad take you to the park?'

'I'll be quiet Mum, I promise,' she replies in a grump, and gives Jonathan Lightfoot a cold look. Yep, she's already learning a deep seated mistrust of anyone behind a camera. I look forward to attending court proceedings in fifteen years after she kicks Steven Spielberg in the testicles.

'Excellent,' Lightfoot says as Dad takes Poppy over to the couch. 'Shall we get started?'

It comes as something of a surprise when the first question out of the producer's mouth is 'What makes you both laugh?' I was expecting a question about the actual job of writing comedy, but it seems Lightfoot is more interested in the emotional response that comedy has on people, rather than the mechanics of how it's created. It's rather a refreshing change, to be honest.

'Two answers for me,' Jamie replies. 'The intelligent, adult answer is the juxtaposition of the commonplace with the absurd, but in reality I just like it when people fall over and hurt themselves on YouTube. Hilarious.'

I roll my eyes. Jamie is obviously in one of those moods today. 'I'm a sucker for a bit of slapstick,' I add. 'That, and when people misunderstand one another. There's a lot of mileage in that.'

'That happens quite a lot in your books,' Lightfoot points out.

'Yeah, it's not quite so funny then!' I tell him.

And that sets the tone for the next hour. Lightfoot continues to ask us a lot of ephemeral questions about the nature of humour, the effect it has on us as writers, and the effect it also has on our readers. I find myself actually having to think about my answers before I give them. Not once does he ask us how many words we write per day, or what it felt like to get our first publishing deal. Instead, he's only interested in getting to the bottom of what Jamie and I believe is the deeper meaning of good comedy, and how we translate it into our work. By the time Lightfoot has finished, I feel like I've been grilled by the Spanish Inquisition - which I really wasn't expecting.

'Phew,' Jamie mutters. 'That was intense!'

Lightfoot looks apologetic. 'Sorry about that. I just don't want to bore you or the audience with the same old, same old.'

'No, that's fine,' I tell him. 'That's the best workout our brains have had in years.'

Lightfoot laughs. 'Well, you were both very good. Why don't you go make yourselves a nice drink while I have a chat with Poppy and Terry?'

'Okay. But I warn you, if you ask Poppy what she thinks the meaning of comedy is she's likely to give you the sweetest look you've ever seen and then answer 'farts'.'

'Mum! No I wouldn't!' Poppy objects from the couch, but there's a look in her eyes that tells me she knows I've got her pegged.

Jamie and I make ourselves a cup of tea while Pete rearranges the camera and lights so that they get the best shot of Dad and Poppy. Pops sits on her grandfather's lap, and gets tickled for her troubles. I can't believe how natural these two look together.

As I sip my tea, I can't help but feel an intense curiosity come over me as I wonder what my father is about to say. I'm assuming Lightfoot will want to know how he feels about his daughter's work as a writer. I'm also fascinated to find out what kind of thing actually makes him laugh. We've never really discussed our books. I know he's read them, but I've never thought to ask him whether he found them all that funny. I guess I haven't wanted to know, just in case he didn't.

I blink a couple of times in surprise. Can it be true? Can I really be worried about my father's opinion of me? That must mean something surely?

'Stop it,' Jamie says, looking at me.

'Stop what?'

'I can hear the cogs turning, Laura. You're going into over analysis mode, I can see it in your eyes. Just let the man speak, and don't read too much into it.'

I smile ruefully. Jamie can read me like a book. I may be worried about Dad's opinion of my writing, but ultimately, the only person in this world whose opinion I really care about is sitting next to me. Right where he's been without fail for almost ten years.

Oh dear, I've come over all soppy. Best not let Lightfoot see, otherwise he'll want to ask me questions about it.

'So then Terry,' Lightfoot begins. 'I know what makes your daughter laugh. What about you?'

For a second, Dad looks a bit stunned, and I'm worried he's going to freeze, but then he smiles and tickles Poppy again. 'This little monster. She always makes me laugh.'

Oh, that's a great answer. And one I should have thought of. I am a terrible parent.

Poppy giggles. 'Stop it Grandad!'

'Anything else?' Lightfoot probes.

'I laugh when other people laugh,' Dad says.

'So it makes you happy to see other people smiling?'

'Exactly.' Dad looks briefly over at me. 'That's why I'm so proud of what Laura's doing. She makes so many people laugh that I just can't keep a straight face.'

Oh dear. The soppiness is increasing. I may have to spend another ten minutes in the bathroom on my mascara at this rate.

Lightfoot asks Dad another few questions, before turning his attention to Poppy. 'And what about you, sweetheart? Do you like what your mum and dad do for a living?'

'Yeah! All the kids at school are dead jealous. Their mums and dads have to go out, but mine are home, so I get to see them all the time.'

Yep. Here come the tears.

'Would you like to be a writer too?'

My daughter crinkles her brow in deep thought for a moment. 'No,' she replies matter of factly.

'And why's that?' Lightfoot asks in surprise at Poppy's answer.

'I don't like it. Mrs Carmoody makes me write lots in English class and my hand hurts.' Poppy leans forward and fixes Lightfoot with a look of wisdom beyond the ages. 'Mrs Carmoody is a poo head.'

'Is she now?' the producer replies, trying not to laugh.

'Sorry about that,' I say to him. 'Poppy has some definite opinions when it comes to her teachers.'

Lightfoot gives Poppy a conspiratorial wink. 'Don't worry Poppy. I agree with you. All of my teachers were poo heads as well.'

And with that profound assessment of the British educational system, the interviews come to a close.

I make us all another round of drinks while Pete starts to pack the equipment up. The rest of us sit round the dining table and watch him work. This probably goes on a lot at the BBC.

'Well, that was fantastic, all of you,' Jonathan Lightfoot tells us. 'We've got plenty of great material.'

'How long do you think we'll be on for?' Jamie asks him.

'Oh, about two or three minutes.'

'Is that all?' I say, amazed. 'We've been at this for hours!'

Lightfoot shrugs his shoulders. 'That's the nature of making a TV show I'm afraid.'

'I think we'll stick to writing.'

He gives me a tired smile. 'I would.'

'When will it be on the telly?' Poppy asks.

'Early next year. Probably March,' Lightfoot says. 'That's the UK broadcast anyway. We'll send the documentary to other countries, so you'll be famous all over the world Poppy!'

Never mind the animatronic version of Simba. Lightfoot has now pretty much produced the real thing and started singing The Circle Of Life. Poppy's eyes light up - and I start saving for counselling sessions.

'All over the world?' Dad says to Lightfoot. There's a note of worry in his voice.

'Yes!'

'America?'

'Oh my yes. That's our main audience outside the UK. I'd imagine it'll get picked up by one of the major broadcasters.'

Dad's face has suddenly gone very, *very* pale.

'What's wrong Terry?' Jamie asks, seeing the instant change that came over my father the second the prospect of the show being aired in the USA came across the table.

Dad looks from Jamie to me, and back to Lightfoot. There looks to be actual terror in his eyes now.

'Dad? What is it?' I ask.

He licks his lips and stands up quickly. 'Er. I don't want to be in the show anymore. I don't... Can you cut my bits please?'

'But what about my stuff Grandad?' Poppy demands.

Lightfoot looks shocked. 'We can certainly edit you out if you feel that strongly about it Terry.'

I stand up too. 'What's wrong? Why don't you want to be in it anymore?'

'Not if it's broadcast in America,' he says, voice cracking.

I'm completely confused. 'Why Dad?'

He backs away from me into the living room. 'Don't... Don't... '

My heart rate has rocketed. Something is going on here. I've never seen my father act like this. 'Dad! Tell me what the hell is wrong with you!'

He stops backing away, and gives me an anguished look. 'I just don't want to be on a TV programme that gets shown in America.'

'Why?!'

'Someone... someone might recognise me. And I don't want that if I'm with you... ' A hand goes to his mouth, as if realising he's said too much.

'If you're *with me?* What's that supposed to mean?'

'If you're on the TV with me, as my daughter, I mean. He might see it, recognise my face, see yours... and put two and two together.'

Okay, now this is getting ridiculous.

'He? Who is *he?*'

My heart rate speeds even faster when I see tears coming from Dad's eyes. 'We're getting on so well,' he says. 'I don't want anything to ruin it.' He looks to the ceiling as if searching for divine assistance. 'Oh God! I'm such an idiot! I've said too much!'

Jamie comes to stand beside me. 'You're not making any sense Terry.'

'Dad! Just stand still and tell us what you're talking about!'

His knees give out from under him and he slumps onto the couch. 'You shouldn't call me that,' he says, looking up into my eyes with an imploring look. 'Please don't.'

'Call you what?'

'Dad.'

'Why the hell not?! You're my father, aren't you?'

He shakes his head back and forth slowly, the tears flowing stronger now. 'No, sweetheart. I'm not your real dad. I'm so, so sorry.'

When the fuck did I step into an episode of Eastenders?

'You're not my Dad? Of course you're my bloody Dad! You may have been gone for most of my life, but that doesn't stop you being my father!'

Dad shakes his head back and forth. 'No, that's not what I mean, Laura.'

Jamie steps forward. 'For God's sakes Terry, start making some sense. We do have a BBC film crew here!'

Dad stands on shaky legs and takes my hand. He gulps loudly and licks his lips. 'You see, your mum needed me, Laura. Because he... he went back home, and she didn't have anyone else. He didn't know she was pregnant, of course. Helen never told him. Your Mum didn't want to ruin his life back in the States, that was why. He had a family there.'

Someone has thrown a cold blanket across my shoulders. 'Who is *he*?' I say from about seven galaxies away.

'Your *real* Dad. He was American. In the army. He was based here in the seventies. They met and fell in love... that's what your mum told me. He was supposed to be getting a divorce from his wife back home, but they managed to patch things up, apparently. He didn't want to leave Helen, but she made him go. Made him go back for the sake of his kids. Never told him she was carrying his child as well, because she knew he'd never have left her then.'

Now I feel like I've been dropped into an icebox. I start to shiver from my feet all the way to the top of my head.

'I only met him a couple of times,' Dad continues. 'In passing, you know. He knew me and your mum had been an item before he came along. It was all... very complicated. Then he was gone, you see. But me and your mum, we went way back, you know? Started seeing each other in our teens, before we split up the first time. And then when she was left alone, after he'd gone back to the States, I stepped in. Tried to be a dad to you, the way he wasn't. The way he couldn't.'

'You *left*, Terry,' Jamie says, rage in his voice. 'You fucking left them both!'

Dad looks distraught. 'I know! I couldn't take it! Your mum never really stopped loving him. Never looked at me the way I wanted her to... because of him. I had to go!'

I try to speak, but have to swallow the nausea boiling in my stomach before I can get the words out. 'Mum never told me any of this.' My voice is weak, faint, horrible.

'She didn't want to hurt you any more, sweetheart. You had one father leave you already. You didn't need to know about another one!'

'Why didn't you say anything when you came back this year?' I ask. 'Why didn't you tell me the truth then?'

Dad's face crumples even more. 'I was going to! Really I was! But then I saw Poppy... saw the life you all had together, and I wanted to be part of it. Besides, if Helen didn't tell you, what right did I have?'

'Excuse me?' Jonathan Lightfoot pipes up awkwardly from behind us. 'Should we, er, leave?'

'Shut up!' Jamie and I both snap at him in unison.

I look back at my father. 'You're not my dad?' I feel Jamie's hand grasp mine tightly.

'No, sweetheart. Your real dad is an American guy. That's why I didn't want to be on TV in the States with you. Just in case he saw it and recognised me. He might have seen you too, and realised who you were.'

'That's a bit of a fucking stretch, Terry. I doubt the guy is Sherlock Holmes,' Jamie argues, quite rightly.

'I know! I'm an idiot! I should have just kept quiet. Everything would have been fine!'

I feel a small hand take mine, so both of my family are standing either side of me. 'Mum? What's going on?' Poppy asks. 'Why are you talking about America?'

Jamie moves around and picks her up. 'Let's let Mum and Grandad talk, sweetheart.' He backs away with her and stands next to Lightfoot and Pete, who both look like they wish they were anywhere else - even at ITV.

'*Grandad*?' I hiss. A sneer forms on my lips as I look back at my fathe - sorry, *Terry*. 'What's his name? What's this mystery man's name?' I order.

'Lawrence. She called him Laurie though,' Terry replies.

Of course she did.

'Laurie what?'

Terry shakes his head. 'I don't know! I never asked more about him, and your mum never told.'

'So, you don't know where he came from?'

'No.'

'Just that he was called Laurie and was in the army?'

'Yes. I think he might have come from Boston, or somewhere like that.' Terry swallows hard. 'She loved him Laura. Loved him in a way she never loved me!'

Words fail me. *Utterly.*

Here is this man who I thought was my father, who left me as a little girl, standing here now and looking at me with a combination of fear and self pity on his face that makes me want to punch him in the mouth.

'Get out,' I order, discovering that words don't fail me after all, it's just that they're not very nice ones. 'Get out *now*.'

'But Laura - '

'Get the fuck out of my house!' I scream.

A few silent moments pass. Terry then gives Jamie and Poppy a last, regretful look, and walks out of the lounge and towards the front door.

I hear it slam behind him as he goes, and turn to look at my husband and child, both of whom have tears in their eyes. 'Don't cry,' I tell them. 'He's not worth it.'

'Oh honey,' Jamie replies. 'We're not crying for him.'

I open my mouth to say that I'm not even going to cry for me, so why should they, but realise that the tears are already flowing down my cheeks.

'What do you want to do, baby?' Jamie asks gently.

I think for a moment. 'I want to punch him,' I say with a sniff.

'What?'

'I said I want to *punch* him.' My hand curls into a fist. 'I'm *going* to punch him.'

I'm headed for the door in pursuit of Terry before Jamie or Poppy can say another word.

I should just let the old man walk away - that would be the mature thing to do, but I'm so fucking angry at him that the mature thing can go take a long walk off a short pier.

I fling the front door open to see Terry walking slowly down the driveway, his head hanging.

'You!' I holler.

He turns to see me barrelling towards him. 'Now wait just a moment Laura!' he says, arms held up.

I will do no such thing. I will however punch him in the face - or at least try my best to.

Sadly, my aim is off thanks to all that anger and betrayal, so I end up whacking him on the forehead, and therefore probably doing more of an injury to myself than him.

Given my ineptitude when it comes to fisticuffs, I resort to slapping like a mad fishwife at dawn. I can feel pain rocketing up my right wrist every time I do, but the adrenaline is powering me through it nicely at the moment, and I won't realise I need hospital treatment for another few minutes.

One thing to bear in mind here is that Jamie and I live in a nice residential area, where the inhabitants are not used to seeing a fully grown woman beating up an old man on one of the less well manicured front lawns in the street. Even through my rage I can feel the eyes of the neighbours turn swiftly in my direction to see what all the fuss is about.

And I'm not the only one who sees this.

'Laura! Sweetheart! Just stop!' Jamie cries, walking across the grass towards me, head darting around at all the nearby windows.

But I can't. I so want to, but I can't.

Terry is putting up no kind of defence now, other than one raised arm that I'm still slapping at in impotent fury. My hand hurts, my face is streaked with tears and I feel dizzy, and yet I can't stop hitting this stupid man. He's taken my feet out from under me in the worst possible way in the last ten minutes, and I want revenge, damn it.

Then Jamie says the one thing that does get me to stop.

'Laura! Poppy is watching this! You're scaring her.'

The anger drains completely out of my body in a split second. I turn to look at my daughter, who is hiding behind Jonathan Lightfoot's legs. The BBC producer has trailed out behind my family, and is looking on aghast at my actions. Pete, obeying some kind of universal journalistic law, is filming the entire exchange on his camera.

I see the upset expression on Poppy's face and hold my hands out to her. 'Poppy, it's okay honey. Mum's just a bit angry with Gran - she's just a bit angry right now.'

Poppy gives Terry a grave look and my heart sinks. She should never have had to watch any of this. I am a terrible parent. But then so is my not-father for lying to me all this time.

'He's not my Grandad then?' Poppy asks in a low voice.

'We'll talk about it later, Pops,' Jamie says, moving to stand by her again.

That is one conversation I doubt either of us is looking forward to. Trying to explain the cruelty and stupidity of adults to a child must be one of the hardest parts of being a mother or father.

Which reminds me...

I turn back to Terry. 'Leave. Just leave,' I say, all the passion and rage now gone from my voice.

The old man moves towards me, hands out again. 'I'm sorry, Laura!'

'Stop saying that. It means nothing.' I'm acutely aware that my right hand is throbbing like mad. I'm dog tired now as well. Funny, I was so full of happy energy just ten minutes ago, thinking the interview had gone really well. If anyone ever tells you that life is easy to predict, they are comprehensively lying to you.

'Just go, Terry,' Jamie orders, one finger pointing down the road.

Unbelievably, as the old man trudges away, Pete the cameraman moves to follow him. I step in his path and instantly fill the camera's field of vision. 'Pete, unless you want the next shot you get to be the inside of your own colon, I suggest you stop filming right this instant.' The camera drops to his side in a heartbeat. A skinny, clumsy woman I may be, but I wouldn't mess with me either right now, given how I look.

I hold out my arms to my daughter. 'Come here baby,' I tell her. 'I'm so sorry about all of this. It's all going to be okay.'

Now some children would be frightened of their mother right about now, having seen her so enraged, but if you've been paying attention properly, you'll know that my Pops is no ordinary child. She runs into my arms, and I gather her up, wincing at both the pain in my hand, and under the strain of her rapidly increasing size. 'So, my Grandad isn't him then?' she asks, her perfect little brow knitted in thought.

I could lie. I could sugar coat. But this is a girl who thinks nothing of entertaining a room full of complete strangers with a bad rendition of Umbrella. Her bravery is undeniable. 'No Pops. It turns out that he isn't.'

'No,' she confirms, as much to herself as anyone. 'My Grandad is somebody called Lorry. A man from America with a funny name.'

I stroke her hair. 'That's right honey.' And if I ever find Lorry, I'm going to drive him round the bend.

Now my hand is *really* hurting, so I give Poppy to Jamie and look round at Lightfoot. 'Jonathan. I think we're done here for the day.'

'Yes, I believe we probably are,' he replies, trying to sound nice and neutral. Disagreeing with this apparently psychopathic writer wouldn't be in his best interests - or the best interests of his documentary, which lest we forget, is supposed to be about comedy.

'I trust that you will cut any mention of that man from your interview with us?' I say.

'Absolutely.'

'And you won't say anything about my horrendously complicated family life either, will you?'

'No Laura, I won't.' He offers me a sympathetic smile. 'I'm so sorry.'

I roll my eyes. 'Don't be. I didn't even know that man a year ago. It's no loss.'

Oh, but it is. It really, *really* is.

'Jamie,' I say to my quiet husband, as we watch Lightfoot and Pete drive away, no doubt delighted to be escaping this strange soap opera in suburbia, and looking forward to getting back to the safe haven of central London.

'Yes, sweetheart?'

'There are two things I need at the moment.'

'What is it?' he asks intently. 'Anything you need Laura!'

God bless him. I have one reliable man in my life, and that's probably all I need when you get right down to it.

'A hug.'

'Of course!' He wraps his arms around me.

'And a lift to the casualty department.' I hold the offending limb out as Jamie pulls away. 'I think Terry may have done me some damage.' The tears are back. 'In more ways than one.'

Luckily, it's just a bad sprain, rather than a break. A friendly nurse called Christina wraps a bandage around my wrist, and sends me on my way with a prescription for painkillers, and advice to let Jamie do the fighting for me from now on.

Back home, we sit in silence over tea, watching Poppy play with Winklehoven on the floor. We let her eat the turkey dinosaurs again tonight, and didn't complain once when she wolfed them down in a minute and left all her peas. It only seemed fair enough. Jamie didn't even complain when Winklehoven bit his finger. Both of us are just too shell shocked after the events of this afternoon to react much to anything.

The lassitude that has come over me is understandable, but not very productive. There must be something I can do to shake myself out of it.

A thought occurs as I'm slowly chewing on a mouthful of peas I can't taste.

'I think I'll do some writing this evening,' I tell Jamie after I swallow.

'Really? You think that's a good idea, baby? After what's happened today?'

'Yes. I need to do it. It'll make me feel better. I want to get all of this down. It'll help me clear my head.'

Jamie regards me with doubt in his eyes. 'Okay. I'll keep Poppy and the hellhound amused then. But call me if you need anything.'

'Thank you, sweetheart.'

I rise from the table and give him a kiss. I also hug Poppy, and tickle Winky behind one ear, before making my way slowly up the stairs.

I feel apprehensive as I do. Nauseous, in fact.

Why?

Because I'm about to sit and talk to the one person who needs to hear what I have to say following today's revelations. The one person I'm actually angry at - possibly for the first time in my life.

You, Mum.

How could you keep it from me? How could you let me think that idiot was my father? How could you never tell me the *truth*? Not even when you were *dying*? Not even when you were *leaving me too*? You didn't think it would be a good idea to let your bloody daughter know that her father was actually some Yank in the fucking army? Some man you had a brief fling with, before letting him sod off back across the Atlantic to be with his real family?! Why didn't you put up more of a fight, Mum? Why didn't you *care*??

And so here I sit, raging at the keyboard, and pouring my heart out to a woman who died of cancer years ago... a woman I thought I knew everything about!

I can hear Jamie downstairs right now, telling Winky off for biting his toes, while my glorious daughter giggles at the top of her lungs, and all I want to do is go and join them. But here I sit, tears coursing down my cheeks as I write, trying my hardest to understand why my dead mother would have kept me in the dark about something so important... and knowing that it doesn't matter how many words I type, or how many times I ask, because *I'm never going to get an answer!*

Why, Mum?
Why?

I love you, but I don't miss you at all today,

Laura.

Jamie's Blog
Wednesday 3 November

Snore.
'Jamie!'
Snore.
'Jamie, wake up!'
Snore.
'Jamie! For crying out loud, wake up!'
Sno -
Smack!
'Ow! Whasser matter? What? Whas going on?'
'Are you awake?'
'Fuck me no! I'm sleeping. Or I bloody was.' I sit up in bed, groaning as I do. That's when you know you're getting old, when just the simple act of sitting up in the most comfortable place on Earth is accompanied by a groan. 'What is it, baby?' I ask my wife, rubbing my eyes and looking at the clock. It reads 6.17am.

In the dim pre-dawn light I see that Laura is wide awake, her hair wild. There's a twitchiness about her I don't like one bit.

I'm sure yesterday was one of the worst days of her life, and I was rather hoping a good night's sleep would do her the world of good. From the looks of things though, she hasn't slept a wink. I guess I shouldn't be that surprised, losing a father for the second time, and discovering you're the illegitimate child of another man, would be enough to rob anyone of a proper night's kip.

When I went up to find her hunched over the computer and crying last night, it was the most heartbreaking thing I'd ever seen. I was almost in the car and driving round to Terry's to see if I could break my hand on his face too, but Laura persuaded me it would be a pointless thing to do. She told me she wasn't really angry at him anyway, and showed me what she'd written to her mother through all those tears.

When I'd finished reading, I put my arm around her and gave her a kiss. 'It's well written, but I don't think we should end the next book with it, baby,' I said with a rueful smile. 'It'd be a bit of a downer.'

'Very funny,' Laura replied, wiping her eyes. 'I can't delete it though, not yet. She doesn't deserve that.'

And who can blame her for feeling that way?

I'd be angry at my mother too, if she'd kept something like that from me. Hell, I generally *am* always angry at my mother for one thing or another, but nothing this bad. Booking a barbershop quartet that tells you you're going to die horribly is one thing, but it pales in comparison alongside keeping your real father's identity a secret all the way to your grave. I never knew Helen McIntyre, but by all accounts she seemed a wonderful woman. It's disconcerting to know she was capable of keeping such secrets from her own daughter. And if I'm disconcerted, then Laura must feel a thousand times worse.

Is it any wonder then, that at 6.17am, my wife is wide awake and looking at me with a wild look in her eyes.

'I've had an idea!' she says animatedly, sitting up on her knees in front of me. I notice her iPad is on and open on the bed beside her, its light bathing the ceiling in an eerie white glow.

'Does it involve sleeping?' I say, bleary eyed. 'Because any plan involving going back to sleep would get my vote.'

Laura takes my hand. 'I want to go to America.'

'You want to what?'

'I want to go to America, Jamie. Boston. In Massachusetts.'

'I know where Boston is. But why?' I ask, with a sinking heart, knowing full well what the answer will be.

'Because I want to find him.'

I grimace. 'Your real dad, you mean?'

'Yes! This Laurie person.' Her face darkens. 'I have questions, Jamie. Many, many questions. Mum can't answer them, but maybe this man can. Maybe he can tell me why I was lied to.'

'But we don't know anything about him. Terry said he didn't know more than his first name, and the fact he was in the army.'

'Exactly!' Laura crows with excitement. 'He was in the army... and he came from Boston.'

'*Might* have come from Boston.'

Laura flaps her hand. 'Yes, yes, alright, he *might* have. But it's still a lead.'

'Not much of one.'

Laura picks up the iPad. 'There's a veterans centre in the city. We might be able to find out more about Laurie there. Where he lives maybe. If he's still alive, there's a good chance we can track him down.'

I sigh. I have a horrible feeling that my wife is clutching at straws here.

But then I remember reading those heartbreaking words she'd written to her mother about needing answers, and can fully understand why Laura wants this so much.

How can I tell my wife that there may be *no* answers for her? Here, or in the USA? That finding this man will be like finding a needle in a haystack. A very large haystack of 50 states, with an obesity problem and a relaxed attitude to gun control.

I can't do it though. I can't let her down.

This is the woman I love - and sometimes, when love is involved, you just have to clutch at those straws and hope they hold.

'Okay baby,' I say with a grin.

'Okay? You mean we can go?'

'Yeah. Sure. If that's what you want to do.'

Laura throws her arms around me. 'Thank you, Jamie!'

'My pleasure.'

And it really is my pleasure, because *oh my God*, how could I ever deny this woman anything? In the dim white light cast by the iPad, with her hair dishevelled, and her vest pulled down slightly so one of her nipples is poking out, she looks absolutely *beautiful*.

Laura has given me everything. A daughter I adore, a career I love, a life I enjoy. How can I refuse her anything?

I would walk through Hell for Laura Newman. A manhunt across America should be no trouble at all.

There's a knock at the bedroom door. It opens to reveal a yawning Poppy Newman holding a stuffed Nemo, and looking decidedly unhappy about being woken up at this time in the morning by her excited mother.

'What's going on?' she asks, rubbing one eye. 'I was sleeping.'

'Poppy!' Laura exclaims. 'Would you like to go to America?!'

Never underestimate the ability of a seven-year-old to go from half asleep to wide awake in a nanosecond. 'America! Yeah! That'd be great!' With a smile of pure joy spread across her face, Poppy jumps up onto the bed and throws her arms around us both.

And there you have it. Even if we don't find Laura's real father, then at least we'll make our little powerhouse of a daughter happy. Which, when you get right down to it, is the best reason to do anything, as far as I'm concerned.

...also, we'll probably have to put Winklebastard in a kennel while we're away.

Don't worry, I'll make sure I pack something familiar from home, so that the dog can think about us fondly while we're gone. It's made of cardboard and Border Terrier shaped.

Next stop then, is the United States of America.

Hold on to your hats, folks. It's going to be an experience none of us are likely to forget!

The End.

...for now.

Will Laura find her real father?
Will Poppy eat her own bodyweight in donuts?
Will Jamie look good in a Stetson?

Find out in the next book:

Love... Across The Pond.

About the author:

Nick Spalding is an author who, try as he might, can't seem to write anything serious.

Before becoming a full-time author, he worked in the communications industry, mainly in media and marketing. As talking rubbish for a living can get tiresome (for anyone other than a politician), he thought he'd have a crack at writing comedy fiction - with a very agreeable level of success so far, it has to be said. Nick has now sold over half a million books, and still can't quite believe his luck.

Nick lives in the South of England with his fiancée. He recently had to turn 40 - and is rather annoyed at the universe because it gave him no choice in the matter; he also suffers from the occasional bout of insomnia, is addicted to Thai food, and still thinks Batman is cool.

Printed in Great Britain
by Amazon.co.uk, Ltd.,
Marston Gate.